FRIENDS
OF ACPL

SACRIFICE

D1069357

SACRIFICE

BOOK 2 IN THE DEMON HUNTER SERIES

by
TL GARDNER

Q-Boro Books
WWW.QBOROBOOKS.COM

An Urban Entertainment Company

Published by Q-Boro Books

ISBN-13: 978-1-933967-38-7
ISBN-10: 1-933967-38-2
LCCN: 2007923278

First Printing April 2008
Printed in the United States of America

10 9 8 7 6 5 4 3 2 1

Cover layout/design by Candace K. Cottrell; Photo by Ted Mebane
Editors: Candace K. Cottrell, Latoya Smith

Q-BORO BOOKS
Jamaica, Queens NY 11434
WWW.QBOROBOOKS.COM

*This book is dedicated to the memory of
Johnniemae Smith.*

R.I.P.

But you have changed your works, and have not done according to his command, and transgressed against him; (and have spoken) haughty and harsh words, with your impure mouths, against his majesty, for your heart is hard. You will have no peace.

They (the leaders) and all . . . took for themselves wives from all that they chose and they began to cohabit with them and to defile themselves with them; and to teach them sorcery and spells and the cutting of roots; and to acquaint them with herbs. And they become pregnant by them and bore (great) giants three thousand cubits high . . .

THE DEAD SEA SCROLLS

REFLECTION

As I look back on the events of the last year, it is with mixed emotions that I have come to accept this fate that has been given to me, for it is beyond my meager understanding. Learning that my entire life has been one long, orchestrated drama to prepare me for this moment in time was overwhelming to say the least. Although I can say that I do enjoy releasing the rage built up within my heart upon the demons I have encountered here. Demons . . . the word rings of fantasy still to my ears. Once they were only images I created in my imagination, in my dreams . . . the reality of their true existence should have shocked me, but given the state of this sinful world we live in, perhaps nothing can be unexpected. Yet with the undeniable proof of their realness also comes a reality that I must now come to terms with. A reality that I have spent many a night worrying myself to tears over. A reality that I have battled with, denied, accepted, and denied time and time again. A vicious circle. The reality of God.

Merely the thought brings tears to my eyes as I sit here scribbling upon this pad. Perhaps it is guilt that brings forth these tears. So many times I have turned my life over to Him, confessing and promising to live a righteous life in His name, only to fall deeper into a sinful life of lust and greed. It was only during times of desperation that I would turn

to Him, when I was in some sort of trouble with nowhere left to go. With all of the surreal events that
have transpired in my life within the recent past—
losing Taysia, the woman who finally gave me happiness after a lifetime of disappointment, having her
die in my arms, killed by a bullet meant for me . . .
placing the barrel of a 9 mm into my own mouth
and pulling the trigger, finally ending the foolishness that was my life . . . being torn away from my
own personal heaven after my death was so rudely
interrupted by Gabriel and his heavenly plans . . .
battling demons with the twin blades humming in
my hands . . . meeting Ebonee Lane . . . Ebonee, my
heart skips a beat at the thought of her. The moon's
beauty is flawed when compared to her. Her love
was something I never expected to know, a true
blessing. A blessing flawed only by my own fears
and insecurities, for one image haunts me deep in
my soul. The image of my beloved Ebonee, bloodied and beaten, tortured, hanging upon that cross
below the underground complex in Southeastern
Pennsylvania as bait. Bait to draw me near.

But all of that pales in comparison to the deeper
struggles within my soul. For I now know that the
Lord is real. I cannot deny that any longer. I must
come to terms with this reality knowing that I am
still but a human, flawed and subject to sin, a slave
to it. It is my fear that I cannot break away from the
yoke of iniquity, throw aside my doubts and obvious foolish thinking. For even with this new proof
of God, I still find myself skeptical and still I am disturbed by the opening passages of the book of Job.
Perhaps Father Holbrook can help me come to
terms with my troubled soul. . . .

PROLOGUE

Elijah Garland staggered backward under the relentless assault, his twin blades, Enobe and Soul Seeker blurring in their frantic attempts to keep the enemy weapons at bay. How many would come? How many had he already slaughtered this night?

His slender black hands sent the twin blades into a spectacular dance, the ring of steel on steel echoing in his ears like thousands of tiny church bells being rung in his head.

Rage spurred him on.

A wickedly barbed spear tip came in from his left, too fast to be deflected by his preoccupied blades. Elijah spun as soon as he felt the pressure in the left side of his abdomen, and the tip of the spear drew blood but continued on its forward plunge, its blade now past the swift moving Protector. Elijah brought Soul Seeker down hard with his right hand as he finished the spin, slicing through the heavy wooden pole, ignoring the pain from the new wound as Enobe followed in Soul Seeker's wake, her tip exploding into the foul demon's stunned face and continuing through its black brain. The remnants of the spear clattered to the blood soaked earth, the demon defeated, dead before it hit the ground.

It was replaced by three more.

Elijah's taut and chiseled muscles burned from fatigue. How long had he been here? How long had this battle raged? One demon howled madly, charging forward, seeking to bury the Protector under its weight. Elijah sneered, accepting a glancing blow to the back of his shoulder as he turned to face the advancing fool, dropping low to one knee, Enobe slicing through the air in a wide arc. The demon's large, pupil-less black eyes went wide as it fell forward, finding it suddenly had no leg below the knee cap to support its vicious charge. Elijah was up then, darting past the falling creature, Soul Seeker taking its head from its shoulders even as Enobe came up to block another attack.

The Protector's movements were a blur. He was rage incarnate. He was the hate amassed within his own heart. He was death.

His stark white hair, hanging below his shoulders in thick locks, was bathed red with blood, some his own, most not. *I am dreaming again.* It had to be a dream. The same dream. Sleeveless black leather armor fit snugly over a platinum chain mail shirt which hung down below his waist, split on both sides. Thick metal bracers, glinting red with blood, protected his bulging biceps, and armored leather gloves covered both hands up to his forearms. *Yes . . . a dream.* He was aware of the cavern then, dark and sinister, shadows seeming to cover every inch of the place.

With awareness came clarity. This place was his domain . . . created years ago as a sublet for his sorrow. He would come here often; to give back the pain of heartbreak and loss, to repay the unseen demons within the material world into which he was born—a world he knew he did not belong to.

Enobe and Soul Seeker ceased their defensive dance, their razor-sharp edges dripping red with the blood of his attackers. Elijah's light brown eyes flared, and now seemed to glow with a fire that burned within his soul. A single movement brought the twin blades to a reversed hold within his hands, their slightly curved blades extending along both arms up to the elbow.

The nearest demons, their elongated, sinewy arms carrying cudgels, swords and spears, seemed to take note of the subtle change in the Protector's movements. Their disgusting faces, huge elongated maws filled with rows of wickedly sharp teeth, seemed doubtful, almost afraid . . . and justly so.

With a heart-wrenching, lustful cry, Elijah tore into the surrounding horde of demons. Soul Seeker and Enobe sliced through arms and pierced black hearts, decapitating and impaling demon after demon. *Yes . . . this is my place . . . this is my pain.*

Elijah felt a surge of pleasure wash through his body, like a never-ending orgasm. It saturated his being, causing his heart to flutter. Warm tears found his cheeks as the feeling continued to engulf him. His nostrils flared and he again reversed his grip on his blades, spinning in a breathless dance of death and destruction. *Take it back!* Elijah released the pain. He released the suffering.

The smell of sulfur suddenly became thick, and the air around him seemed to develop heaviness.

His arms slowed in their dance. Demons scampered away from the Protector now, tripping and falling over the dead, which numbered in the hundreds. Elijah stood within the center of a circle now, his feet stumbling about the slippery ground, stepping on arms, legs, and torsos.

His heart was still pounding in his chest and his knuckles ached from the death-like grip with which he held onto his twin swords.

Slowly he watched a narrow path open up as the minor demons tripped upon each other to get out of the way. Their misshapen bodies cringed and hustled quickly away, their strange eyes searching in the direction the narrow-forming path led to. Elijah could taste the silence it was so complete. It laid upon the wide cavern like a thick wool blanket, suffocating all sound.

His light brown eyes narrowed to thin slits, and his demeanor darkened further as he felt a powerful presence at the end of the path. Enobe and Soul Seeker at once began a vibrant hum, transmitting the truth of the unnatural evil through the hilt of the enchanted blades and into the palms of his hands.

Nothing changes here.

This battle had played out hundreds of times in his mind. Always it was the same, the weak demon fodder sent first to test him, to weaken him perhaps. Elijah again reversed the grip of his blades and waited for the powerful demon he had named Reality to show himself and launch his attack.

His muscles tensed in anticipation; he longed to hack away at the powerful demon, to allow Enobe and Soul Seeker to feed off of its life force. The blades continued to hum, sensing the rage within their wielder. A grin found its way to Elijah's full lips, his thin white goatee framing it nicely. *Yes, come to me, Reality.* Confidence oozed from his aura, a confidence borne of repetition. He could never lose to this beast here, not in this place that he had created—not in his dreams.

He stood there waiting for what seemed to be an eternity. He could sense the demon's presence, but it had yet to manifest itself. Elijah grew tired of waiting. His purposeful steps took him down the center of the sea of minor demons, along the narrow path. They stared at the Protector, fear in their eyes. Some of them had tasted the bite of those terrible blades.

Elijah faltered halfway along the trail, his sure-footedness stolen away as a wave of unexpected dizziness washed through him. His eyes batted rapidly as he dropped to one knee, supporting his weight upon the tip of Soul Seeker. *What's this?* Confusion stole some of the bravado from his body. There was a flaw in his resolve, a weakness he knew well, but could not place. Elijah growled the wooziness away and resumed his march. He could show these beasts no fear.

The sea of deformed, grotesque demons closed the path behind him as he continued forward, their hissing snarls suddenly floating upon the thick, dank air as they momentarily sensed his trepidation. The path narrowed in on him, the closer creatures forced to come within range of Elijah's thirsty blades by their eager companions behind them who had not yet tasted their sting.

A flash of steel left three of them headless, and the path again widened. *Mindless fools.* Elijah frowned at the cowardly response of the beasts. He was approaching the source. The path before him angled upward, a slight slope within the cavern, leading up to a flat, rocky plateau. Around the flat elevated area, the sea of demons writhed—hundreds of them, thousands. . . .

And there was Reality. A great and mighty beast of a demon, shoulders black as pitch and wide as a house. The demon stood nearly twice Elijah's six-four height, and was almost just as wide. Its monstrous legs bulged with knotted muscles. A flaming sword, longer than Elijah was tall, lit up the area with bright orange flames. Ram-like horns sat upon the creature's grotesque, canine-like head, and its teeth were like daggers.

Elijah ignored the inherent fear the creature's image triggered within his very soul—an image meant to stun its prey, to paralyze them. The terrible monstrosity's eyes burned blood-red as it stared at this Protector who continued up the path, unfazed by the demon fear it projected.

Enobe and Soul Seeker led the way, their hunger for this demon's soul undeniable. Elijah gave into their pull, forgetting the momentary lapse of resolve he had experienced a moment before. His heart pounded with the anticipation of battle as he closed the last few feet between himself and the creature. Only then did he notice the tiny form lying at the beasts hoofed feet.

Elijah's blood ran cold within his veins like ice water, his heart seized, and he was paralyzed. A low chuckle echoed throughout the cavern as Elijah fell to his knees, his eyes locked with those of the woman kneeling prostrate at the demons feet.

Ebonee's tears glistened upon her cheek.

The rage flew from Elijah's being like thousands of animals fleeing a burning forest. *No!*

The fiery blade fell swiftly.

Stunned, and motionless, Elijah watched Ebonee's head bounce along the rocky path toward him. It came to a stop at his feet, her lovely brown eyes wide, staring up at him. Her lips moved.

"*I love you, Elijah.*"

Elijah screamed in denial, his hands releasing their grip on his only protection, his only comfort. Enobe and Soul Seeker clamored to the stone and were trampled by a thousand demon feet as they swarmed on the unarmed Protector, claws gouging, teeth biting.

Their snarls echoed all around him, and he could hear their desire to take his life. He felt the pain, felt his skin being torn, felt the many clawed hands upon his body, and he knew then, as darkness settled over his bloody corpse and the demons fed upon his remains, the weakness in his resolve. He knew the one chink in his armor. That weakness . . . was love.

"Elijah! Elijah! Wake up!"

Ebonee Lane cradled her lover's head in her arms as she called out to him. His naked body was covered with sweat and his skin felt like it was on fire. Her eyes darted around the cool hotel suite's bedroom fearfully as she continued to attempt to shake Elijah from his sleep. Kneeling in the bed, she reached over to the nightstand and tapped the brass lamp, her eyes turning to avoid the sudden bright light that illuminated the room at her touch. Her fear intensified as she saw the line of rich crimson snaking from Elijah's nostrils. "Elijah!"

Her eyes fell upon the telephone and she thought briefly of calling 9-1-1. She dismissed the notion without a second thought. No hospital could help her Elijah. She forced herself to remain calm; her hands trembled as she snatched her purse from the nightstand, retrieving a small compact make-up case. She said a silent prayer as her nervous hand held the tiny mirror beneath his nose.

Elijah was not breathing.

"Elijah! Wake up!" She was in full panic now. Desperation brought her tiny fists down hard on his still chest. Her tears blurred her vision and her sobs filled the room. She could not lose Elijah—not now, not ever. His love was her life, and she would not live without it.

Her sorrowful sobs slowly shifted to angry grunts. "Don't you do this to me!" She could not see past the moisture clouding her vision, but her fists continued to fall until she could no longer handle the pain. Her head fell upon his abdomen and her tears began to pool in his navel. Her body trembled as her emotions wavered back and forth between anger and sorrow. She turned her head at the sound of a sudden deep inhalation.

Elijah's eyes flashed open.

Ebonee quickly scooted forward on the sheets, her full lips peppering her lover's face with joyful kisses. Elijah remained silent, the remnants of the nightmare still clouding his mind. He felt the moisture on his face as her tears fell, only to be whisked away by her loving lips. His head was in her bosom then, the softness of bare breasts speeding the memories of the dream away. He exhaled heavily as if cleansing his soul of the thoughts completely. His eyes closed within the warm embrace as she lay beside him, positioning herself next to him and pulling his body over to rest upon hers.

His lips brushed her nipple gently and a chill filled the void vacated by the departing fear. Ebonee moaned softly as she felt his arousal against her thigh. Her tears continued to flow even as her own arousal was evident between her legs. Elijah trembled as he felt her nipple stiffen, becoming erect within his mouth. Never had he desired a woman like he desired Ebonee. The nightmare was a mere memory now, a leaf blowing in the winds of autumn. His lips glided slowly, sensually up to her slender neck, tasting the saltiness of her tears as they continued to flow down her cheeks and to her throat.

Her body shuddered; anticipating his sweet kiss as his lips hovered momentarily over hers, so close, grazing, teasing . . . He knew how to drive her wild, like no man before him had ever done. Every nerve in her body screamed out for his touch, her sorrow was forgotten, replaced by a hunger only he could inspire in her groin. She was an animal now, instinctually driven, her legs parted as her hands found the back of Elijah's head, forcing their lips together in a savage, passionate kiss. No . . . she could never live without this.

Elijah's eyes rolled up in the back of his head as he tasted of her soft succulent lips. No matter how many times he kissed Ebonee, the effect was always the same. He eased up, allowing their lips to remain touching, sliding together gently as he savored the intoxicating feelings flowing through his body from the connection.

Ebonee's eyes closed as she basked in the unbelievable pleasure. She felt his body slide downward an inch at a time, and her walls clenched uncontrollably, memories of his skillful tongue dancing upon her swollen clitoris. But not this time. She had to have him now. Her hands embraced him, gliding over the well-defined muscles of his shoulders; her legs pulling him back up and into her groin and into a passionate kiss. His engorged member found her tunnel like a heat seeking missile. The orgasm that racked her body as Elijah pushed into her awaiting vagina was like no other. Even before he had buried his length deep into her as far as he could, her legs were trembling, her moans escalating.

Elijah swooned as he felt the soft wetness contracting like a pump around his member, pulling him in deeper, and accepting every inch of his love. They came together, Elijah growling a primitive exclamation as he drove his seed deep into her, Ebonee clawing at his back hungrily, her legs spread wide, devouring his offering as her moans of ecstasy reverberated off of the walls.

As the last drops of Elijah's emotion flowed into her, he opened his eyes, staring down into his beautiful Ebonee's light brown eyes. He was taken aback to see tears still streaming down her cheek. She was shaking, her throat constricting repeatedly as if she were having trouble swallowing the emotion building up inside of her mind.

"No, no, baby don't," Elijah whispered, pulling her close as he rolled over onto his back, keeping her in his arms as her body continued to convulse. "It's okay. Everything is okay, baby." His hand stroked her head lovingly as he spoke the comforting words.

His soothing words, spoken with a voice as smooth as honey, only brought more tears to the young woman's eyes. "Don't you leave me, Elijah." Her words came out between heavy sobs. "I was scared."

"Shhh, I can't leave you, baby, you know that." Elijah ignored the tickle upon his cheek as his own tears began to fall. "I searched my whole life for you, Ebonee . . . and I'll never lose this . . . never, baby."

Ebonee's head came up after a moment, and her glowing brown eyes, glistening with moisture, found his. She sniffled softly. "Cherry pie?"

Elijah's smile brought a never-ending stream of tears bursting forth from the well of happiness within his heart as he heard the words. He pulled her close. "Apple kisses," he responded, completing the lover's phrase the two had playfully created when they had first began seeing each other. Then they both finished the saying as they held each other close in the darkness.

"Everythang is cool."

CHAPTER ONE

Acceptance

A crisp autumn breeze accompanied the dark
dressed man along the cracked city sidewalks
of South Philadelphia. His steps were light and mea-
sured, silent as cotton falling to the earth. Also like
cotton was the color of his hair, white dreadlocks
pulled into a ponytail that hung down between his
slender shoulder blades, resting upon the fine
leather of his black trench coat, its tail billowing in
the wind like a flag upon a flagpole in a wintry Chi-
town.

Not many things would bring a man out at this
time of night on the rough streets of South Philly.
But this was no ordinary man. In fact, he was no
man at all, but Nephilim. Born of the Arch Angel
Gabriel and the human woman Eva Garland, Elijah
was a pawn—a pawn in a game larger than life itself. A game that had been carried out through all
of history, an ancient game—between good and
evil. Troubled thoughts accompanied him on his

walk. The dreams were getting worse. He had left Ebonee back at the hotel in Center City after experiencing yet another nightmare.

Brown eyes scanned the dark, vacant lots and shadowy empty two-story projects known as Tasker Homes. Elijah could not remember the last time fear had run through his veins, but the gentle hum of Soul Seeker and Enobe bolstered his courage tenfold. A rare smile found the Protector's dark features as he let his hands fall to the hilts of his trusted weapons. The four-foot, diamond-edged blades had been a gift, blessed by Saint Michael himself and given to the Protector almost a year ago this day.

A heavy sigh left Elijah's full lips, lips framed by a meticulously trimmed goatee, which, like the color of his hair, had also turned white upon his rebirth. For a moment he went back to that moment, when he had placed the chrome 9 mm into his mouth and pulled the trigger. His death was a short victory for him, for he had lost the one thing he had searched for his entire life—true love. Taysia had been killed by a bullet meant for him, fired by a gun resting in a jealous husband's hand. She had died in his arms. It was an event that signaled the end of life, and also the beginning.

"Yo!"

Elijah did not look up at the hostile voice that shattered his revere. He simply stopped walking, lowering his head with an almost sorrowful sigh. He had picked up the two young men at least three blocks back as they shadowed his trail, hoping they would not be foolish enough to approach him. But, this was South Philly, and he knew the odds were stacked against that hope. A single figure walking alone on the streets at 3AM? More like a single victim.

"You lookin for somethin', man?" came the heavy voice again.

Elijah remained perfectly still, feeling the owner of the voice as he brushed by him roughly on his right, and came to a halt in front of him. His companion silently set himself up behind Elijah.

His eyes remained closed for a moment longer; he imagined the shocked look on the young thug's face as he stared at his white locks and white goatee. A slight grin found his lips just before he cracked open his eyes to stare at the man. He was short and stocky, dressed in an oversized Eagles jersey and baggy blue jeans. His face was flat and darker than the night below a half-plaited head of hair.

"Yes, I'm looking for God," Elijah said softly.

The thug swallowed hard, confused by the Protector's words. The second man, becoming nervous at his partners hesitation, edged around to stare at Elijah, brandishing a glock 9 mm pistol as he did so. His eyes went wide immediately.

"Oh shit!" he exclaimed in a hushed whisper. "You that dude that was all up in tha news last year!" His eyes darted back to his partner who had pulled his own glock now.

Elijah waited patiently, silently.

The second thug continued, "You remember that shit, man? The FBI and shit was lookin for dude!" he offered to his partner to refresh his memory.

"Man, fuck that! I don't give a shit who he is. What you got, nigga?" the flat-faced man exclaimed, shoving the barrel of the weapon toward Elijah.

Elijah smiled.

"Fuck you smiling for, muthafucka? I said what the fuck you got?" Flat-face reiterated. He cocked back the hammer as if to emphasize his point.

"*Pain.*" The word was followed by an almost sinister chuckle as Elijah's hands closed on the hilts of his twin blades.

"Man, fuck this!" Flat-face exclaimed, bringing the weapon up to fire.

For a moment, Flat-face thought that it was perhaps the darkness that had prevented him from seeing the dark figure draw the twin blades, which he was now slowly sliding back into their sheaths at his sides. But what he could not figure was why his gun had not fired. Confusion rattled his brain and he realized that he had not yet pulled the trigger. He blinked, pulling the trigger, just as the barrel of his weapon, sliced cleanly to the trigger guard, clanged loudly off of the cement sidewalk.

Elijah retained his grin as his fingers deftly snapped the weapons back into place, his stare slowly turning to Flat-face's accomplice.

The man's eyes were wide in awe; his hands went up reflexively, swallowing hard. "I . . . I . . . It's cool, man . . . y . . . you got it," he stuttered, backing away. Abruptly, he turned and ran, leaving Flat-face alone with the whitehaired "nigger ninja."

WHOOOP!

The sound of the short siren blare and the flashing lights shook the remaining hood from his shock. He dropped the remains of the glock and stared at the police, throwing his hands up in the air as two officers rushed between the parked cars onto the sidewalk, guns trained on both Elijah and the thief.

"Hands up, buddy!" one of the officers announced, staring at Elijah as his partner roughly forced Flat-face onto the ground to cuff him.

Elijah laughed, making no move to comply, recognizing the cop immediately as Officer Jones from a year ago. He was one of the two cops who had tried to restrain him in the hospital after his rebirth.

Jones slowly let his weapon down as he recognized the Protector, although reluctantly.

Elijah chuckled again, seeing there were still hard feelings from their little run-in last year.

"It's okay . . . he's a Fed," Jones announced to his partner.

"There were two of them, the other ran off in that direction, Officer Jones," Elijah said calmly, stepping up to the taller Jones.

"What the hell?"

Elijah and Jones both looked over as the other officer picked up the cleanly sliced barrel of the gun.

Elijah chuckled once more. "By the way, Jonesy," he asked, smiling as he turned to walk away, "how's the arm?"

Jones scowled after the dark dressed man, his coat tail flowing up behind him with the light sound of his laughter as he continued his walk along the dangerous South Philly streets. Jones rubbed his arm absently where it had been snapped out of joint by the slender man upon their last meeting, turning to help his partner get Flat-face into the patrol car.

Elijah walked on for several blocks, snorting derisively every time Officer Jones and his partner, still with Flat-face in the backseat, cruised by him at a crawl, eying him. After several more blocks, they were gone, leaving him again alone to contemplate his goal. He stared up at the street crossing sign, memories flashing back to him as he read the words there. *Bainbridge Street*. He was close to his old apartment, but more importantly, he was close to the Protestant Church that his Grandmother had raised him in.

A wave of emotion suddenly blasted through his soul. He wavered on his feet as he approached the dark steps of the church, draped in shadows by a row of large trees that lined the sidewalk here. He stumbled to his hands and knees at the ferocity of the emotions which brought moisture to his eyes. Gritting his teeth, he swallowed back the tears, forced the unwanted feelings to be buried beneath a wall of denial, shutting his eyes tight, refusing to bear witness to the images of his grandmother's dead body, lying still in her casket. Growling, he rose from the cracked concrete steps.

His suddenly serious glare found the wide red church doors in the gloom. The paint was old and flaking away, just as he remembered it. A blast of crisp air whipped his locks and trench coat up as a car sped down the tiny one-way street, its loud engine setting off sensitive alarms near the next corner.

Elijah stared at the large arch-shaped doors for a long moment, trembling as yet again the fierce emotion rived through him, bringing tears to his eyes. His nostrils flared as he battled back the guilt, fought away the sorrow and the tears, his hand snatching Soul Seeker from its sheath, sending it slicing through the center of the doors, severing the locks.

His breaths were ragged as he stood, his blade still at bear, staring at the half open door and the darkness beyond. His heart pounded within the confines of his chest, the restrained emotions threatening to explode through the wall of denial he had in place. And for the first time in what seemed to the Protector to be an eternity, he felt fear. As he stared into the darkness of this holy place, he was afraid.

Slowly the scent of the pine trees that lined the short city block drifted up into his senses, releasing those locked away memories of times long ago, when he had ran through these same doors without a care, laughing happily as a child, oblivious to God, to Lucifer, to the world. He drew courage from these memories, and silently slid Soul Seeker back into its sheath. Standing erect, he drew in a deep breath of the memories to take with him, and walked through the doors into the darkness.

He did not need to see the short flight of stairs that he knew were there. He skipped up them just as easily as if it were broad daylight, coming to a halt at the entrance to the huge sanctuary. His eyes adjusted to the darkness quickly as he reached out a hand, touching the swinging wooden doors with small cross-shaped windows centered on each of them. Slowly, he pushed them open, his feet dragging as if they were reluctant to enter this holy place.

The sanctuary was as he remembered it, minus the normal sunlight that would grace the large room with warmth and brightness on any given Sunday. The weak light of the overcast October skies did little to alleviate the sinister shadows that now danced in his peripheral vision, muted further by the stained glass windows depicting varied biblical scenes and Saints lining the upper walls of the church just below the high domed ceiling with its intricate carvings and designs.

A single tear found his cheek, drawn forth as his

eyes roamed over the old wooden pews, memories again flashing into his mind. Elijah forced the lids of his eyes closed tightly. A strained smile tempered with sorrow forced his lips to part as he gasped for air. His own childlike giggles floated upon the darkness as if it were yesterday, and he felt his throat constrict as he could virtually feel the sting in his thigh from his grandmother's patented "Twist Pinch."

Elijah slowly blinked his eyes back open, licking his lips as he let the images fade away. Calmness fell over him as he stared to the sanctuary's pulpit and the life-size crucifix which dominated the circular area. His pulse quickened as he took a tentative step down the center aisle, his knees weak. Silent steps across the thin red carpet brought him to the front of the church, just below the image of Christ. Elijah found his gaze going to every fixture upon the circular pulpit except for that Holy representation. Deep shadows clung to it. The weak light, muted already by the stained glass windows which arched around the top of the cubby, helped little. He could feel the sadness of his soul trying to break free as he stood there, trembling. He kept his head down and turned to the right, staring at the small table upon which sat rows upon rows of tiny candles, each line higher than the next. He studied the tall, golden candelabrums, glimmering faintly, each the height of a short man, stationed in various positions upon the carpeted pulpit. He marveled at the magnificent organ with its huge pipes extending up into the rafters of the hollowed dome along the left wall.

You are a sinner, Elijah!

His knees buckled immediately upon hearing the

whispered voice echo in his mind and the waves of sorrow flowed forth from his closed eyelids in rivers. He sobbed heavily for a long while, trembling upon his knees, prostrate before God. He thought the voices had gone, for it had been a year's time since last he had heard them shouting whispered words of degradation into his fragile and tortured mind. Always pulling him toward one goal, insisting his life was worthless . . .

His return here had awoken them. For this place was indeed his torment. "Lord, please!" His voice shattered the silence, reverberating in the dark reaches of the domed ceiling eerily. He fought through the deep sobs, tasting the strong scent of frankincense and myrrh that clung to the room and everything in it. Another scent slowly joined that one, one he had never associated with this place, the slight, almost imperceptible hint of sulfur.

"Lord, I trust in You," he whispered softly through his tears. He searched for the words to convey his inner most feelings, longing to be rid of the guilt which had ensnared him. "But I can't do this without You. Help me, please."

His sobs increased as he thought of the many times in his past that he had turned his life over to the Lord, only to fall heavily back into sin, reveling in lust, even going as far as to doubt his Father's existence.

His manicured nails dug into his palms, leaving moisture there as the blood flowed. Always he would return to God, desperate and seeking forgiveness, but only when his life seemed unbearable, and his sins had buried him in a hole he could not dig himself out of. The guilt brought a new wave of tortured

moans from his full lips. Elijah's body began to tremble violently in the darkness below the crucifix, his
conscience eating away at his attempts to seek shelter from The Almighty. He leaned back on his
haunches, head bowed and eyes closed, the sobs
slowly abating as the darker part of his soul, the side
that agreed with the condemning voices, assumed
control.

Why serve a god who cares nothing for you?

Elijah's sniffling echoed off of the walls of the
dark sanctuary as he gritted his teeth, his soul re-
futing the words whispered in his mind.

*Do you recall Job? And how he was the most just
and upright man who served God?*

"No! Shut up!" Elijah threw his hands up to cover
his ears, his eyes shut tightly.

*Yet he was struck down by your merciful God! His
children killed, his land and all his possessions
snatched away from him! Inflicted with lesions and
sores, cast down to a worthless beggar!*

"Leave me alone!" Elijah quivered as his angry exclamation returned to him over and over again in
the silent shadow filled sanctuary. Blood splattered
his white locks and flowed down the sides of his
ebony skin as he pressed his palms against his ears,
ignoring the sudden vibrations emitted from the
blades at his sides.

His skin crawled with thousands of tiny goose
bumps as an electrifying chill ran through his body.

*And for what, Elijah? What reason did your merci-
ful God have for this ruthless torture?*

"No!" Elijah exclaimed in rage. His hands dropped
to his sides, balled up tightly into fists that trembled with fury. His eyes flared open and suddenly—

his breath held. A wave of dizziness washed over him as he stared open mouthed at the heart stopping sight before him.

A small pool of crimson liquid had formed beneath the crucifix.

Elijah watched as a drop seemed to fall in slow motion before his eyes, sending undulating ripples through the small pool. The sound the drop made upon contact with the liquid seemed to ring out into his ears, drowning out the ragged, wispy breaths he was now drawing through parted lips.

Slowly he lifted his gaze to the shadow-enshrined figure upon the cross, to the bronze feet and the stake impaling them to the wood. A dark line of blood ran across the spot and down to the toe, resuming in a quicker flow as the dripping increased. Elijah traced the snaking line of crimson up the crucifix's leg to the open wound in his savior's side. Blood flowed from this wound also.

The dripping increased in the darkness as his eyes continued to climb upward, until he stared into the face of the statue. Confusion caused his face to twist into an unknowing frown. He didn't remember the statue's head ever facing down; always it had been up, its unliving eyes locked upon the domed ceiling. Those eyes were now closed, as blood flowed from the thorns encircling the statue's head. Then Elijah's world fell into terror.

The eyes opened.

Black pits of coal stared down at him as he fell back onto his behind, unable to tear his gaze from the blasphemous sight. He became aware of the violent vibrations at his sides now, Enobe and Soul Seeker warning of the proximity of evil, but he could not move, frozen in unbridled horror by the vileness before him. He watched as the emotionless face of Jesus Christ slowly began to twist and blur, transforming into a nameless evil. An elongated neck stretched forth from the cross, bringing with it the body of his savior, tearing bloodied hands from the stakes in the darkness.

Your soul shall burn in hell for the rest of eternity!

The foul evil dropped from the cross before the terror-filled Protector then, hovering, rather than standing, for Elijah could not see its feet any longer.. Its mouth opened, and Elijah swooned at the foul stench that washed over him. He could not find the strength to move as the thing loomed over him. Wider the dark orifice stretched, threatening to swallow him whole as it approached his head. He heard the faint sound of screams riding upon the wave of putrid air as if the souls of thousands were crying out from within the beast's belly.

Elijah gave in to the terror, conceding to the utter hopelessness that seemed to radiate out from the dark mass itself. He closed his eyes as the black void descended over his white locks.

Suddenly the shadows gave way, wilting like soft snowflakes upon the sun's approach. From the front of the church came a definitive twill—three arrows of brilliant radiance lanced forth, impaling the darkness, jerking it back with angry shrieks.

"The Lord rebukes thee!"

Elijah heard the words clearly, somehow rising above the heart piercing cries of the darkness that writhed before him. He wanted to turn back to see from whence the holy barrage and voice had come from, but the twisting black void held his gaze. The wounds inflicted by the shafts glowed brightly, burning the creature unmercifully. But the terrorizing wails died quickly and the blackness closed in on itself, blotting out the burning gashes. Elijah watched, transfixed by the spectacle before him, as the demon took note of its assailant, rushing over Elijah with a howl of vengeance.

Elijah watched as three more arrows streaked through the darkness, seeking to impale the demon once more. This time, the demon was ready, its body phased in and out, allowing the shafts of light to pass through it harmlessly.

Elijah saw the Angel then.

Magnificent wings, as white as the purest snow, stretched out from its back, a brilliant golden breastplate rested upon its upper torso, shining radiantly. A large bow rested in its hands and a quiver filled with what Elijah could only see as light was anchored to its back. Its face was shrouded in light, too bright for Elijah to hold his gaze to. A second light pulled Elijah's eyes to his right, behind the demon as it floated toward the first Angel. This second Angel was as splendid as the first, but in its hand it held a mighty golden javelin.

The demon turned at the arrival of this second enemy, but too late. The Javelin split the darkness like a ray of light, a bright laser burning through a bank of snow. It struck the creature center mass, continuing through its dark form and coming to a halt a foot into the cement floor.

Elijah sat in open-mouthed awe as the Angels converged on the darkness. He heard them speak words he could not understand as they grabbed the suddenly solid form of the demon with strong hands. He watched as it spat curses at them in a language older than time itself. He watched them bind the creature in chains, their magnificent wings stretching out, scattering the shadows within the sanctuary. Then, with a mighty downward swoosh; they bore the demon skyward, disappearing into the darkness of the hollowed dome above.

Elijah sat in thick silence, his eyes affixed to the domed ceiling. Again he felt the rolling emotions flow through his body, bringing tears to his eyes. He swung back to the crucifix, dropping prostrate below the shadow covered symbol.

Elijah would never doubt his God again.

CHAPTER TWO

How long will you simple ones love your simple ways? How long will mockers delight in mockery and fools hate knowledge? If you had responded to my rebuke, I would have poured out my heart to you.

Proverbs

Ebonee Lane's eyes fluttered open, a string of muttered curses pouring forth from her sleepy lips as she stirred in the suddenly uncomfortable bed—uncomfortable only because of the absence of her partner, lover, and friend.

Soft moonlight slid into the room through thick burgundy drapes pulled closed in front of the balcony of the hotel suite's bedroom. She rubbed at her eyes, yawning as she swung her feet out over the floor, searching for the ringing telephone that had awakened her. Ebonee inhaled deeply, reluctantly preparing to push herself up from the edge of the bed when she realized the phone had ceased to ring. A chill shook her naked frame as she brought her hands together, tucking them between her thighs. A smile found the beautiful FBI agent's face as thoughts of Elijah and his skillful tongue ran through her mind. Her head hit the soft pillow a second later, her mind easing back into dreams of her lover.

Before Ebonee could pull the quilt back up to

cover her nakedness, the phone rang again, chasing the lewd, yet satisfying thoughts from her mind. Growling angrily, she flung the quilt away, standing in the shadows and walking over to the small desk in the corner of the room.

"Hello?" she answered. She turned to the balcony as her director's voice returned to her on the other end of the line. Her fingers pulled back the heavy material, affording her a view of the parking lot below.

She listened to Director Moss's instructions and then hung up the phone, her eyes lingering on the single motorcycle sitting below. *Where are you, Elijah?* Sighing lightly, Ebonee stepped over to the large closet and pulled out a pink silk robe, wrapping it around her as she left the bedroom and entered the living room, going directly to the workstation and her laptop.

They had been in Philadelphia for the last week, spending time with Elijah's family. A warm smile found Ebonee's cheeks as she caught sight of the plain black suit thrown carelessly across the cushions of the living room couch. Her smile turned as she lifted the laptop open, Director Jason Moss's face appearing instantly. Moss was the head of a dual department in the FBI which handled both unexplained phenomena and internal affairs. Ebonee had had no other bosses, working directly for him since her graduation five years ago. Ebonee served under the latter branch, investigating corruption within the vast federal police force.

"Sorry to bother you this late, Agent Lane—"

"You mean early," Ebonee corrected him, glancing down to the taskbar on the lower right of her screen to see the time.

Moss rolled his eyes behind his thin, wire-framed spectacles. "Where's your partner?"

It was Ebonee's turn to roll her eyes. "Okay, I'll play your game. Where is he?" she said bluntly. She knew full well Moss had trackers on the motorcycles the two of them were given to test.

"The bike is at," he paused, his face turning as if he were checking data. "Twenty-ninth and Tasker. Do you know where that is?"

Ebonee sighed lightly. "His sister lives near there, why, is something wrong?"

"I need the two of you to report in at the field station downtown, not far from your location. I have an assignment for you that needs attention ASAP. Go get him and get down there right away. You'll be given a physical when you arrive."

"A physical?" Ebonee asked, surprised.

"No big deal, routine quarterly exams; everyone has to have one."

"But what about Elijah? You know he won't submit—"

"I'm sure you can handle him. Don't worry; he won't be required to give blood. I've already spoken with the department head there. He'll update you on the mission once you're done with the testing," Moss said.

Ebonee frowned as the Director closed the line and she was left staring at a blank screen. She flipped the laptop closed and grumbled as she got dressed, tossing on a pair of black sweats and her white Allen Iverson jersey, which was a gift from Elijah. She sat down lightly on the edge of the bed, dropping her black Timberlands to the floor next to her feet as she flipped open her cell phone to call Kenyatta.

Cradling the phone against her shoulder, she tied her boots, waiting for someone to answer.

"Can I speak with Kenyatta please?" Ebonee asked politely as a male voice answered the telephone.

"Hello?"

Kenyatta sounded like she was half dead. Ebonee smiled. "Sorry to wake you crazy, but is your crazy-ass brother over there?"

"Hold on, bitch," Kenyatta replied sleepily.

Ebonee shook her head with a chuckle as she waited for Kenyatta to return to the phone.

"His bike outside, but he ain't been over here. Now I'm going the fuck back to sleep. Bye!"

Ebonee had already hung up before she could hear Kenyatta's angry exclamation. She was starting to get used to Elijah's family, and Kenyatta had been the first. Having practically saved Ebonee's life last year, the two had grown quite close. Although Kenyatta's gutter mouth and don't-give-a-shit atti-tude still made Ebonee shake her head at times, she realized it was just a front.

A few moments later Ebonee pulled her own black and chrome colored motorcycle into the half-abandoned, half-lived-in housing projects. She circled Elijah's bike once and revved her engine, staring up to Kenyatta's second story bedroom window. Keny-atta appeared a second later, resting her arms on the ledge of the window as she stared down at her brother's partner.

Ebonee shut the engine to her bike and pulled off her helmet, running a hand through her short, brown-tinted hair.

"What's going on?" Kenyatta called down from the dark window.

"Any idea where he might be?" Ebonee called up to her.

At that moment the front door to Kenyatta's unit opened and two figures stepped out. "Man, that shit was crazy, I'm tellin you, yo! This nigga cut Pug shit in half, man!" a slim man, dressed in a plain, extra large white T-shirt and baggy jeans spoke as he walked in front of a second man who wore a striped black and blue polo shirt, also extra large, and a pair of faded Sean John jeans with a white doo-rag underneath a blue Phillies cap.

"Where you going muthafucka?" Kenyatta shouted down from the window to her boyfriend Maurice.

The man with the cap turned to stare up at her. "Yo, I be back, boo. Pug got locked the fuck up with mah shit."

"Fuck you gonna do, go git locked up with him?" Kenyatta frowned.

He sucked his teeth. "I be back!" he said, turning to signal his friend to get into the parked BMW sitting in front of Kenyatta's house.

"Man, this muthafucka had white hair!"

Ebonee's eyes lit up as she overheard the man's words. Kenyatta too had heard him.

"Yo, what y'all talkin' about?" Kenyatta shouted before Ebonee could ask.

Maurice sighed heavily as he clicked a button on his key ring, triggering the alarm to beep twice as it disarmed. "Why?" He turned to stare up at her.

"'Cause y'all talkin' about mah fuckin' brotha! You need to stop smoking that weed, then maybe you would remember what the fuck is going on around here!" Kenyatta yelled down.

Maurice's eyes ballooned. "Oh shit yup! Das right, I forgot ya brotha had white hair and shit!"

"Where did you see him?" Ebonee asked, rolling the bike over in front of him.

Maurice stared beyond her to the other bike. "Oh shit, boo! His bike out here too!"

Kenyatta rolled her eyes. "No shit, numb nuts. We figured that out already. Ask dickhead where he saw him."

"I ain't gonna be too many more dickheads, Kenyatta!" the other man shouted.

"Shut up, dickhead, and answer the question. Damn!" Kenyatta exclaimed, annoyed.

Maurice sighed and eyed the man. "Where you see him at, man, so we can git the fuck up outta here?"

"He was walkin down Bainbridge last I saw him after po-po scooped Pug," he answered.

Ebonee dropped her jet-black helmet back over her head.

"Yo! Somethin wrong, Eb?" Kenyatta shouted.

Ebonee lifted the clear visor from the front of the helmet. "No! We just got called in, that's all. Thanks, Kenyatta!" she shouted, waving as she slapped the visor back down and hit the ignition. Her black trench flared up behind her as she gunned the bike out of the large parking lot, waking more than a few of Kenyatta's neighbors as dogs barked in her wake.

She followed Bainbridge Street for several blocks, spotting the white-haired, dark-dressed figure sitting upon the shadow-covered steps beneath the thick pine trees lining the block. Parking her bike in between the parked cars, she dismounted, leaving the helmet sitting upon the seat. Her eyes went up to the church doors, seeing the broken locks. Elijah's head was down, arms folded across his knees. Her heart skipped a beat as she slowly approached.

"Elijah?" she called out to him, but he did not respond.

As she alighted upon the first concrete step in the darkness, she saw the blood in his hair. "Elijah!" Ebonee ran up the steps, falling to her knees before him, her hands grasping him by both shoulders.

"What happened? Are you okay?" she asked quickly.

Elijah inhaled the familiar scent, keeping his head down as the woman's hands ran across his locks lovingly.

"Baby?" Ebonee stared at him, attempting to lift his head with her hand.

Slowly his eyes came into view, and the sight of them caused her fears to deepen. She saw a sadness there, a look she had only seen once before in her lover's eyes. It was back in the underground chamber, where she had been hung upon the cross as bait. She remembered clearly the look of defeat that had etched itself onto Elijah's handsome face upon the sight of her suffering because of him.

Ebonee swallowed back her emotions and sat softly next to him. "Found some of your little uglies in there?" she whispered, forcing a smile to her face.

Elijah's eyes remained forward and his lips pursed tightly shut. Ebonee sighed heavily, unable to hold back her words any longer, she spoke bluntly. "Elijah I can't do this anymore." She paused to get her thoughts straight. "I know you only want to keep me safe, but every time you run off alone, it kills me inside . . . the reality of what you're running off to face, the definite possibility that you may never return to me. . . ." Her words trailed off as her gaze joined his on the dark trees.

A silent tear rolled down Elijah's cheek.

"Do you ever think about heaven?" he whispered.

The question tossed Ebonee into a sea of confusion without a raft or life vest. "Heaven?"

A moment of silence passed between the two.

"Yes . . . do you ever wonder what's going to happen when you die?" Elijah offered again.

Ebonee sighed heavily again, her thoughtful gaze focusing on the swaying leaves. "I guess, I mean sure . . . sometimes."

"And what do you think of?"

Ebonee was silent for another pregnant minute. "I think of God, I think of a beautiful place . . . happiness, you know,"

"No. . . . I don't."

Her eyes flashed over to his. "What's going on, Elijah? Please talk to me,"

She watched as Elijah finally broke down, his tongue running across dry lips as he turned to face her with a warm smile.

"Never mind, everything is okay now that you're here," he said softly.

"Never mind?" Ebonee echoed, staring at him in disbelief. "Did you hear anything I just said?"

Elijah stood, taking her hand in his as he turned to face her, standing on a lower step so they were face to face. "I heard every word and I understand," he said, bringing a hand up to run along the side of her cheek softly. "and you're right. I won't run off without you anymore."

Ebonee's expression was one of shock. "Just like that?"

"Just like that." Elijah embraced her and stared her in the eye. "It's foolish of me to leave you behind when I chase these demons. I was only worried for your safety ... but I realize now that fate will come as it may ... the Lord's will cannot be changed by me or any other person for that matter."

"The Lord's will?" Ebonee asked, perplexed.

Elijah sighed heavily before letting a smile stretch across his lips. "Yes, the Lord's will. Now what made you come looking for me?"

"But, Elijah, what happened in there?" Ebonee asked, her hand touching the side of his hair where it was still matted with blood.

Elijah pulled her down the steps toward the bikes just as dawn approached the eastern horizon.

"I'll tell you later." He moved to jump on the bike. "I'll ride you back to my bike—"

Ebonee shoved him lightly out of the way, hopping on before he could protest. "This is my bike, baby. I'll ride you."

Elijah stared at the beautiful woman as she pulled the black helmet down over her hair. "Even better," he said, grinning as he stared at her behind arched up on the seat.

Ebonee laughed. "Freak! Get on!"

Elijah complied and jumped on behind her, his hands reaching around her and finding both breasts in an attempt to hold on. She squealed and slapped his hands down to her waist, shaking her head as she pulled off.

Elijah lifted his head into the wind, squinting as his white locks flowed behind him. He wondered if he truly believed his own words back there. Could he really face the undeniable consequences of his Ebonee losing her life in an attempt to aid him?

He would soon find out.

CHAPTER THREE

LUXOR, EGYPT.

The sun was just beginning to set on the vast, dry, mountainous region to the west of the Nile River known as The Valley of the Kings. Tourists were being led back to the flowing vein of life to cross over to the city of Luxor. There were so many splendors to see for average travelers, mystical treasures and ancient tombs of Kings and Princes. The great pyramids, the Sphinx, and wondrous works of architecture from ages past were just a few of the spellbinding attractions in perhaps what is the most illustrious place on earth.

But it was just a hot, dry bed of sand and dirt to Sam Rayborn. The forty-five-year-old bachelor had lived there for the last six months working for a contractor out of New York City. He was born and raised in Detroit, Michigan, and used to cold weather, so the heat was no factor. He loved his job, because the money was good, living quarters were super-band paid for, as were the meals.

"Sam! We hit something!"

Sam dropped the water canteen from his thin lips, wiping his brow once more with his handkerchief before turning to look down the shaft to his friend and co-worker, Jeffrey Otterman.

"What? More dirt?" he quipped, chuckling as he slapped at a bug that had landed on his muscular chest. He frowned, seeing the stain left on his white tank top amidst all the other dirt and grime. Sam adjusted his Pistons baseball cap, also filthy, and stepped to the side of the scaffold to let a worker climb past. Sam realized that Jeffrey was serious when more workers below him began to climb up at his friend's command.

The narrow shaft was now at least two hundred yards deep and about fifteen feet in diameter. Light fixtures were erected along the scaffolding every twenty feet, where supports were built to prevent cave-ins. An electric conveyer ran constantly in the center of the shaft, used to relay dirt and rocks from the excavation and also as an impromptu elevator for the workers. Circular landings were also built every twenty-five feet or so for safety reasons.

Sam double-checked his gear and quickly climbed down to the last landing just above Jeffrey's head.

"Stone . . . flat and smooth," Jeffrey stated calmly as he looked up to Sam.

Sam stared down at Jeffrey; he too was covered in grime and his angular face always made Sam think of rodents. "Natural?" he asked.

Jeffrey shook his head vigorously as he pulled up his dingy blue jeans to lean over and point out his findings. "No way . . . this slab was placed here. I

can see the edges, and. . . ." He picked up a small
ball-peen hammer, tapping it once on the cleared
area of stone. "It's hollow . . . no dirt on the other
side."

Sam had worked with Jeffrey long enough to know
that he knew his rocks. "Better let Michael know," he
said as he gave the tunnel floor one last glance. He
then climbed back up to the next landing, retrieved
the imaging device, and pulled a two-way radio from
his belt. "Mr. Corvalis, we got something you may
want to see," he said into the radio. He didn't wait
for the reply as he reached out a hand and grabbed
the lowering chain of the conveyer, placing his right
work boot into one of the large circular links to ride
back down.

Jeffrey's eyes went wide as he stepped back, seeing Sam's large body jump the last few feet from the
end of the conveyer. "Damn it, Sam!"

Sam smiled, giving his friend a light shove as he
knelt down to investigate the shaft's floor, his broad
shoulders covered with dust and grime.

"Did you not just hear me say the damned thing is
hollow? Meaning there may be nothing below us except this slab of stone?" Jeffrey exclaimed just as
Michael's voice came across the two-way.

Sam waved a hand over his shoulder to silence
Jeffrey.

"Let's see what you have, my friend," Michael
said.

Michael Corvalis crossed his arms over his chest
as he sipped at a cup of coffee, his eyes focused on
the monitor sitting upon a desk in front of him.
Next to the desk in the dimly lit tomb was the sarcophagus of Tuthmosis III. Behind him, in the center
of the room surrounding the circular shaft where

Sam and Jeffrey were doing his dirty work, the low hum of the generators that powered the conveyers and lights filled the large chamber. The walls were covered with hieroglyphics and ancient drawings. To any other man the setting would be rather unsettling to say the least; after all, it was a tomb.

But no curse or eerie feeling could unsettle Michael Corvalis. He was a man of science, born in Cairo to wealthy English parents and spending several years in Great Britain where he attended college to study archeology and ancient Egypt. His jet-black hair was slicked back in a ponytail bound by a single rubber band. His khaki pants and white button-down short-sleeved shirt were free of dust and grime.

"Focus," he said into the radio, watching as the image slowly came into view. He paid little attention to the local workers around him as they began to clean up for the night.

"They've found something, dear?"

Michael never turned from the screen as a beautiful woman stepped into the chamber's entrance, ducking to avoid the low archway.

Bridgette Corvalis raised an eyebrow to her thirty-two-year-old husband as she walked across the dust-covered rock floor to come and stand beside him, her eyes too going to the images on the monitor. "What is it?" she asked, seeing the definite edges appear as Sam brushed dirt and stones away from a corner of the floor.

Michael remained silent, staring intently at the screen.

"What the hell?" Sam stopped shoving the dirt away suddenly, his eyes focused on the area below his feet.

"Careful, you idiot! Use the air gun!" Michael scolded across the radio.

Jeffrey shifted uncomfortably, holding the small camera as he knelt next to his friend in the suddenly tight confines of the shaft. For some odd reason, he was beginning to feel unsettled.

Sam's hand had brushed something upon the floor, something flat and loose covering the stone. "Hand me the hose Jeff."

Jeffrey complied. Reaching up, he pulled the air hose free of the pneumatic drill and handed the end to Sam. His voice came out in a croak. "What is it?"

Sam eyed Jeffrey curiously as he quickly pulled the small air gun from his belt and attached it to the hose. "You okay?" he asked.

"Feels a little creepy, that's all," Jeffrey said after swallowing and licking moisture back to his lips.

Sam paused at his words, a chill sending goosebumps along his grime-covered skin. He stared up the shaft, which now for some reason seemed darker than usual. And the silence, even the continuous rumble of the conveyer seemed muted.

"Let's go! What are you waiting for?" Michael's voice exclaimed over the radio, startling both men.

Sam frowned, shaking away the eerie feelings as he turned back to the stone with the air gun. Slowly he began to clear away the dust and loose dirt.

"Looks like some sort of material," Bridgette offered, nudging closer to her husband as she too felt a sudden coldness flow over her tanned skin. She brought her hands up to rub at her bare arms beneath her short-sleeved blouse. "Do you feel that?"

Michael's attention remained on the image as more dirt was cleared away.

Jeffrey trembled as another chill shook his narrow body to the bone. "It looks like skin!" he shouted, seeing the edge of the placemat-sized material flap under the force of the pressurized air.

Sam swallowed hard as he finished clearing the dirt away from the rectangular area. Jeffrey was right; it did look like skin. "There's some kind of writing on it," he said, kneeling closer.

"Give me a close-up, gentlemen," Michael announced.

Sam sat back on his haunches as Jeffrey lowered the camera over the find with trembling hands. Sam stared at his friend, feeling his own heart rate increase as the air in the shaft became thicker, making it harder for him to breathe.

"Amazing," Michael whispered as the parchment came into view. He recognized the material immediately along with the inscriptions upon it. Most likely it was goatskin, or perhaps sheep. His black eyes narrowed behind his wire-framed glasses as he clicked a button on the keyboard in front of him, freezing the image and saving it.

"What is it, dear?" Bridgette asked curiously.

"This doesn't make any sense," Michael said absently, studying the image, his fingers working the mouse, clicking and enlarging sections of the image one at a time.

"Do you recognize the script?"

Sweat had begun to bead upon Michael's forehead and he appeared flustered to his wife for the first time in ages.

"Y . . . yes," he stuttered, staring at the image. "If I'm not mistaken, it appears to be some form of ancient Hebrew."

Sam couldn't take it anymore. His chest was heaving and he could barely draw breath in the tight confines. "I gotta get some air, Jeffrey," he wheezed, dropping the air hose and climbing up to grab a hold of one of the large rings.

Jeffrey looked up, his eyes wide. "W . . . what? Hey don't leave me . . ."

Jeffrey fell silent as the air hose banged against the side of the shaft, jolting loose the air gun and sending a blast of air to the floor with a loud hiss.

The parchment fluttered as the air caught below its edge, sweeping it away from the flat stone.

Sam let go of the ring at the next ledge, staring down as he hunched over, hands on his knees, wheezing.

They both froze. Silence filled the shaft, muting out the loud hum of the machinery. Sam felt the tunnel stretch out before his eyes and he wavered on his feet, dizzy.

Jeffrey could not pull his eyes from the carving in the stone that had been covered by the parchment.

"I have to report this to our sponsor," Michael was saying as he clicked on the mouse to bring the live image back up. "Gentlemen I need you to—" His voice seized in his throat as the image danced wildly across the screen. Jeffrey was climbing back up with the camera on his belt.

Michael's eyes tripled in size, and his wife stared at him fearfully. "Dear? What is it?" she asked, her gaze darting back and forth from the image on the screen and her husband's shocked expression.

Michael was numb and all he could do was whisper. "*The mark of Gabriel . . .*"

Sam reached out a hand as he felt the world going black around him. He had to get out into the open. He needed oxygen. He had no idea what the symbol etched into the stone upon the shaft floor meant, but he felt a need deep in his soul to be far away from there. His hand missed the metal rung and he flailed his arms wildly, falling off of the ledge. Somehow he managed to catch the next rung and his body jerked to halt violently, dislodging the heavy metal sledgehammer from his belt along with several large drill bits.

Jeffrey had never known fear like this in his life as he scrambled up the ladder. His hand slammed down on the first ledge just as he glanced up the shaft to see the drill bits plummeting toward his face. He reacted naturally, throwing both hands up as he ducked his head, releasing his hold of the ledge, and the ladder.

The fall was a short one, but enough to knock the wind, and the sense out of him for a split second as the drill bits clattered around him. He moaned as he opened his eyes, just in time to see the hammer dropping.

Instincts took Jeffrey's body into a roll and the hammer missed him by inches, slamming directly into the center of the symbol.

Sam could only watch helplessly as the tools fell, unable to draw enough air to shout a warning to his friend. He breathed a sigh of relief when he saw his friend roll out of the way just in the nick of time. He was confident Jeffrey would be okay. It took every bit of strength Sam had to hold onto the metal rung now, where his energy had gone he had no idea, he had never experienced anything like this ever before, and he had worked many sites. He was just about to lift his gaze to stare up the shaft when his blood froze in his veins.

He watched the tiny crack slowly spread through the center of the symbol.

Jeffrey remained motionless upon the stone slab, his eyes closed tightly. He had felt the subtle vibrations seconds after the hammer had landed. He feared to even draw a breath as he heard the faint grating of rock as the crack slowly stretched across the rectangular slab.

The tremors increased, sending dust falling to floor of the shaft from the walls. Sam found his voice then. "Jeff! Get out of there!" he shouted, swinging off of the conveyer to fall upon the passing ledge. He felt tears upon his face, but thought it was sweat.

"What's happening down there?" Michael's voice came across the radio.

Jeffrey refused to move, afraid that the slightest shift of his weight would send him falling through the slab of stone.

Then suddenly, the tremors ceased. Jeffrey waited until he heard the last pebble fall around him and he was bathed in the thickest silence he had ever known before opening his eyes.

Sam could see the tears upon his friend's face and hear his sniffling sobs. It was the only sound he heard. Perhaps his mind had become so accustomed to the vibrant hum of the machinery that it did not register. Slowly he eased himself up to his hands and knees. He would help his friend.

Jeffrey stared straight up the narrow shaft, paralyzed with fear. His eyes caught the movement of his partner, Sam. Time moved in slow motion for him then. He watched Sam's foot brush against the drill bit that rested half on and half off the ledge. It fell, and he fancied the fact that he could see each twist, each flip it made in the air upon its descent. His eyes batted closed as he blinked, and when he opened them the bit was still falling. He followed its tumble, watched as it bounced off of the slab, once, twice . . .

Then his world crumbled apart in a rush of grinding stone and mayhem. The floor fell away beneath him, the symbol and the slab disappearing into the darkness beyond. Jeffrey cried out then, his hands grasping out for the ledge and catching it as a rush of foul, putrid, warm air blasted into the shaft.

Sam gagged as the wave of air hit him in the face, stinging his eyes and causing his nose to run.

A tremor shook the shaft, dislodging a light fixture below Sam. It fell downward until its cord was pulled taught; it dangled next to Jeffrey's swinging feet.

Jeffrey's knuckles ached, and he knew he would not be able to hold on for much longer. "Sam, help me! Sam!" he cried.

Jeffrey dared to stare down into the darkness as the light dangled beside him, its shaft of light dancing wildly on what he could see was the floor of an underground chamber nearly fifty feet below. He caught the brief glimpse of what he assumed was a statue as the light continued to jerk erratically. It was a strange statue, nothing he had seen before. It remained in his mind as the light continued its wild dance. He kept his eyes trained on the spot, waiting for the light to flash over it again. It had what appeared to be four arms and great wings stretched out from its back. Four heads sat atop each long, stiff neck, looking like they belonged to an insect. They faced all four compass points, still and motionless.

The light flashed over the statue again. Jeffrey stared at it.

It stared back.

A terror so complete jetted through his veins as he hung there in the darkness, fear forcing tears to his already watering eyes. "SAAAAMMMM!" he cried in desperation.

Sam felt a chill run through his body upon hearing the horrifying shriek from below. "Hold on, Jeff! I'm coming!" he shouted down the shaft.

Jeffrey's fingers ached as he clung to the narrow ledge of the stone slab. A sound fluttered close, just beneath the swaying light. It was short-lived, but very distinctive to Jeffrey's tortured mind. Wings . . . wings fluttering in the darkness.

"Jeff, grab the line from the light and I'll pull you up!" Sam shouted down as he released his hold on the metal rung of the lift, dropping heavily down to the circular ledge just above his friend. He grabbed the line, swinging it so that it came within Jeffrey's reach.

Sweat rolled from Jeffrey's head in rivulets. He concentrated on the line, focusing his will. He reached out with one hand and caught it on the first attempt. He heard the fluttering sound again. This time it sounded like there were several more of them. He ignored it as he grabbed hold of the line with both hands. "I got it!" he shouted up.

Sam maneuvered the line over to the lift, wrapping it through one of the large metal links. Slowly Jeffrey's head rose above the broken floor.

The fluttering sound below him increased ten fold and he stole a glance into the gloom.

A brown leathery wing swooped past the swinging light and then disappeared.

Jeffrey's eyes grew to the size of saucers. He screamed in terror as the beating sound suddenly filled his world like a thunderous rain storm and hundreds of the creatures swarmed over his body.

Sam stared in paralyzed confusion, watching as the black mass engulfed the lower section of the shaft and began an upward climb. He slammed his hands over his ears, trying to shut out the tumultuous din. "Jeff!" he cried. But he couldn't hear his own voice. The dark mass of chaos continued to rise. Common sense and self preservation took over in Sam's mind then, and he swiftly jumped up into the center of the shaft, his hands grabbing a hold of the lift's rings. The first of the creatures overtook him. Bats. Thousands of them. Sam closed his eyes and buried his face in the crook of his arm, screaming as the darkness surrounded him. He felt the leathery wings beating against him, thumping into him. All he could do was hold on for dear life. A sharp pain stung the back of his neck and he realized one of the creatures had bit him. He hunched his shoulders and cried out, but accepted the pain, knowing that to release his hold of the lift would be certain death.

"Michael."

Michael Corvalis ignored the whispered words of the mother of his two children as he continued to download the images from the monitor to his laptop.

Bridgette stood at the edge of the large hole in the floor of the tomb behind her husband. Other workers had gathered around her, sensing that something was going on.

"Michael . . . something's wrong," she said softly, her eyes glued to the long shaft. The dots of lights extending down its walls seemed to converge deep below her into darkness.

A blast of putrid, warm air suddenly blew her blond hair wildly about her head as she leaned over the hole. One of the local workers standing along-side her reared back at the nearly poisonous fumes. A second local held his gaze down the shaft, noting the line of intermittent lights getting smaller as the darkness rose. His eyes went wide suddenly. Brid-gette stared at him as he uttered a prayer in his own language, and ran from the tomb.

The other workers followed him.

Bridgette saw the darkness rising then. "Michael! You have to see this!" she exclaimed.

Michael, torn from his study of the image by the fleeing and shouting workers, turned to regard his wife. Curiously he stepped over to stand next to her in the gloomy, poorly lit tomb. His head cocked to the side as he tried to comprehend exactly what it was he was seeing. He winced, inhaling the foul warm air as the darkness continued to blot out the trail of lights, climbing ever toward the mouth of the shaft. A spine numbing electric jolt traversed his spine as the chaos neared the top of the shaft.

"What could it be?" Bridgette asked innocently.

"Get down!" Michael tackled her to the ground just as the madness rushed from the mouth of the shaft. Leathery wings beat hysterically, some crash-ing into the walls, others flying straight and true to the exit.

Michael could barely make out his wife's terrified screams over the rush of sound. His heart froze in his chest for what seemed to him to be a lifetime. Slowly the sound dissipated as the flock of awak-ened vampire bats found their way through the maze of tunnels and to the outside world, a black cloud pouring from the tiny entrance of the cave, alive and soaring high into the night sky in search of food. Workers stopped to behold the spectacle, some whispering words of prayer, others simply hurrying away.

"Are you okay, Bri?" Michael asked, climbing to his feet and wiping at the guano left upon his clean clothes with a frown.

Bridgette stood, her hand going to her thigh below her beige shorts. "A few bites, but I will live, dear. How about you?"

Michael fell to the ground as a straggler bat rushed out of the shaft and buzzed past his head. "Bloody winged rats!" he growled, returning to his feet to retrieve the radio.

"Sam . . . what happened down there?"

Sam's voice was shaken. "I think Jeffrey is dead."

"Dead? Are you quite sure of this, chap?" Michael asked, his eyes turning to his wife's with a shocked expression upon his face.

"I'm pretty sure . . . the floor caved in . . ."

Michael and Bridgette turned as the voice came from the mouth of the shaft. A ragged Sam Rayborn climbed over the edge, not slowing as he stalked past the stunned couple. Blood ran down his cheeks and soaked his dingy tank top.

Michael found his voice. "W . . . w . . . where are you going?" he asked in stunned confusion as Sam stepped by him.

Sam paused long enough to turn and toss the radio Michael's way. "I quit. Whatever it is you've dug up down there, I don't want a part of it."

"You can't quit! There is still work that must be

done!" Michael shouted, catching the radio awkwardly. "I'm sure our sponsor will pay you handsomely for this wondrous discovery."

Sam spat on the dusty floor. Wondrous," he muttered. His friend was dead, and he had left his own heart somewhere two hundred and fifty yards down that dark shaft.

"I'll double your salary," Michael shouted at Sam's back. But the man kept walking. "Triple!"

That brought Sam to a halt. He turned and stalked silently back to snatch the radio back from Michael's hands. "What about Jeffrey?"

Michael raised an eyebrow. "Accidents happen . . . it is not the first time life has been lost on a dig. Why do you think we pay you so well?"

Sam pursed his lips and exhaled heavily through his nose. "Well, guess I better get to work setting up a screen at the entrance. Them damn bats may try to return home."

"Yes . . . yes do that," Michael said, turning to scoop up his laptop from the small desk. "Dear, I have to report this discovery to Mr. Glennville . . ." His face suddenly became twisted in thought.

"What is it dear?"

"I'm curious," Michael began, talking more to himself than to his wife. "How could Mr. Glennville possibly have known exactly where to dig?"

Bridgette sighed. "Have you even met the bloke face to face yet?"

Michael seemed to snap back from whatever world it was that he had just drifted off to. "Hmm? No . . . no I have not."

"What you really need to be asking yourself is how in the world this mystery man got the Antiquities Counsel's okay to dig inside of this tomb," she walked over to stare at the mysterious writing upon the screen. "He must be a very influential man."

Michael turned for the exit abruptly. "Yes, influential . . . Be a sweetie and take care of things until I return tomorrow. Do not resume work until I contact you. I would like to translate these inscriptions before going any further."

"What about Jeffrey? Shall we leave the poor bloke until then?" Bridgette asked.

"I don't think he'll mind, dear," Michael said before turning and ducking through the low entrance.

Bridgette watched him until he disappeared around the bend in the darkness. Then she quietly walked back to the shaft. As she stared down into the dim tube she wondered what could possibly be buried at its end. A sudden chill rived through her like a crisp arctic wind, shaking her to the core. Her hands came up to rub at her bare arms as she continued to stare down into the gloom.

They would find out soon enough.

CHAPTER FOUR

Ebonee brought the high-powered motorcycle to a gradual halt, stopping beside its twin in front of Kenyatta's unit. She waited as Elijah hopped off the back of her bike and grabbed his own jet-black helmet to slide down over his thick, white locks.

"Should we stop at the hotel first?" he said into the microphone implanted within the helmet.

Ebonee's image appeared in a small box inside of his visor as he twisted the key in the ignition, gunning the throttle to bring the sophisticated BMW engine roaring to life.

"I don't see the need. Supposedly, Moss has an assignment for us at the sub station. I figure we could just go to the hotel after we find out what it is, where it is, and when it is," she said.

Elijah eased up next to her. "Cool."

"We can wake up the priest when we get back; shouldn't take too long, and you know he likes to sleep in," she grinned inside of the smoke tinted visor.

"A'ight, after you,"

Ebonee waved him forward. "This is your town. I have no idea where to go. 1601 Market Street is the address."

Elijah nodded. "Try to keep up this time!" he said into the intercom. Then he released the clutch and shot off through the parking lot with Ebonee right behind him. Neither of them saw Kenyatta with her head sticking out of her bedroom window, shouting obscenities at their backs.

There was hardly any traffic on the roads at that early hour in the morning, so they made excellent time, hopping on the expressway and exiting after a quick two-minute ride into Center City. Elijah came to a stop at a red light and lifted his visor as Ebonee pulled alongside him to do the same.

"There's no parking on the street, and I would hate to get Moss's toys towed by the good city of Philadelphia's Parking Authority." He rolled his eyes. "There's an underground loading dock. Maybe we can park there."

"If you say so." Ebonee smiled.

Elijah returned her smile and slapped down the visor, gunning the bike across the intersection when the light changed green. They entered a small tunnel a few blocks down and followed its curving lanes around to a series of loading docks.

"It's the last one . . . I think," Elijah announced, trying to recall his days of working as an express mail driver in center city.

The narrow subterranean street ended with a lowered gate and a small shack. A single guard exited upon their approach. "Can I help you?"

Elijah lifted the visor on his helmet as he brought the bike to a halt. The engine seemed to be extra loud in the closed-in area. He kicked the engine into neutral and sat back, retrieving his ID from a pocket in his trench. Ebonee did likewise.

"FBI . . . is there a place we can—"

"Go through the overhead and follow the signs," the guard announced, cutting Elijah off as he took a quick glance at their identification.

Elijah watched as he then returned to his booth and hit a button, raising the gate. The two riders proceeded through and watched as a large metal door slowly rolled upward to their right. Inside, bright halogen lights lit up a cavernous parking area. Between the supporting columns, black SUV's and plain unmarked vehicles were parked randomly.

Ebonee chuckled inside of her helmet upon seeing the cars. *Jump outs.* That's what Kenyatta had called the unmarked vehicles. She motioned Elijah over to the far corner and a set of stairs that led up to a short loading dock and they both eased the powerful motorcycles into the empty spaces below the edge of the dock.

Elijah sat with his engine idling for a few moments, staring up at the single man dressed in a black suit standing in front of what appeared to be the entrance. There was only a single, however large, swinging, grey metal door with no handles. The man, tall and appearing to be rather young with his Ben Affleck hair and square chin, spoke as he watched the two figures. He paused in his report as he considered Elijah, who had yet to remove his helmet.

"You coming or what?" Ebonee asked, running a hand over her hair as she walked past him.

Elijah frowned behind the opaque visor, hating that he had ever accepted the position with the FBI. With a deep sigh he pulled the helmet from his head to let his white locks, still stained with blood, fall down to his shoulders, and then he cut the engine to the bike.

He quickly caught up with Ebonee as she trotted up the short flight of cement steps below the bright lights of the dock.

"You know I had a nice job before all this shit happened," Elijah began as they neared the single sentry. "Worked right out of the comfort of my own home . . . no boss, no set hours."

"Sounds boring," Ebonee smiled, again producing her badge for the sentry to inspect.

Elijah did likewise, again sighing with a roll of his eyes as the guard stared at him.

"I should dye my hair back to black," he said after the sentry waved them in. He really was getting tired of the open mouthed looks of amazement he got everywhere he went.

"Nooo . . . I like it like that . . . it brings out your eyes," Ebonee laughed.

Elijah twisted his lips as they walked down a narrow hall of smooth black and white marble, their footsteps echoing loudly off of the shiny walls. A large marble desk sat at a 'T' intersection ahead of them. On the floor before it was the huge logo of the FBI. Above them was a ceiling of black glass. Track lighting ran along its edges, with all of the lights turned toward the logo. Behind the desk sat a single female in a black suit jacket and white blouse. Her face was pale and freckled, and her hair was red, pulled up into a tight bun that sat on the back of her head like a spare tire.

"Good morning, Agent Lane. Agent Garland," she announced, never looking up from her monitor.

Ebonee smiled as she stepped up to the waist-high desk. "Morning," she said brightly.

Elijah sighed yet again as he caught her eyes staring back at him, and he shook his head, frowning. He disliked doctors almost as much as he disliked working for the FBI, and now he would be suffering through both.

"Can we just get this over with?" he said, avoiding her eyes.

"Agent Lane, you can proceed to exam room four. Doctor Lazinger is waiting for you. And Agent Garland . . ." She paused, staring at the screen peculiarly. "You can proceed to exam room seven at the end of the hall to your right. A doctor . . ." She had to pause again to read the unfamiliar name. "Pokalman?" she offered, sounding almost as if she were asking. "Yes, Dr. Pokalman will see you."

"Are you sure?" Elijah asked sarcastically.

The receptionist looked up then. "Hmm? Oh yes . . . he must be new, never saw his name before that's all."

"Great," Elijah muttered.

"When the two of you are done with your required check-ups, then you can wait in the lounge which is next to exam room four. Director Halfrey will be in by then," the receptionist added.

Ebonee laughed lightly as she turned to Elijah and pulled off her lightweight black leather trench and draped it across her arm, noticing his foul demeanor. "Come on, it won't be that bad," she teased with a wink.

"Long as it ain't no needles involved, I'm cool," Elijah answered calmly, removing his own trench.

Ebonee let out a boisterous laugh, her voice echoing in the smooth halls. "But a huge spear going through your gut is okay?" she exclaimed, bringing a raised eye from the receptionist.

Elijah had to laugh at that one, remembering the incident in the church back in New York very vividly. "Yeah, but I was allowed to hit back in that case." He smiled as he turned to walk down the other hall. The memory of the battle in the church brought a rush to his brain. The demon Dalfien had put up quite a fight, and it had been some time since he had run into any demons of that caliber. His words ached for some action.

His hand went absently to the hilt of Enobe, which sat in its sheath on his right hip. The soothing hum sent comforting warmth through his body as his slender fingers closed on the smooth pommel.

Black eyes flashed open, staring down from the face of the crucifix into his soul.

Elijah wavered on his feet as the image flashed into his mind, and his eyelids batted rapidly to clear his vision as he leaned up against the smooth wall. He swallowed hard as a man in a black suit walked past, pausing to extend his hand to him. Elijah had not even seen him coming.

"You okay?" he asked.

Elijah exhaled heavily as he pushed himself away from the wall, waving the man on. "Yes . . . thank you."

He took a deep, steadying breath and continued down the suddenly busy hall. Agents were now walking about; some dressed in sweats, others in the same old tired suits.

"Agent Garland?"

Elijah turned, still blinking rapidly, his vision not quite clear. He saw a tall bald man with glasses wearing a white labcoat over his blue dress shirt and black slacks standing in a doorway. Slowly his vision cleared and he could make out the tiny pockmarks covering the man's tanned, oval face.

"I'm Dr. Pokalman. This is exam room seven," the man announced, smiling as he extended his hand.

Elijah shook his hand and stared up at the doorway, seeing the small plaque there that indicated that this was indeed exam room seven. "I walked right past it," he smiled.

"No problem. I still get confused down here sometimes," the doctor said, waving Elijah into the room. "You can have a seat on the table and I'll get this over with," he said jovially.

Elijah hopped up onto the plain vinyl table, trying not to tear the sheet of paper drawn across it. "What's all this?" he asked curiously, nodding at the large donut shaped machine that hummed softly at the head of the table.

The doctor smiled. "That's my nurse; does all of my work for me." He walked over to the machine and punched in a few commands on the tiny keyboard inlaid on the machine's flat surface. "Takes your temperature, reads your vitals . . . among other things," he explained.

"Long as it doesn't give needles we cool," Elijah joked.

"Oh nooo. I do that," the doctor answered with a smile as he pulled out a small needle from his lab coat pocket.

"I was told I would not have to give blood."

"You don't. This is just a harmless dye. We have to stick this in you to allow the machine to see the flow of your arteries—make sure there are no clogs or anything like that. Now, can you take off your uhhh," he motioned to Elijah's top.

"It's called chain mail," Elijah sighed as he slipped the blessed armor shirt over his head and dropped it to the table beside him.

"That's good, now just lay back facing the machine, and we'll get you out of here and on your way. You'll feel a slight—"

"Ouch! Dammit!"

". . . prick." The doctor smiled.

Elijah wondered just how funny it would be if he took Enobe and shoved it up the jovial man's ass without any warning. He growled the thought away, watching as the blue liquid emptied from the syringe and into his veins. He shivered slightly, feeling the coldness of the liquid as it spread through his system.

"Now, that wasn't so bad, was it?"

Again the image of Enobe poking into the man's butt-cheek drifted into Elijah's mind. "No . . . no it wasn't." Elijah smiled, and he really didn't know why he was smiling. His eyes batted closed slowly as he heard the doctor saying something, but it sounded like a different language. The hum of the machine grew louder in his head, and he again blinked his eyes closed, and again he could not help but smile. His lids drifted open once more to stare at the blank white ceiling, seeing the doctor's cratered face as it came to hover over his. He chuckled again, seeing the doctor hold up a scalpel.

Again Elijah closed his eyes, this time he decided it was too much work to open them up again, and he let images of Ebonee Lane remain upon the back of his eyelids. In no time at all, the room was filled with loud snores.

"Elijah. Elijah, wake up!" Ebonee frowned as she shook Elijah's arm, he was still snoring loudly, lying on the table in room seven.

Elijah heard the heavenly voice and his eyes fluttered open with a smile. "Hey. I was just dreaming about you," he said slowly.

"Where's the doctor?" Ebonee asked.

"The who? Oh . . . I guess he must have had to make a house call," Elijah chuckled. "I guess I'm done . . . Damn." He winced as he sat up. "How long have I been asleep?"

"I've been waiting in the lounge for an hour,"

"That's it? An hour? Feels like it was longer than that." He accepted his shirt from Ebonee.

"Well, the Director is waiting for us. Come on."

Elijah pulled the soft, supple, metal chain shirt over his head and watched as Ebonee walked to the door.

"I don't like that shirt," he commented, referring to the basketball jersey, which effectively hid the view of her behind.

Ebonee chuckled as she stepped into the busy hallway, turning to wait for him. "I thought you liked A.I.," she said.

"A.I. ain't got nothing to do with the view," Elijah flashed her a smile as he walked past her with his trench draped over his arm.

Ebonee sucked her teeth, slapping him playfully on the arm as she took up pace beside him. "Freak," she muttered.

The two walked back to the receptionist's desk where a short, grey-haired man stood, leaning over the desk talking to the receptionist. He wore a grey suit and in his hand he held a manila folder. He glanced up as the two approached. His eyes were surrounded by crows' feet, yet their bright blue sparkle showed no signs of his age.

"Agent Lane, I see you've found your partner," he said, extending a hand to Elijah. "Hello, Agent Garland. I'm Director Halfrey, nice to meet you."

Elijah took the man's hand, shaking it firmly. "You too."

"So . . . if the two of you will just follow me, I'll get you up to date on your assignment," Halfrey offered, turning to head back down the left hall.

They followed the short man to a large, carpeted office at the end of the hall where they both took seats in the two large soft leather chairs that sat before a large black marble desk. The entire floor was below ground level, so there were no windows at all. Pictures of former directors and the current chain of command up to the President of the United States graced both side walls. A large mural of an ocean vista dominated the rear wall behind the high backed black leather seat in which the director flopped down in with a heavy sigh. Filing cabinets lined both sides of the room below the pictures.

"Director Moss sent these in for you," he began, extending the folder across the cluttered desk to Ebonee.

Ebonee accepted the folder as she cut her eyes over to Elijah, who was frowning as he rubbed a hand across the back of his neck beneath his white locks.

"Accident?"

Elijah looked up to find both of them staring at him, Halfrey nodding to his bloodstained hair.

"Oh. Yeah, nothing serious," he said, forcing the strange stinging behind his ear away and dropping his hand into his lap.

Ebonee held her gaze on him for a moment longer, feeling that something more was going on in his mind. Whatever had happened in that church was more than, "nothing serious."

"Dr. Pearlman give you a hard time?" Halfrey said, smiling.

"Who?" Elijah asked.

"Dr. Pearlman, he gave you your physical,"

Elijah frowned. "I thought his name was Polkadot-man or some crazy shit,"

"Dr. Pokalman," Ebonee offered, remembering the strange name clearly.

Halfrey's grey bushy eyebrow rose. "Pokalman? That's odd, I don't remember anyone by that name on our staff . . ." He glanced at Ebonee. "Are you certain that was his name?"

"I'm positive . . . at least that was what the receptionist said. Maybe she got it wrong," Ebonee said.

Elijah opened his mouth to clarify the point, the doctor had introduced himself as Pokalman, but before he could speak the receptionist's voice came across the intercom.

"Director, the head of the secret service is here to discuss the security plans for the president's visit next week."

"Thank you, Natalie. Have him wait in the lounge, I'll be with him in a minute," Halfrey said. "Okay, this is recent surveillance footage taken at a PHL security checkpoint."

Ebonee and Elijah both watched as the director

pushed a button on his desk and turned around in his seat as a small screen lowered over the mural behind him.

"This man here," Halfrey clicked another button, freezing the image, "dressed in Arabic garb."

Elijah studied the frozen image in which several figures stood waiting in line to pass through a metal detector. The man Halfrey indicated wore tan-colored robes, and two narrow black bands held down the material upon his head. He also wore dark sunglasses on his bearded face and carried a black briefcase.

"Glenn," Ebonee voiced, seeing through the disguise almost immediately.

Halfrey cocked an eye at her. "Yes . . . the former director of operations here in Philadelphia, and ring leader of the Order of the Rose, which the two of you were successful in bringing down."

Elijah could see the anger building in Ebonee's eyes as she stared at the image. Glenn had nearly succeeded in having her assassinated, and had slipped through their fingers a year ago when they had brought down the hate organization of which he was the head.

"One of our operatives spotted this on a routine check of the airports surveillance operations," Halfrey continued. "We did some digging and found out some useful information."

Ebonee swallowed the anger building in her heart. "Where?" she asked simply.

"Well . . . the name he was traveling under came up blank, nothing to trace . . . but we found other records of his travel. The hub of these trips is LaGuardia."

Halfrey paused as he hit another button to bring up a single photo of another man.

"This is Michael Corvalis, a leading archeological

investigator and interpreter from Great Britain. We intercepted several emails from an account under his name going to a Mr. Alfred Glennville, which is the alias Glenn is using. Michael is currently on a dig somewhere in Egypt, and we believe he is connected to Glenn in some way, but we don't believe he is aware of Glenn's true identity."

Elijah shrugged silently, his face holding a bored expression as the director laid out some papers on the desk before them.

"These are records from different hotels in Manhattan where Glenn has stayed under the alias of Alfred Glennville. As you can see, they're random . . . but we have people there now, waiting for him to show up again." He stopped, his eyes going to Ebonee with a serious expression. "Moss requested the two of you to be on this, and I agreed. Your tickets will be waiting for you at the airport."

Elijah rolled his eyes with a deep sigh, leading the director's gaze down to the hilts of his twin blades.

Halfrey smiled. "Not a problem. You're FBI now, remember?"

"Who's our contact in New York?" Ebonee asked, standing.

"Director Moss." Halfrey answered, rising to walk them to the door. "Hey Garland . . . you ever think about dying your hair?"

"Yeah, I was thinking blond would be nice," Elijah frowned.

"I mean not that white isn't a good color for you, but you do seem to stand out. Just a bit," Halfrey said as they stepped into the hall.

"I'll keep that in mind, Director," Elijah answered, shaking his head as he followed behind his swift-walking partner.

They reached the intersection and turned right, heading back toward the dock amidst the curious stares of other agents. Elijah could only shake his head and think perhaps the director was right.

Elijah almost had to take up a jog to catch up to the fast-moving Ebonee Lane as they made it to the dock. "You okay there, speedy?" he asked, staring at her as she swung her trench coat on and picked up her helmet.

"Are you?" she snapped, pulling the helmet on without even a glance his way.

Elijah was not surprised by her sudden attitude. He knew how she felt about Glenn, and he also knew what else was bothering her.

"Look, I'll tell you everything that went on in the church when we get to the hotel," he said into the helmet's intercom system as he started the motorcycle. "I just wanted the priest to hear too." Ebonee's shoulders slumped slightly as she revved the engine inside of the underground parking garage. She turned to look at him, lifting her visor.

"I'm sorry, baby . . . I just let things get to me for a moment there . . . Glenn—"

Elijah cut her off with a wink. "I know, silly. It's cool. If you can put up with me and my bullshit, then I can certainly handle a little of yours," he said, smiling as he slapped the visor on her helmet back down. "Now, a hundred bucks says I beat you back to the hotel!"

Ebonee shook her head as they guided the bikes over to the metal garage door that would lead them to the tunnel and the outside world. He watched as she stopped next to him and threw open her trench. Taking the bottom of her jersey, she tied it in a knot so that it left her hips and backside exposed.

Elijah grinned, his eyes straying from her helmet down to her shapely waist and the tattoo on the small of her back in the shape of a flaring sun, his eyes went wide. "Hey! I didn't know you were allowed to have tattoos in the FBI! And when the hell did you get that?" he said, unable to pull his eyes from her shapely behind. He could see her pink thong just below the tattoo and just above her sweat pants' elastic waist.

Ebonee smiled behind the smoky visor. "Who says we are? And don't worry . . . you'll get to see a lot more of it on the trip back!"

Elijah was still staring after her as she took off through the half raised door, ducking to miss the bottom of it. He laughed to himself as he took off behind her, more than happy to pay a hundred dollars for this losing ride.

Dr. Alfred Glennville paced lightly across the carpeted floor of his suite in the Radisson Inn in downtown Manhattan. His black eyes continued to hold the image displayed upon his laptop that sat upon the oak desk near the window. Michael had found it, he was almost sure of it. Just what it was that he had found, the former FBI head had no idea. He only knew that his employer would pay handsomely for whatever it was. Glenn sighed lightly as he walked over to the bar and poured himself a scotch, dropping two ice cubes into the short crystal goblet.

"I wonder just how handsomely you will pay?" he whispered into the golden colored firewater, just before sipping.

He decided to find out. Never had he met with this invisible contact in person, he figured now was as good a time as any. He would have to assume a disguise, which seemed a bit ridiculous when he actually thought about it. This "contact" had found him almost two months ago, and considering the fact that he was already in hiding from the FBI, this person or persons definitely knew more about him than he knew about himself. It was odd, for they had even contacted him using his real name, Alexander Glenn.

Perhaps they were old contacts from the Order of the Rose—who knew how deep those ties went? A frown found his lips at the thought of his former glory and the inevitable downfall, a downfall initiated by that damn female agent, Ebonee Lane and her freak friend, Elijah Garland.

Glenn swallowed the rest of the scotch and slammed the glass down on the bar as thoughts of revenge filled his heart. When the Order had collapsed in on itself, Glenn had lost a lot of his contacts. Fear of association haunted his every step, and he survived for a few months on offshore bank accounts under false names, but that money soon ran out. Luckily he was approached by Enoch—that was the alias the contact went by—and offered a very lucrative proposition. Revenge upon Ebonee Lane and Elijah Garland was not an option for a long time because of his struggle to remain hidden on limited funds. But now . . .

His eyes lit up in the onset of an epiphany as he quickly poured himself a second drink. "Enoch," he whispered into the glass, turning again to stare at the image of the ancient writing on the screen of his desktop. "How deep does your well descend?"

Very deep. Any organization powerful enough to obtain a permit from the Egyptian Antiquities Organization to unearth ground in the sacred tomb of an

Egyptian King had to carry some weight. And if Enoch and his group knew his identity as an FBI agent . . . perhaps they also knew Ebonee Lane.

Glenn gulped down the remaining liquor and began to dress, donning one of his less favorable identities. A New York cop. He smiled as he pulled the blue cap down over his salt and pepper hair. It was time to milk the cow.

Outside of the busy hotel he found a payphone and made the call, telling Enoch of his possible discovery and his desire to arrange a meeting. Hanging up the phone, Glenn lifted the cap from his head to run his fingers through his graying hair in the abnormal heat of the October afternoon. His mind struggled to make sense out of the strange location Enoch had given for the meeting. Why would he want meet at the Archdiocese of Philadelphia?

Michael Corvalis hurried down the narrow, repaired, stone stairway that would take him to the corridor leading to the tomb of Tuthmosis III. He had spent the night reviewing and translating what he could of the ancient parchment found on the slab deep beneath the earth. He ignored passing workers as they greeted him with slight bows and nods of their heads. His wife had not been outside, so he expected to find her in the inner tomb, probably already at work preparing the equipment to enter the newly found subterranean chamber.

But upon his entrance to the small resting place of the Egyptian king, he found only Sam, standing beside the mouth of the shaft, radio in hand and eyes peering down into the vertical tunnel. The lift had already been replaced by a sturdy wench, which Michael noted was in operation. A thick rope lowered as Michael silently stepped over to the small portable table where various archeological instruments were sitting.

"What's going on, Sam?" His English accent was almost drowned out by the loud wench. "I did not see my wife on my way in—"

"She's down there," Sam announced, looking over his broad shoulder.

Michael sighed lightly, he expected nothing less from his curious and sometimes adventurous wife. "What has she found?" he said excitedly, dropping his laptop and backpack onto the table to rush over to the shaft.

Sam let out a deep sigh as Michael joined him. "Nothing yet. She just went down."

Michael stared down the shaft and could just make out the tiny figure dangling from the thick length of rope that descended down the center of the shaft. He took the radio from Sam.

"Dear, I am not surprised that you could not wait for me to explore our find," he said.

A moment passed as Bridgette pulled the radio from her hip. She could see the darkness of the entrance a few yards below her as she slowly descended, sitting in the harness attached to the mechanical wench. "Hello, dear. I am glad to see you have returned safely. Did you find out anything about the parchment?" her light accent echoed from the radio.

"Actually, I was hoping you would be able to assist me," Michael said, turning with radio in hand to retrieve his backpack. "I sent our discovery ahead to Mr. Glennville, who, by the way, has informed us to *not* proceed any further." He smiled as he paused to pull his notes from his pack, returning to stand next to a frowning Sam Rayborn. "Anyway . . . I translated what I could from the ancient Aramaic writings, but I don't understand it . . . It appears to be similar to the writings found in the caves of Quhmran."

Bridgette's eyes widened at the mention of the caves where the Dead Sea Scrolls had been found. She had done extensive research on the highly volatile and debated artifacts. She adjusted herself in the harness as it lowered closer to the dark entrance, bringing her bright flashlight to bear. She could not wait to see what wonders lay in the chamber. Slowly her feet inched into the darkness.

"What does it say, dear?" she asked, her eyes roving the areas of the chamber floor where her bright light touched. She was just below the entrance now, in the chamber itself. The foul, putrid odor remained, and the air was humid. The shadows around her seemed thick, like the darkness had weight.

"I figured you would know what it means, considering all the research you have done on the subject. Are you familiar with Enoch?" Michael asked.

"Sam, stop!"

Bridgette's sudden shriek sent a chill through Sam as he quickly hit a button to stop the wench's descent.

Bridgette held her breath as she let the light remain focused on the terrifying sight below her on the sandy floor of the black chamber. She swallowed her fear back. "I found Jeffrey," she whispered.

"Oh . . . yes well, as I was saying . . . the script refers to Enoch, and then it goes on about some great misdeed, and sons of God. Then it says an Angel was punished, buried . . . I believe the name given is Shemhazai?"

Bridgette felt her blood run cold upon hearing the name. Suddenly the darkness around her felt as though it were alive. Chill bumps raced along her skin, causing her to tremble violently in the harness.

She knew the ancient story well.

"Sam! Pull me up now!" she cried fearfully.

Tears began to blur her vision, and she continued to tremble. Her eyes went to the light of the tunnel above; no longer was she curious to find what mysteries lay in the shadows below her. She only wanted to be out of that darkness.

"Faster! Please hurry!"

Michael stared at Sam in befuddlement as the man cranked the wench into high gear. "What is it, dear?" he asked into the radio.

Bridgette's voice was broken when it returned, her sobs heavy. "Please . . . just hurry!"

Her very soul trembled within her being as she felt something within the darkness, something horribly powerful. It had no substance, yet she thought if she were to reach a hand out, she would be able to touch it. Her eyes closed tight, refusing to lay eyes on anything the straying light touched. Her tears fell freely now, and she buried her face in the crook of her arm, only a few feet away from the entrance. The powerful malevolence touched her spine, sending a riving chill up the vertebrae, causing the hairs on her neck to stand. Her body jerked as her head ascended into the light. Numbness entered her body through her feet, which still dangled below in the darkness.

She screamed.

"Get her out of there now! Faster, damn you!" Michael felt his own goose bumps as his wife's chilling scream flowed from the narrow shaft into his ears.

Sam cursed to himself as he stared down the shaft. The wench was moving at its highest speed. No amount of money in the world was worth this. His soul had screamed out for him to leave this damned place the moment the seal was broken, but greed had overridden that feeling. Now, staring down at the slow moving rope, it was all he could do to not break into a run and flee the cursed place, leaving Michael and his wife to fend for themselves.

CHAPTER FIVE

Father Thaddeus Holbrook heard the loud roar of the powerful twin motorbikes as he sat across from the hotel in a small diner having breakfast. Craning his neck to see the front window from his booth near the back, he quickly grabbed up a napkin to wipe a smidge of jelly from his grey beard. Unfortunately it rolled right down onto his white shirt.

"Dear me," he whispered, frantically wiping at the purple mess until it became a long, dark, sticky spot.

"Making a mess are we, Thaddeus?"

Father Holbrook glanced up at the lighthearted voice to see Carla's bright smile hovering over him.

"Yes . . . yes so it seems," he replied with a deep sigh, his hand going into his pockets to get his wallet.

"Don't worry," Carla smiled, her wrinkled skin stretching around her brown eyes. She was sixty-eight, and had worked in the diner for the last fifty years. "It matches the tea stain," she laughed as she leaned over him, removing his plate from the table.

Father Holbrook's bushy grey eyebrow rose as the smell of peaches, lilacs, and bacon wafted up into his nostrils. His memory clicked at the strong odor, and he forgot about Ebonee and Elijah, who had already pulled into the parking lot of the hotel. "Might I inquire as to the name of that glorious fragrance?" he asked, his blue eyes wide behind his thick bifocals.

Carla stood back and placed a hand on her hip while balancing three soiled plates easily on her free arm. "Peaches and Lilac . . . from Avon." She smiled wide.

Father Holbrook found himself staring up at her, admiring her full head of salt and pepper hair, which was styled in a neat bouffant, appearing to be the reverse body of a high flowing wave. He knew where he remembered that scent. "*My Mirabel*," he whispered.

"What's that, handsome?" Carla turned as she heard his muttered whisper.

"Oh . . . nothing . . . I said it smells wonderfully pleasant," he stammered, his eyes watching as her full body twisted beneath the long, pink, checkered dress she wore.

"Compliments will get you everywhere, Thaddeus." She smiled as she walked behind the long counter to his left, depositing the dishes in a low sink.

"Better watch it, old man. I got my eyes on you. Be comin in here distracting my waitresses."

Father Holbrook turned to look up at Marcus Hicks, the head cook in the small diner, smiling down at him as he dropped a hand on his shoulder.

"How was breakfast? Better than London?" the heavyset white man asked. His arms were hairy, and his white apron covered with grease and other foodstuffs. He appeared to be in his middle years, perhaps forty or so.

"Well . . . you have managed to keep me coming back on a consistent basis for the last week," Father Holbrook answered, sliding his round belly from the booth to stand.

Marcus let out a hearty laugh. "Carla's managed to keep you coming back!" he roared.

"Damn sure wasn't these runny-ass eggs!" a patron shouted from the counter, causing the rest of the staff to break out in laughter.

"Watch it, Slim! You gotta come back here for lunch!" Marcus laughed.

Father Holbrook, blushing heavily, pulled the check from the table and left a five-dollar bill in its place before following Marcus toward the front of the diner.

Slim, as he was called, by everyone in the place, glanced at him and winked. "I see you musta had the grits too . . . he's turning red!" he laughed. Slim was a nice fellow with a scraggly grey beard, and was always bringing a smile to everyone's face. His black skin was marred by pockmarks.

Father Holbrook laughed with him and slipped another five on the counter in front of Slim.

"Thank you, Father. God bless you," Slim said softly, his smile turning serious as he slid the money into the pocket of his well-worn grey flannel pants. "'Cause your gonna need it if you ate them eggs!"

Father Holbrook smiled warmly, baffled at how

quickly he had become attached to the small group of friendly people.

"Hey, old man."

Father Holbrook turned as he heard the familiar voice enter in through the glass front door.

"Hey, hey, hey," Carla said slowly, fixing Elijah with a chastening glare. "You know we don't use that word in here Elijah."

"Oh, mah bad . . . *experienced* man," Elijah corrected, smiling as he came up to stand next to the priest in front of the cash register. "Figured we'd find you in here," he added, looking to Father Holbrook.

"Yes . . . yes young Protector, I was just about to join you. Heard the two of you pull in."

"Hi, Carla!" Ebonee strolled into the diner, her smile bright in the morning sun.

"Hi, Eb. You guys gonna eat?" Carla answered.

"I guess so, might as well before we hit the road," Elijah announced as Ebonee joined them.

Father Holbrook found himself staring at Carla as she stood there behind the large, old-fashioned cash register.

"Olm—" Elijah caught himself with a glance at Carla. "Priest, join us . . . there is something I need to discuss with the two of you."

Father Holbrook nodded silently, his eyes still fixed on Carla. He noticed his friends walking toward the rear and turned to join them.

Carla winked at him.

"Come on, old—" Elijah let the words fall from his lips as he watched Father Holbrook trip over his feet to go sprawling to the diner floor.

Ebonee's hand shot up to her mouth, trying to stifle the explosive chuckle that came to her lips as she watched the old man quickly sit up, his eyes glaring down at the floor mat accusingly.

"You okay, Thaddeus?" Carla rushed from behind the counter to kneel down next to him.

"Hmm? Oh . . . yes, yes, quite fine actually," he said, slowly climbing to his feet. "But I think Marcus should get those troublesome mats replaced."

Elijah stared at Ebonee hard, trying to keep a straight face. She knew what he was trying to do, and it was working. Her body convulsed slightly as she continued in her endeavor to control the laughter behind her upraised hand.

She was almost to the point of tears when Father Holbrook took a seat next to her in the booth.

He stared at both of them alternately. "Did I miss something?"

Ebonee fell out then, her tears flowing forth as she dropped her head to the table, giggling madly under the befuddled gaze of the accident-prone priest.

"Are you gonna eat again, handsome?" Carla stepped up to the table to stare at Father Holbrook with a smile, her pad in hand.

"No . . . no . . . I'll have a spot of tea please," he answered.

Ebonee sat bolt upright in the leather booth. "What did he just say?"

Elijah shook his head, smiling.

Father Holbrook continued to stare at them curiously. "What? Is there something amiss?"

"A cup of tea?" Ebonee repeated suspiciously.

"Why yes. Do you disapprove?"

Ebonee caught the smile on Carla's face as she stared at Father Holbrook. "Ummm, no . . . no, of course not." Her cheeks were sore from laughing. "I'll have two eggs, grits, and sausage."

"Over medium, right?" Carla asked.

"Yes."

Carla scribbled the order down and then sighed, looking down at Elijah, who was perusing the menu thoughtfully. She started to wait for him to order, then simply snatched the menu from his brown skinned hands. "I'll just keep bringing food out until you tell me to stop, okay?"

Elijah chuckled and nodded.

"I just don't understand where it all goes," Carla said, dropping her hand to her hip as she stood there, pondering her thoughts. Then she glanced over to Ebonee. "Gotta be burnin' those carbs some way." She winked as she turned away, with Father Holbrook's eyes glued to her backside.

Elijah noticed the dreamy look in the old priests stare. "Everything okay over there, pops?" he asked.

Father Holbrook snapped his head around as if being awakened from a dream. "Hmm? Oh . . . yes . . . now, what is it you want to converse about?"

Elijah shared a curious glance with Ebonee; he could practically see the old man's heart jumping from his body to run behind the waitress. Shrugging his shoulders with an arch of his white eyebrows, he decided to let it go.

"Something happened to me last night," Elijah began, his hands folding in front of him upon the table as he glanced alternately from Ebonee to the priest. "Before all of this happened to me," he spoke softly, his eyes now on Father Holbrook. "Before I came to your church in London . . ." he paused to get the right words. "I was a sinner."

Father Holbrook smiled softly. "That is nothing to

be ashamed of, my son, we are all born into sin," he said, sounding like one of the many preachers Elijah and Ebonee had had the pleasure of talking to in their final search for Glenn.

"I know that . . . but, I don't think I have come to terms with my sin. I mean, I still have questions," Elijah tried to explain.

Father Holbrook eyed Elijah for a moment, his expression intent. "It is not sin you have a problem with, but rather your faith?"

Elijah shrugged. "I guess. I just don't know what He wants from me."

"What happened in the church, Elijah?" Ebonee asked.

The two of them listened intently, interrupted only momentarily by Carla bringing out their breakfast. Elijah related the events in detail, not withholding anything.

At the telling of the demon coming down from the crucifix, Father Holbrook's hand trembled slightly, and his teacup clanged down onto the saucer. "You say the Angels bound its hands and feet?" he asked, leaning forward.

Elijah shrugged between forkfuls of scrambled eggs. "Yes . . . with heavy chains."

"Interesting. Now you say it was as black as the night itself? And you heard moans?"

Elijah nodded.

Ebonee sat back in the booth, chills flowing through her body as she pictured the scene in her mind.

"Father I'm just afraid that if I turn my life over to Him again, I'll only fall back into sin again . . . I just feel so guilty . . . And then there are my doubts . . .

Like the book of Job. I will never understand why God did that to—"

"*Azazel*," Father Holbrook whispered, cutting Elijah off. His eyes were far away, locked in whatever thoughts he was having.

"What's that, Father?" Ebonee asked, seeing the look of frustration on Elijah's face.

"One of the fallen Angels spoken of in the book of Enoch," the old man explained.

Elijah sighed. "There is no book of Enoch in the bible," he said.

"No . . . no there is not, but this book was found only a few decades ago. Are you familiar with the Dead Sea Scrolls?"

Elijah shook his head.

"I know that they were supposed to be writings from the same period as the original books of the bible. They were found near the Dead Sea, right? In caves?" Ebonee said.

Father Holbrook leaned forward, suddenly full of enthusiasm. "Yes, yes. A very controversial find indeed. I have studied them, for the church—"

"What in the hell does this have to do with my faith?" Elijah interrupted, looking at the two of them curiously.

"This demon you described has a name," Father Holbrook explained. "In one of the books of Enoch, he describes the events that led to the great flood, the time of the so called Watchers or Guiding Angels, whichever you prefer." He cleared his throat before continuing. "You see, the divisive books told of stories that can be directly correlated to actions that took place in the bible as we know it."

Elijah rolled his eyes as Ebonee leaned forward,

pushing her plate across the table. "What about this demon? You said he has a name," she said.

"Yes. Azazel," Father Holbrook said. "You see, in one of the writings of Enoch, he gives the names of the leaders of the fallen Angels."

"Fallen Angels?" Ebonee asked.

"You see, my child, there was a time before the flood of Noah's age, when, according to the book of Enoch, and briefly mentioned in Genesis, when Angels walked the earth. According to Enoch, a group of two hundred Angels decided to go and teach man in ways of righteousness. But when they saw the daughters of man, and their beauty, they desired them . . . this is a very controversial point because we as Christians have always believed that Angels were without gender—"

"Get to the point," Elijah said, again rolling his eyes.

"Yes, yes . . . Enoch goes on to tell of a vow made by these Angels, a vow that would bind them all to whatever punishment was handed down upon them for their deeds. They then proceeded to take man's daughters as wives, sleeping with them, bearing children, which we call Nephilim. The Nephilim were giants, and brought great terror to the earth, devouring the birds, the animals, everything, for their appetites were double that of man, and soon, when there was nothing left for them to eat, they began to war amongst themselves, stripping the flesh of man and of their brothers, slaking their thirst in rivers of blood. Meanwhile, the leaders of the two hundred, Azazel, Arakiel, Barakel, Shemhazai, and others whom I can not remember their names, began to show their wives the secrets mysteries in the earth, teaching them sorcery, showing them how to form weapons from the minerals in the earth, taught them to make paints and other make-up effects to wear as rouge upon their faces and other secrecies they were afore ignorant of.

"Eventually the cry for mercy from mankind was heard by the Archangel Gabriel, who relayed Enoch's plea for deliverance from the Nephilim to the Lord. The Lord then sent Gabriel, Uriel, Michael, and Raphael . . . I believe, my memory is not what it once was . . . to deliver His punishment upon the fallen angels. One by one the leaders of the Watchers were gathered and, for their part in mankind's corruption, they were forced to watch the slaughter of their offspring before being cast into a heavenly prison, some sort of 'Abyss of Fire.' The Archangels Gabriel and Raphael then took Shemhazai, chief of the fallen angels, and bound him hand and foot, casting him into the darkness of a desert then referred to as Dudael. Upon him were placed jagged rocks, and Gabriel set four Sephilim to guard over his spirit. There he would stay until the Day of Judgment, where he will be cast into the lake of fire for his sins. Azazel and Arakiel shared this same fate."

A moment of silence sat between the three friends as the priest took a sip of his tea. Ebonee inhaled a deep breath and stared at him curiously.

"Wow . . . but what does that have to do with what happened in the church with Elijah?" she asked.

Elijah sat forward. "Are you trying to tell me that that 'thing' was one of those imprisoned Angels? How can you know that?"

"Enoch writes that Azazel, one of the leaders of the Fallen Angels, taught his wives sorcery and dark arts, and also how to form weapons and instructed them in killing. Many men fell to these tricks and to these weapons, their souls swallowed up by Azazel's dark heart."

Elijah sat back, staring at the priest suspiciously. "If that's all true, then how in the hell did Azazel get out? I mean, what? Did he get parole or something?"

Ebonee chuckled lightly as she awaited the old man's reply.

"I have no idea," Father Holbrook admitted. "But by your account, his spirit has been bound once more before it could find a human host to cover its presence."

"Okay," Elijah dropped an exasperated look on him. "I take it this has some sort of hidden meaning."

Ebonee glanced down at her watch, noting the time.

"No meaning, young Protector. But it does raise the question: How was the demon freed in the first place?"

Elijah shook his head, thoroughly fed up with the conversation. "I'll get the check," he said, reaching for his wallet. "Maybe you can offer me some spiritual guidance when your head is clear of distractions," he finished.

But Father Holbrook's attention was once again upon Carla as she stepped over to the table to take Elijah's credit card.

"We're going to New York, Father Holbrook. We have an assignment there," Ebonee began as she nudged the priest to stand so she could vacate the booth.

"Do you need me to—"

"Stay here by all means, pops. Get ya mack on," Elijah interrupted with a grin.

Father Holbrook looked confused. "My mack on?" he repeated, staring after the two FBI agents as they moved toward the front door.

"Elijah, didn't Director Halfrey say something about a Michael Corvalis being an archeologist?" Ebonee said as Elijah retrieved his credit card and they proceeded out of the front door onto the busy Chinatown street.

"Yeah, so what?"

Ebonee stood next to him as they waited for the traffic to break on the one way, two lane street, her mind working. "Father Holbrook said something about that thing being buried in the desert."

"You think there may be a connection?" Elijah asked, pulling her by the hand as he took off across the street, ignoring the stares he received from pedestrians and drivers alike.

Ebonee sighed lightly as they alighted upon the high curb in front of the hotel. "Do you?"

Elijah turned to her with a wide grin, his hand going to Soul Seeker's hilt. "I hope so."

The two made their way into the hotel lobby and Elijah slowed as they passed a wall-length mirror. He studied his reflection intently as they made their way to the elevator. "I think maybe your director was right."

"And just what was *our* director right about?" Ebonee asked, reaching out to push the call button.

"Maybe I should try to dye my hair. Shit, maybe all these fools will stop staring at me then," he said.

Ebonee could not argue with him. "Well, our flight doesn't leave until later on this afternoon. Go get it done,"

"I think I will," Elijah said as he stepped onto the elevator behind his partner, already contemplating where he would go to get his hair done.

After a quick shower, he changed his clothes, donning a pair of faded blue jeans, his chain mesh vest, which he wore under a long-sleeved, button-down, diagonal blue and white striped Guess shirt. As always, he slung his black trench coat on to cover the twin blades hanging from the belt around his waist. He paused as he realized how completely idiotic that was when he again stared into the mirror at his reflection. He laughed aloud, wondering what difference it would make for the blades to be seen.

"The plane leaves at six PM . . . so we should get to the airport at around four," Ebonee called to him from the bathroom.

"Okay, I'll be back in a few hours," he shouted over his shoulder as he stepped out into the hall.

Ebonee sighed as she glanced down to her wrist watch, wondering where Elijah could be. It was 3:30 PM and their flight would depart at six, which meant they would have to get to the airport no later than five PM. Her eyes scanned the lobby of the hotel as she began to pace on the red carpet in front of the large windows looking out onto the busy street. Her hands went to her hips as she spotted Father Holbrook, walking into the lobby's main entrance with a wide grin on his lips. Beside him, hanging onto his elbow, was the waitress from the diner across the street, Carla

His eyes lit up when he saw her. "Ebonee, I thought—"

"Have you seen Elijah?" Ebonee cut him off as he and his friend stepped up to her.

"He isn't with you? I thought the two of you were leaving for New York," he answered, his English accent strong.

Ebonee sighed, turning away from them to stare

out of the window. "Our flight leaves at six," she said.

"Well, no need to fret; it's only half past three. I'm sure he will be along shortly," Father Holbrook offered with a smile. He cocked his head to the side as he watched her, noticing her troubled demeanor. "Is everything okay, dear?"

Ebonee forced a deep breath through her nose and uncrossed her arms, turning to look him in the eye. "I don't know," she replied, her eyes downcast. "Something has been bothering me every since I found Elijah on the steps of that church this morning, but I can't figure out just what it is," she admitted.

Father Holbrook nodded. "It has been some time since the Protector has had work," he said softly, feeling he knew what was bothering the young woman. He excused himself from Carla with a polite smile and gently led Ebonee a few steps away so they could talk in private. "My dear child, the two of you have been through quite a lot in your young romance." He paused to gently lift her chin so that he was looking her in the eye. "With his line of work it is only natural for you to worry."

Ebonee sighed deeply, looking away. "It's more than that . . . sometimes I feel like he's so far away, like he just closes off," she said, speaking slowly. "I mean, it makes me think he doesn't trust me or something."

Father Holbrook chuckled softly, drawing a somewhat angry glare from Ebonee. "Forgive me, dear," he said, swallowing away his amusement, but continuing to smile as he held her gaze. "For the last year I have watched the two of you together, and I must say," he paused, swallowing hard as a wave of emotion washed through him. Ebonee could see the sudden moisture build in his clear blue eyes.

"I remember once when I was just a lad of twelve summers, I had the most dreadful fear of flying." His smile disappeared as he thought back, caught up in his latest revere. "My mother and I were to take a flight and visit her family in Northern Ireland. I must say, I believe I kept my eyes closed for almost the entire flight. I remember sitting there next to her in the window seat, my fingers plastered across my eyes protectively, ignoring my mother's instructions to look out of the window. But curiosity proved to be stronger than my fear, and slowly I let my fingers slide away if only a fraction of an inch, just far enough for me to see the grandest sunset I had ever witnessed. It was breathtaking; the way the bright, soft orange ball of light sat nestled in between two layers of fluffy white clouds...I was spellbound, and to think, if I would not have overcome that fear, I would have missed the most beautiful sunset ever."

Ebonee stared at the priest with an upraised eyebrow as his eyes remained focused on the window and the sky beyond, probably still basking in his amazing sunset of the past. But she had to give him credit. In his own weird way, he had spelled out her problem for her. She sighed lightly, her shoulders slumping beneath the light brown blazer she now wore. "I think I understand," she whispered.

"Hmm? Understand what?" Father Holbrook announced, snapping out of his trance to stare at her curiously.

She shook her head in dismay, chuckling softly as she realized he was truly serious. "Nothing, Father Holbrook. Thank you," she smiled, leaning close to place a kiss on his chubby cheek.

Ebonee realized that she would just have to trust in Elijah. After all, he was a big boy, and more than capable of taking care of his problems in his own way. Maybe in a way she was jealous, jealous because there was a part of Elijah that he kept from her. Yes, that's all it could be. She would just have to put her fear aside, like Father Holbrook did on that plane, and hang on for the ride.

"Hey, you two. Waiting for me?"

The duo turned in unison, both of their faces holding curious expressions as they stared at Elijah.

"Okay," Elijah sighed, rolling his eyes. "Before, it was the strangers staring at me like I was a leper . . . now it's you two."

Ebonee smiled and threw a warm hug on her partner, her hands going up into his locks—his jet-black locks. Even his facial hair had been trimmed neatly and died black. His goatee was gone, revealing a firm, rounded, brown chin.

Elijah smiled as Ebonee kissed him on the chin. "Well damn. I would have done it a long time ago if I would have known I would get this reaction!"

Father Holbrook continued to stare at Elijah, his eyes focused on the Protector's long black locks.

"So? What do you think, old man?" Elijah asked, looking up from Ebonee's bright smile.

All Father Holbrook could do was nod silently.

Ebonee could see the priest's mind already fast at work and she laughed. "I think grey suits you, Father Holbrook," she chuckled, pulling Elijah's arm around her waist. "Don't you think so, Carla?"

Father Holbrook's intent gaze was pulled away as Carla stepped up beside him, nudging him with her wide hips. "I think it's sexy," she said, winking at him.

Elijah and Ebonee smiled as they turned away. Heading for the exit, they could overhear the priest behind them, rambling and stuttering about the color of his hair as Carla reassured him that it was fine.

"So how do we get to the airport? Ride?" Ebonee asked, motioning to the parking lot where their bikes were parked as they stepped out into the warm evening air, stopping just outside of the sliding glass doors.

Elijah smiled, looking down to her brown pumps, visible below the hem of her brown dress slacks. "In those?"

"Why not?" she shrugged.

"No, we can take a taxi, it's easier."

Ebonee nodded and waited as Elijah informed the bellman to get them a taxi.

"Elijah," she sighed softly as he returned, her hand going to his. "I just want you to know that I'm here for you."

"I know, baby," Elijah replied, a slightly confused expression on his face.

"You can talk to me about anything," she added, her eyes coming up to find his with a soft, serious gaze.

Elijah smiled. "This is about the church, isn't it?"

"Well . . . yes," she said, looking down at her toes. "But I don't want you to feel like I'm trying to pressure you or anything,"

"Look, baby," he gently lifted her face with one hand, bringing her sad gaze up to meet his own, "what happened back there . . . well," he paused, struggling with what he was about to say, "it scared the hell out of me," he finally admitted.

Ebonee looked shocked. "A demon scared you?" she asked, frowning with disbelief.

Elijah chuckled. "No, not the demon, but the reason that I was there in the first place. That's what scares me."

Both of them looked up as the bellman waved his hand to them and opened the door of a taxi that had pulled up into circular driveway.

Once inside, Elijah continued with his confession. "I went to that church because I'm afraid. All of my life I've battled with my spirituality. I was so confused, not knowing whether I believed or not . . . afraid to not believe . . . and knowing that if I did believe, then I would surely be sent to hell for all of my sins."

"But that's why Jesus died on the—"

Elijah cut her off with a chuckle and an upraised hand. "Yeah, I know all of that. It's deeper for me . . . I don't really know how to explain it."

"Try . . . for me," Ebonee said softly.

Elijah took a deep breath and turned to stare out at the landscape, his eyes focusing on Lincoln Financial Field, home of his Philadelphia Eagles. "Well, I guess the real problem began when I first read the book of Job." He paused, adjusting Soul Seeker's hilt that was digging into his side causing him slight discomfort. "It just didn't sit right with me."

"What didn't?" Ebonee leaned to the side, crossing her legs as she stared into his light brown eyes, which were glowing brightly in the setting sun's golden rays.

"The first couple of verses," he explained, shaking his head and shrugging his shoulders as he brought up the words in his mind. "I mean, it begins saying that Job was a just and upright man who loved the Lord, and served him. I mean, don't quote me, but that's what I got out of it,"

"Okay, so he was tested," Ebonee agreed, trying to pull Elijah along. She could feel his uneasiness with the subject, and also his zeal.

"Yeah, he was. But why? I mean, Job had done nothing to warrant any of the terrible things that God allowed to happen to him, did he? I mean, damn . . . yeah, he restored him several times over, but folks died! You can't replace that. That make any sense?" he asked, staring at her hopefully.

Ebonee had never really thought of it that way. "I can understand how you're thinking, but who are we to question God?"

"I know, but it still just ain't right. I mean, to me, it sounds like the devil came to God and made a bet, and God took the bet," Elijah replied. "I feel like shit for feeling that way too. That's why I went to the church. That's why I'm afraid. See, I know that God is definitely real now . . . and me feeling like this . . . I can't see anything good coming my way when the time comes for me to be judged."

"You want to know what I think?"

Elijah sighed, nodding as Ebonee sat up straight in the backseat of the taxi to fix a serious gaze on him.

"I think you have the same problem that Job and the three, was it three?" She paused, trying to re-member the story. "Well anyway, they were so caught up in trying to rationalize what happened to Job, they missed the whole point of it all, which is really quite simple to me. Who are we to question God? We are here because he willed it to be. What happened to Job was a message for all of us. Like it says in the last verses of the chapter: How can we question the Creator? How can we know his will? He who created the leviathan and the great beasts of the sea." She chuckled. "Don't quote me, but you understand what I'm saying?"

Elijah stared at her, his heart pounding in his chest. He actually understood what she was saying. For years no one had been able to make any sense out of his problem—no priest, no Sunday school teacher—no one had been able to explain Job to him in a way that left him feeling safe about his beliefs. "Wow, I guess you're right," he said softly, turning to stare out of the window again. A chill suddenly washed through his body, giving him goose bumps. "Why does that make me feel even more afraid?" he whispered.

Ebonee's face twisted up in confusion as she stared at him. "Don't you get it? You are supposed to be afraid! I know I am! You *should* fear God. Mountains tremble at his command, seas part, Angels bow down before him!" Ebonee was excited now, her voice clear and true as she realized perhaps she was helping him achieve understanding.

"But why should we fear someone that we are supposed to love?" Elijah asked curiously, and Ebonee could see moisture building in his eyes.

"You love your father, don't you, but you also know that if you messed up when you were little he would put his foot up your behind, right?" Ebonee asked happily, thinking she had found a perfect simile to help him understand.

He didn't reply at first, and the back of the taxi was suddenly deathly quiet.

"I don't have one of those, remember?" he said softly.

Everything was a little clearer to Ebonee then. "Well, I guess that explains everything," she said, reaching out to hold his hand in hers as his tears began to fall.

"How do you figure?" he asked, forcing his words through his emotions.

"What terminal, sir?"

Ebonee looked forward as the driver spoke, her eyes going to the large blue signs with listings of airlines and their respective terminals. "*F,*" she announced, her hand squeezing Elijah's comfortingly. "We'll talk some more on the plane, okay?"

Elijah swallowed away his tears and regained his composure, smiling as he stared at her. "I love you," he whispered softly.

Ebonee returned his smile with a wink as the taxi slowed to a halt in front of Terminal F. "Cherry pie," she said, reaching for the handle of the door.

Elijah laughed. "Apple kisses," he replied happily, watching her as she stepped out.

"Everythang is cool!" they both finished, laughing together as they stepped out of the taxi and embraced each other with a warm hug.

They stepped through the revolving door into the mayhem that was the Philadelphia airport. Crowds of people stood in line at the ticket counters; others hauled large suitcases behind them as they made their way to the first of many security checkpoints. Children cried, others laughed and played. It was a sort of controlled chaos. They found the counter for their flight and got in the rather short line, compared to some of the others. As they approached the front of the line, Ebonee's cell phone rang.

It was Director Halfrey.

Elijah listened and watched her as she got their

instructions over the phone. He saw the sudden change in her demeanor, and knew something was up before she clicked off the phone and dropped it back into her purse.

"What's up?" he asked.

"Change of plans . . . Glenn is here," she stated, moving quickly out of the line.

"In Philly? Where?" Elijah asked, easily pacing her as she headed toward the closest set of monitors displaying the status of inbound and outbound flights. "He's in the airport?"

"Yes, Flight 729 out of LaGuardia. Shit!" she exclaimed, finding the listed flight on the screen. "It's already here. Come on. Terminal A!"

Elijah quickly took the lead and bolted for the exit. "This way!" he shouted as he turned abruptly, heading up a long escalator.

Ebonee followed, hot on his heels.

They reached the next level and Elijah turned, running full speed down the crowded hallway, jostling people roughly as he shouted apologies. He spotted an airport transport vehicle used for the elderly and handicapped and quickly ran it down, forcing the driver to stop.

"Get us to Terminal A now!" he shouted in the bewildered drivers face. "FBI!" he added, flashing out his badge as Ebonee climbed into the back.

"Wait a minute! What's all this about?" the driver asked, not making a move to comply.

"It's a matter of airport security! FBI dammit! Now move!" Ebonee shouted from the back, pulling her suit jacket aside to flash her holstered 9 mm. "You have a radio in here?" she asked as the driver swallowed hard and took off down the wide hall, honking the vehicles horn at slow-moving travelers.

"Yes! It's right here!" he replied, taking a hand off the wheel to pull a microphone from his belt.

"Get on it! Find out if Flight 729 out of LaGuardia has unloaded its passengers yet!" she shouted, holding on as the driver swerved to miss an elderly couple.

She listened closely as the driver communicated with his superiors, her hopes of finally catching Glenn rising when she heard the man on the other end announce that he had already received a call from the FBI headquarters downtown. Her hopes deflated a second later when he explained that they had gotten the call too late, and that the plane was already unloading.

The small vehicle slowed as they neared the security checkpoint for terminal A, the crowds too large for the car to pass through with any speed.

Ebonee wanted to shout for people to get out of the way, but knew to do so would likely incite madness in light of all the recent terrorist activity and the war in Iraq. The small vehicle edged through, veering to an opening directly ahead and to the right of the mass of people, where a group of security guards were waving them through.

They picked up speed once beyond the checkpoint, finding guards already making a path through the sea of people.

Elijah kept one hand on Enobe at his waist and the other on the side of the car, bracing himself as they sped through the terminal. His eyes scanned the many faces whisking by, looking for anyone that looked out of place or that fit the description last given to them by Director Halfrey. Eateries and lounges whizzed by in the background to his right, on his left, seating areas were a blur, pasted against

the large windows and the scenes of airplanes taxi-
ing on the bright cement.

A violent chill suddenly racked his body, and his
hand felt the undeniable vibrations in the hilt of his
diamond edged blade as goose bumps traveled
along his skin.

A demon was about.

Standing in the front of the vehicle, Elijah turned.
"Keep going!" he shouted to the driver as Ebonee's
eyes focused on him from the back. "Get Glenn . . .
I'll catch up!"

Ebonee's head twisted around as she watched his
lithe body jump into the air, landing in the wake of
the vehicle in a crouch, his eyes already searching
the crowd. "Two way!" she shouted after him, hoping he had heard. Then she reached into her purse
and slid on the designer glasses that served as a
communications device.

Ahead of her, the end of the terminal quickly approached, she focused her attention on the many
travelers who had already debarked from the plane.
At the gate itself, she found more security guards
and flight attendants milling around the open door
that led to the long chute like tunnel attached to the
plane. She found they had succeeded in halting the
unloading of passengers. However, almost half of
the passengers were already off, and the other half
was growing restless, still lined up in the narrow
tunnel. She instructed the guards to let them through
one at a time, praying that Glenn was still on board.

Elijah growled as he stalked slowly back along
their path, his eyes scrutinizing every traveler as he
held the hilt of Enobe at his waist, letting the vibrant hum guide him closer to the source. He stopped
and stared to his left at one of the gates, and a seat-

ing area situated in front of the large glass windows. Outside dusk was falling over the city, and
the sunlight was fast waning. People stood around,
talking amongst themselves, wondering what was
going on as guards ushered them into the waiting
areas and out of the wide hall. Whatever was here
was in this throng of people. But there were too
many of them, and he had no way to single the possessed individual out without inciting a riot. Growling angrily once more, Elijah spun around, walking
quickly back toward the end of the terminal to join
up with Ebonee as he slid on his blue tinted shades.

Alexander Glenn heaved a sigh of relief as he
stepped from the bathroom stall, adjusting
his NYPD uniform as he stepped in front of the large
mirror and the sinks, ignoring the other travelers
going on their way. He smiled, running his hands
beneath the faucet, his blue police cap tucked beneath his arm. Then with a grin, he ran a hand
through his thick head of grey speckled hair and
headed for the exit of the restroom. When he stepped
into the large carpeted hall, his eyes caught the com-
motion directly across from the bathroom at the
gate where he had only moments before debarked
from his flight. He spotted Ebonee Lane immediately.

His pulse tripled as he turned, walking briskly
away from the gate, trying his best to look incon-
spicuous, mixing with the sparse crowd flowing in
the same direction. It appeared his old friends at
the FBI had caught up to his alias, Dr. Glennville, the
name under which he was traveling. He would have
to find a new one, but first he just had to get out of
the airport and meet his unknown accomplice. He

quickened his pace, walking behind a young couple and their young child.

Elijah studied every face he passed, his steps quickening as he approached the gate where Ebonee Lane stood with a group of security guards, checking the travelers as they stepped through the door.

He passed a single soldier, dressed in his army green uniform, walking briskly, an older couple, tourists from the looks of them, a younger couple with a child, an elderly looking NYPD officer . . .

Elijah began to jog lightly as he neared the gate, and then froze in his tracks. NYPD? He turned and stared behind him, his eyes falling on the back of the quick walking policeman. Something nagged at Elijah, what was NYPD doing here in Philly? He kept the man in his sight, his eyes narrowing as he got farther away. Then the cop looked back over his shoulder.

Their eyes locked for a long moment, and Elijah could see the nervousness etched onto the man's face. If he would not have looked back, Elijah probably would have forgotten about him.

"Ebonee! NYPD! It's him!" he shouted, taking off after Glenn.

Ebonee turned and spotted her partner, his black trench flaring up behind him as he sprinted off, her eyes traveled further down the hall to see the running officer and she too took up the chase.

Elijah closed the distance rapidly, dancing skillfully through the crowd, running flat out. He watched as Glenn continued to stare over his shoulder as he ran, bowling over anyone who got in his way.

He was almost in range, only a few feet away from the fleeing man as they came to the area where Elijah had felt the presence of the demon. Elijah reached out a hand as he caught up to Glenn, aiming to grab the man by the shoulder and bring him to a halt.

Abruptly, the air was slammed from his lungs and he felt the burn of broken ribs in his side. Enobe and Soul Seeker vibrated wickedly as he was tackled to the ground by a large man dressed in a fashionable black suit. The force of the impact sent both men careening across the carpet. Elijah agilely sprung to his feet, his hand grasping at his cracked ribs as he watched the man roll and get up. His eyes were mad, and his face twisted in a scowl as he circled the Protector.

Ebonee slowed when she saw the two squaring off, fighting through the small mob that was gathering around them. Her eyes darted back and forth from the fleeing cop and her partner.

"Go! Get Glenn!" Elijah shouted, seeing her hesitation.

Ebonee obeyed, pushing through the other side of the crowd just as Glenn hit the security checkpoint and disappeared down an escalator.

Elijah's hands went immediately to the hilt of his blades as he circled the possessed businessman. All he had to do was say the words to bring the thing out of his body and then take its head. He didn't care who saw it at this point.

The crazed man charged him with an angry howl. Elijah sidestepped the wild rush and grabbed one of the man's arms as he passed, twisting it up behind his back as he moved in behind him, throwing his own momentum into the charge. They slammed into the black tiled wall, dislodging the small black ceramic pieces, which shattered when they hit the floor. Elijah kept the man's arm pinned into his back between their bodies, and growled as he struggled against the man's enhanced strength.

"*Anel Nathrak*—"

The words to bring the demon forth fell off of Elijah's stunned lips as the man suddenly screamed out in pain, and his strength left him, allowing Elijah's grip to wrench his arm up out of socket.

The hum was gone from his twin blades; the demon had gone. He dropped the man to the floor, unconscious as security guards ran up to take him into custody.

"Take it easy on him. I'm not going to press charges," Elijah informed one of the guards before taking off once more to catch up with Ebonee.

"Where are you?" he asked as he ran. The sensitive communication device transmitted his voice vibrations through the glasses to Ebonee's ear.

Ebonee panted heavily as she exited the baggage claim area, nearly knocking over a skycap that was in the process of gathering the suitcases knocked over by Glenn. "Outside the terminal's baggage claim!" she huffed, slowing as she ran out into the wide six-lane street, her hand upraised as buses and cars honked, swerving and slamming on brakes to miss her.

She watched as Glenn climbed a fence and stood upon a narrow platform beneath a string of soft glowing yellow lights. He turned, staring at her. She fumed as she pulled her 9 mm, only halfway across the wide street, aiming it in his direction, her finger coming to the trigger. She growled in anger as a bus skidded to a halt, its horn blaring in her ear, the driver's face flustered as the impact knocked her to the side and off balance. Rolling and jumping back to her feet, she brought the gun up again as Glenn smiled, placing his cap on his head and waving at her.

Then he disappeared.

The train came to a halt between her and Glenn, and she took off across the street once more, limping slightly as she felt a dull pain in her hip. She cursed bitterly as the train pulled off, leaving the platform empty.

Glenn had escaped her.

CHAPTER SIX

"Pussy walked right by me," Elijah scowled, his voice barely audible as he sat on the comfortable burgundy couch in the suite back at their hotel.

Director Moss sat quietly at the round table with his back to the balcony, his tie hanging loosely around his neck beneath the collar of his white dress shirt which was unbuttoned at the collar. "You couldn't have known it was him . . . it's amazing that you even made the ID at all," he consoled, pushing up his glasses to rest on his nose. He then ran a hand through his thinning black hair, sighing as Ebonee Lane stepped out of the bedroom, still dressed in her brown business suit.

It was near midnight, and Moss had already been informed of the failed apprehension attempt.

Elijah ignored the director's words, watching as Ebonee gingerly made her way to the table and took a seat, her back to him. Her hip was slightly bruised from the accident, but other than that, only her ego was injured.

"Well, at least you bagged one of your bad guys," Moss said, letting his gaze fall to the oak surface of the table and the drink sitting in front of him.

Elijah let the words simmer in his ears for a moment as he brought up the scene from the airport. "Actually, I didn't," he began quietly, his eyes focused on the floral wallpaper in front of him.

Director Moss looked up curiously. "What do you mean? I thought you said—"

"I know what I said," Elijah replied quickly, his voice rising as he concentrated on the events. He closed his eyes, his face distorting in confusion. "Something's wrong," he whispered.

Moss brought the glass of scotch up to his thin lips and took a swig, dropping it back to the table as he focused his gaze on Elijah.

Ebonee turned in her seat. Somehow she could feel the knowledge that something was indeed wrong with what had went down in the airport. "You never killed it, did you?"

"I never even said the words," Elijah admitted, looking up into her eyes.

Moss let his gaze dart back and forth between the two of them as they continued to stare at each other, their minds obviously hard at work. "So? What does that mean?"

Elijah leaned back on the sofa, slouching as he brought his hand up to his lips, his fingers working over his trimmed mustache. "That's never happened before," he said softly, and it was almost as if he were talking to himself. "Most of your run-of-the-mill, common demons are not too smart." He took a deep breath and released it through his nostrils.

"Once captured or cornered, usually they go down with a fight, cursing you to hell with every fiber of their being, while trying to send you there physically. This one didn't. It just gave up."

"It had accomplished its mission," Ebonee offered flatly. She had first hand experience to the mind of the demon, having spent several hours in the clutches of the powerful demon Dalfien. A chill racked her body as she remembered the torturous pain that tore through her body when he had entered her mind.

Elijah stared up at Ebonee, coming to the same conclusion.

"Wait, let me get this straight. You're saying that the thing was there simply to slow you down?" Moss asked skeptically.

Elijah looked over at him. "Well, it certainly accomplished that, now didn't it?"

Moss frowned at the sarcastic tone. Sitting back, he crossed his arms over his chest, bringing his hand up to rub thoughtfully at his chin. "What does that mean?"

Silence hovered over the trio for a long moment as they tried to figure out the answer.

"Remember what Father Holbrook said about the Fallen Angels, Elijah?" Ebonee said, resting her arm across the back of the chair as she looked at her partner.

Elijah shrugged and frowned. "What about them?"

"Director Halfrey said that Glenn was doing business with this Michael Corvalis, who is now, as we speak, on an archeological dig in Egypt," she said.

Elijah sighed heavily, dropping his head into his hands to rub away the stress. "Look, you two do the thinking. I have a headache, so just wake me up when it's time to kill some demons or catch some bad guys," he huffed lightly, slouching back onto the sofa again, his eyes closed.

Ebonee rolled her eyes and turned to Director Moss. "Do we know just what it is this Corvalis guy is digging up?"

Moss opened his mouth to answer but was interrupted as Elijah sat forward suddenly, just as Father Holbrook walked into the suite.

"I have a question for you, Director," Elijah began, ignoring the priest as he came to sit next to him on the couch, his eyes going around the group, hoping to catch up on the conversation. "Why is it that the government doesn't want me to kill these demons in public view? I mean, it is really a pain in the ass."

"Do you have any idea the amount of chaos it would cause if the people knew?" Moss asked. "Look at our country now. After the incident of 9/11, Americans have enough to worry about!"

"Spoken like a true Republican," Ebonee muttered, chuckling lightly.

Elijah gazed at the director curiously. "I don't know, but it would seem to me, that if they did know, then they would have no choice but to believe that God is real. Isn't that a good thing?"

Director Moss sighed, returning Elijah's gaze. "Elijah, think clearly for a moment. In all honesty, what good could that do for our country?"

Elijah frowned with a low chuckle. "Uhhh, save us all from eternal damnation maybe?"

"Perhaps I can offer a simple answer to this question," Father Holbrook said, drawing their eyes to him. When he was sure he had their full attention he began to speak again. "It is a matter of separation between church and state. If all of mankind lived sinless lives, the Vatican would surely be the seat of power in this world."

"But surely the Vatican knows about these demons. I mean, there's a church in London with a damn arsenal in its basement. Hell, you work for the Vatican!" Elijah interjected.

"I serve only one master, young Protector," Father Holbrook scolded with a grin. "And until He comes to me and tells me otherwise, I will carry out my position as directed to me by the church."

Elijah shook his head, confused. "Okay, I'm lost. Why in the hell would the church not want the people to know that God is real without a doubt?"

"I cannot speak for those who sit above me, but I for one would consider the obvious reasons for them to be cautious about such a thing," Father Holbrook said.

Elijah growled, scowling at the priest. "Old man, you've said simple and obvious one too many times. Just come the hell out and say it!"

All eyes once again focused on Father Holbrook.

"Revelations," he offered flatly.

"Michael, please! You have to listen to me!" Bridgette Corvalis shouted lividly. She was beside herself with fear as she stalked behind her husband who was preparing to venture back down into the shaft.

Sam watched the two of them from his position near the tomb of Tuthmosis III, on the other side of the chamber away from the shaft they had opened in the floor of the tomb. His eyes ventured often to the exit. He was tempted to walk right out in light of the madness of the last thirty-two hours.

"Please, Michael! We have to seal this evil place back up!" Bridgette shouted at her husband's back. She had felt the malevolence deep within the chamber first hand, had felt its vileness upon her skin.

Michael turned to her with a frown as he pulled on a pair of thick work gloves. "Of all the foolishness I've witnessed come from your mouth in our four years of marriage I never would have thought the day would come when Bridgette Corvalis would utter such nonsense!" he said, pushing away her hands as she continued to grab at him.

"Michael, I have studied the scrolls! I know what's down there!" she ranted, her blond hair wild. "You know I am right! Please, Michael!"

"Oh for God sakes, Bridgette! Give it a rest!" Michael cried, grabbing his wife by the arms and shaking her violently. "The only thing in that blasted hole is bats, a dead man, and the glory of newfound archeological wonders!" His eyes were glossed over as he made the proclamation. "Which will exalt the name Corvalis into the history books!"

Bridgette stared up into his almost maniacal expression, snatching out of his grasp. "You're mad!"

Michael chuckled, an eerie sound that reverbed throughout the dim chamber. "You hear this, Sam? A moment ago she is spouting off about evil and dead Angels! Now I am the one who's mad!" He glanced over to Sam, who simply shook his head, crossing his thick arms across his chest.

Michael sighed deeply, stepping again to hold his wife at arm's length, staring down into her terror-filled blue eyes. "Perhaps you should go back to the hotel and get some rest, dear. It is obvious that the lack of sleep is affecting your judgment," he soothed.

Bridgette inhaled deeply, returning her husband's

sympathetic gaze with one of resolution. "Very well," she began, her hands going up to straighten her mussed hair as she tried to regain a bit of her composure. "If you truly must continue with this course of action, against my warnings, then I have no choice but to respect your decision." She picked up the end of the cable that would lower him into the shaft. "Do be careful, dear."

Sam rolled his eyes, his head shaking increasing as he watched the eccentric couple. "Takes a damned fool ta marry a damned fool," he muttered, seeing Michael's smile stretch below his hawk like nose.

"Excellent!" Michael beamed, taking the cable from his wife's hand and quickly attaching it to the body harness. "Sam! We are ready!" he exclaimed, motioning for Sam to come over to the shaft's entrance.

Sam sighed heavily, still shaking his head as he stared at a worker who was eyeing the group curiously. Sam's shoulders trembled as a violent chill shook him right between their bulging blades, traveling quickly throughout the rest of his body. He stalked slowly past the worker, who gave him a dour look just before disappearing through the exit. He wondered if these damned fools would even notify Jeffrey's next of kin, whoever that might be.

"I thought you said *The Man* said not to go in there?" Sam asked in a curious, but sarcastic tone, his hand reaching up to adjust the cranks and pulleys above the shaft.

Michael snorted and didn't bother to reply. He had heard enough from these fools. Of course *The Man* had said not to go inside, but with such a possible historical discovery looming only a few hundred yards down the vertical shaft, Michael could have cared less what *The Man* had said. And besides, he was a world away, and patience was not a Corvalis strong point.

Sam eyed Bridgette as Michael climbed up over the lip of the wide hole; her fear seemed to have been replaced by anger, for she was glaring at her husband with daggers in her eyes.

Bridgette knew her husband could be stubborn as a mule, but this was beyond stubborn. This was just plain stupid, and he would have realized that if he would have taken a few Sundays off and went to mass with her every now and then. But no, Michael did not share Bridgette's religious fervor, so it was that Bridgette's thoughts began to roam. She wondered if their life insurance policies were up to date.

"Okay, slowly," Michael instructed, looking at Sam.

Sam shrugged, hitting the lever with his hand. "Your funeral," he said flatly, ignoring the scowl that Michael shot him as his head lowered past the lip of the hole.

Sam and Bridgette stood silently, the low hum of the generator the only sound in the room as they watched Michael slowly descend into the wide, sporadically lit shaft. Many of the lights had been damaged by the incident with the bats. Sam still couldn't believe that many bats could exist in one place at one time.

"Madame Corvalis?"

Bridgette sighed as she heard the soft words behind her, knowing the heavily accented voice belonging to Jahari, the lead local worker. She didn't even turn to reply.

"Yes, yes . . . all of you can go!" she dismissed him with a wave of her hand. Having the heavy work out of the way, they had already released over half of the laborers.

Jahari bowed once and then shook his head as he stared at Sam, his expression one of pity. Then he turned on his sandaled heel and quickly strode to the exit. The remaining six workers waited just beyond the chamber's low doorway in the shadows, awaiting his return.

Sam rolled his eyes as he heard the elated voices outside of the tomb. "Just what I need . . . alone in a tomb with you two," he muttered, receiving a frown from Bridgette.

Jahari slowed, letting his co-workers rush out into the evening heat of the Egyptian desert. His eyes followed the last of them turning a sharp bend in the tunnel ahead. He then stopped when he himself came to the bend, peering around to ensure that all were gone. Slowly their voices ceased to echo through the labyrinth-like tunnels, until only he could hear the sound of his own breathing and the low hum of the generator back in the main tomb.

Jahari sighed lightly, resting his back against the carved stone walls, his thoughts going immediately to the path that lead to the upper chamber, where treasures awaited for the taking. He was nothing more than a lowly grave robber like his father before him and his father before him. His only problem was how to get whatever goods he could pilfer past the guards stationed at the tomb's entrance.

Silently, Jahari slid down to kneel against the wall, cursing his father for having it so easy in his time. There were no guards with automatic weapons stationed all over the great valley of riches to gun him down or inspect his dung hole! He angrily slapped at a scarab that wondered up his dusty, sand colored robe, cursing it. Pray that it could have been a scorpion! A thousand scorpions for that matter, to sting him to death and rid him of this cursed legacy of thievery he had inherited from his ancestors!

Jahari's prayer nearly came true.

At first he thought the strange vision to be a trick of the lights, stretching around the sharp bend, casting their shadows in strange ways across the dust floor of the tunnel. A second scarab dropped from the ceiling, bouncing off of his covered head.

Jahari breathed in a deep breath, jumping alertly to his feet, his eyes trained on the many black objects crawling toward him from the direction of the main tomb. He swallowed hard, his heart skipping a beat in his chest as he pressed his back against the wall, watching as the procession of tiny beetles continued to come forth from the darkness. He heard the tiny clattering then, as their armored legs clicked off of the hard floor, hundreds of them, thousands! He found himself barely able to draw breath as they closed upon him. Frozen in fear, Jahari closed his eyes, uttering a prayer to Allah, beseeching him to forgive him for his sacrilegious thoughts. Perhaps a curse had fallen upon his head, a curse for thinking to rob the grave of a King of Egypt.

Tears fell from his tightly closed eyes as the clacking sound became almost unbearable. They were on top of him. They had to be! Surely he would feel the sting as they would begin to mince the skin from his cursed bones!

The clacking sound drifted away, leaving him in the tunnel, in darkness, his whined prayer echoing around him. Tears ran down his cheeks as he rocked back and forth against the stone, slowly becoming aware that he was still alive. He cracked an eye open curiously, staring at the last beetle as it scurried to keep up with the mass exodus, turning the corner and disappearing from sight. Jahari swore he would never steal again as he dropped down to his knees, bowing and thanking the gods for their mercy.

He then heard the low shouts from the tunnel's entrance.

Surely the guards had fled.

Jahari wasted no time jumping to his feet, knowing that this would be his only opportunity. His prayers were left behind as he sprinted back toward the upper chamber.

Sam exhaled a tired breath, resting his hands on the lip of the hole as he stared over at Bridgette, who stood with arms crossed, her eyes focused down the shaft. "Lady . . . just so ya know," he said gruffly, as he pulled his grungy Pistons hat down on his head tighter to cover his eyes. "When the time comes ta be headin' for the door," he gave her a serious look, "make sure you ain't between me and it." "Stop!"

Sam huffed, reaching up to hit a lever, bringing the wench to a halt. He kept his eyes on Bridgette as he brought the radio up to his lips. "Havin' problems down there, Captain Courageous?" he teased, enjoying the frown displayed on Bridgette's face.

"Problems? No, no. I'm at the entrance . . . just want to get a few flares down there first," Michael announced calmly. "There, that should—"

Michael's words fell off abruptly. Sam and Bridgette both focused intently on the radio.

Michael's feet swung just above the small opening in the floor of the shaft. His body angled awkwardly to the side as he tried to peer through the darkness, searching for the bright burning flare he had just let go of.

Sweat rolled freely from his forehead in the humid confines of the vertical tunnel, and the pungent odor was still strong in the air. He continued to twist around, his body swinging in circles as he scowled, unable to see through the shroud of pitch black at his feet.

He could not understand why the flare had died. Was there not enough oxygen in the chamber? Was there water perhaps? Maybe the flare was faulty? Or was the darkness just that thick? Maybe his wife was right, maybe—maybe it was not the darkness alone that cloaked the light of the flare.

"Dear, are you okay?" Bridgette's voice startled him as it came across the radio he held in his hand.

He let himself drift slowly around in a circle for a few moments more, staring down into the blackness. Then his eyes went wide, picking up the soft reddish glow of the flare far below him. It was weak, a small five foot diameter globe of frail light that virtually struggled against the overwhelming darkness of the chamber.

A chill caused him to tremble within the harness as his wife's fearful cries sounded in his memory. "I'm fine, dear," he said, forcing the feelings away as he pulled a bright spot light from his belt. "Okay, Sam . . . I can see the floor, looks like about another fifty feet," He inhaled a deep breath, bolstering his resolve. "Take me down."

* * *

Jahari crept silently along the dim tunnel of worked stone until he found the staircase leading up to the secondary tomb. The narrow path inclined steeply at a sharp angle, its stone steps long ago worn away by floods, leaving only curved indentations to climb up. He glanced toward the main tomb's entrance ahead, hearing the muffled voices of Sam and Bridgette, and then darted quickly up the incline, using the smooth grooves carved into the walls, one running the length of the upgrade on each side at about waist height, for leverage to pull himself up.

He was breathing hard by the time he reached the small, circular opening at the top. Ducking low, he stepped into the dark room. He found himself in a dark cubby, set within the floor of the room's entrance and quickly removed a wax candle and a match from the folds of his robe. The soft yellow flame shed its light on the area. The cubby he was in was actually where they had dug into the tomb, below the actual stone slab that had been set in place thousands of years ago.

Jahari could not quell the beating of his heart as he brought the candle up high and stood on his tiptoes, peering over the walls of the cubby into the small chamber. It struck him odd that no matter how many of the tombs he had been in, no matter how often he had frequented them, they still sent fearful chills through his body. There was something about the dark painted walls, something about the ancient craftsmen that had built these graves with their blood, sweat, and tears. It was almost as if their spirits had been forever captured in their creations.

Jahari snorted derisively as his eyes scanned over

the empty room. There was nothing but dirt and empty cubby's cut out in the stone walls, where he was sure once sat valuable pieces of Egyptian art. His dejection overshadowed the fear he always felt when alone in the creepy rooms as his eyes fell upon a single stone sepulcher sitting against the far wall. The lid of the tomb, a heavy slab, leaned against it upon the floor. Perhaps there were jewels inside!

Quickly, he sat the candle upon the floor and climbed up, scooping the candle back up as he rushed forward. He froze in his tracks a few feet before he could see into the crypt. What if the mummified remains were still there? His swallow of saliva was loud in the small room as he inhaled deeply, forcing his feet to shuffle forward. "Am I a coward or a thief?" he whispered, trying to find the courage to continue.

The flame danced softly, casting restless shadows upon the walls, making the painted images seem to move of their own volition. He closed his eyes, stepping up to the side of the grave. He took three deep breaths, and braced himself for whatever he would see in the tomb.

The body was there.

The shock of the sight evaporated quickly, for there were no jewels here. There was nothing, nothing but a dried up, black husk of skin and bones.

The candle flickered wildly.

Jahari trembled as he stared at the flame, watching its wild dance, wondering why it would move in such a way in the silent, breezeless room.

The chill that traversed his spine at that moment caused him to spill the wax onto his hand, releasing the candle to fall. He knew then that he was not alone. He felt the presence behind him, causing the hairs on his neck to stand on end, and when he turned, he saw everything and nothing at all. Fear filled his heart to the point of combustion as the presence settled over him, filling him, tormenting him vilely in a million ways before the candle hit the ground.

Michael's eyes followed the wide shaft of light as he descended into the darkness above the burning flare. He estimated the room to be about as wide as it was deep as the light flashed across the cold, rocky surfaces surrounding him. Jagged outcroppings of stone filled the room, giving it the appearance of a natural cave, not something man made. The floor slowly drew closer, and he saw that it too, was solid, unshaped rock.

A wave of terror flashed through him suddenly as the light passed over something upon the uneven stone floor. "Christ!"

Sam stepped back from the mouth of the shaft as he heard the exclamation, his escape route clear in his mind as he eyed Bridgette, who held the radio.

"What? What is it, Michael?" she shouted, staring down into the hole.

There was a long moment of silence, and Sam inched away another step. Bridgett's hand hovered over the lever that would bring her husband back up the shaft.

"I've found Jeffrey."

Bridgette let out a deep sigh of relief as her husband's words echoed in the chamber; at the same moment a violent chill penetrated her soul.

Sam felt it too, his eyes turning back to the entrance of the tomb curiously, expecting to see a

host of mummies walking in through the low opening.

"He's dead, all right."

Sam swallowed the fear in his throat and stepped
back to the shaft, glancing over his shoulder ner-
vously as he felt the chill lingering in his bones.

"Okay, I'm on the floor of the chamber . . . well,
actually . . . it's not a chamber at all, looks like a
cave," Michael said, his feet straddling the flare as
he shined the light down on Jeffrey's body.

"Wonderful," Sam muttered, shrugging the resid-
ual effects of the chill off as he waved Bridgette
away from the wench, taking the radio from her
hand. "I'm sending down the second harness."

Bridgette accepted the radio back as Sam went to
work. "Do you see anything else, Michael?"

"No . . . nothing but rocks and—" His voice broke
off, and Bridgette's body stiffened. "My God . . . this
is very odd."

Michael tried to hold the light steady, but his
hands were trembling. Something about the statues
he now gazed at unsettled him. Michael stood on a
slightly higher area of the cave and looked down
over a small grouping of large, half-buried boulders. Just beyond the boulders, about twenty feet
away, stood the statues. The small circle of light
danced over them as his hand continued to shake.

He took a deep breath and steadied the narrow
beam, guiding it and his eyes over the strange
grouping. There were four of them from what he
could tell, each standing about eight feet tall. He
couldn't really tell because of the reddish glow of
the flare, but they seemed to be painted a fiery red
color. Michael trained the light on one of the sculp-

tures, letting the light begin at the foot and work its way up to the head, or *heads* he soon realized.

"There are some sort of statues down here," he began, briefly taking his eyes off of his findings to glance up to the hole in the ceiling as he heard the harness hit the edge of the slab when it entered. Then he turned his gaze back to the statues, his face instantly contorting into confusion. "That's odd," he muttered, trying to recall their exact positions.

"What type of statues, Michael? What do they look like? Can you describe them?" Bridgette's voice echoed off of the dark walls of the cave, sending chills through Michael's body.

"I can see four of them . . . I believe they are all the same, or very similar," he answered, again following the light as it roamed over one of the stone figures.

"Describe it to me, Michael."

"Well, it appears to have wings," he paused, squinting. "Six of them actually . . . and four heads . . . grotesque to be certain!" he added, pursing his lips as he silently surveyed the figures details.

The artistry was amazing; a set of lower wings branched out from the back of the torso, folding over to cover its feet, preventing any onlooker from telling whether the creature was coming or going. A second set of wings hid the creature's gender.

Michael took his gaze from them once more to grab the harness as it lowered to within reach. He struggled briefly with the dead body, but finally managed to get the harness around it. "Okay, Sam. You can haul him up."

"Can you see the statue's feet, Michael?" Bridgette

sounded almost as if she knew the answer to her own question.

Michael returned his gaze to the statues, wiping sweat from his forehead. "No, its wings are covering them," he answered.

"*Seraphim*," Bridgette whispered, her face going pale, just as Sam leaned over the lip of the shaft to check on the ascent of Jeffrey's body.

"Poor shmuck," Sam muttered, watching the limp body sway as it reached the halfway point of the shaft. Again he felt the chill, this time stronger than before, causing him to tremble in the weak light of the chamber. His hands gripped the lip of the opening and he was suddenly very afraid. The hair on his neck stood up as if it was electrified, and he found he could not move now even if he wanted to. He was paralyzed by fear.

Something was behind him, and not just Bridgette.

Sam wanted to run then, he wanted to turn and sprint from the tomb as fast as he could, but he could not pull himself to do so. All he could do, as tears began to well up in his eyes, was stare down at Jeffrey's dead body, spinning lazily as it was hoisted through the shaft.

Then the fearful feelings were given physical form.

Sam was a hard man, tall and muscular, and not too many things in this world could make this grown man cry.

But cry he did, as he was suddenly staring into Bridgette's wide eyes. Her head seemed to fall in slow motion, staring back up at him with a horror-filled expression before finally skipping off of the rocky walls of the shaft, tumbling down into the darkness.

Adrenaline rushed through Sam's veins as he realized death was at his back. He turned, his back pressed against the circular well-like wall built up around the hole in the ground. His skin crawled as he stared into the eyes of the local worker that stood before him. His face showed no emotion, but the madness was clear in Jahiri's brown eyes. A bloody machete rested in his right hand.

Sam swallowed hard, preparing to push himself off of the wall and past the mad worker. Somehow he knew there would be no talking to this . . . thing. He could feel the evil thickening in the chamber, causing the lights to dim. No, this worker was not himself. Something foul and sinister controlled him, and Sam had no intentions of finding out what.

Jahari's eyes flickered momentarily as he held Sam in his gaze. Sam brought his right foot up behind him, bracing it for a push that would send him on his way to the exit.

The eyes staring at Sam were not Jahari's, and he felt sickened to his stomach as they slowly ran up and down his body, as if they were assessing him. Then Sam watched as the eyes focused on its own thin, frail body.

Sam bolted. He rushed past the worker, ignoring the chill that ran across his skin as he passed. He didn't look back as he neared the exit, so he didn't see the figure suddenly collapse to the dirt floor.

His heart pounded in his chest as he ducked low in his run, the exit just before him.

Then the strangest thing happened.

Sam watched as the tomb exit suddenly began to

shrink, growing smaller and smaller in his sight. He felt his body stop and turn back to the room, and even that seemed to be dwindling in size, everything was shrinking—or was he falling? And why was everything getting darker? He tried to focus his vision on the sarcophagus to his right, which seemed gigantic now. He tried to force the dwindling feeling away, but he kept falling. The room was enormous now, like a great cavernous cave, the walls seemed miles away and even they soon faded, as the darkness began to settle on him.

Then Sam felt the presence.

Terror filled his soul as he felt it swallowing him up, devouring him. He cried out until his lungs burned, but the darkness swallowed all sound. Sam fought desperately, but soon he was completely overwhelmed by the darkness. He trembled and cried now, huddled in a corner deep within his own mind, his eyes staring out into the tiny window back into reality.

He had no control over his actions, and could only watch as his body methodically walked over to the shaft. Sam could not watch anymore. His last vision was of Bridgette's headless body being tossed into the mouth of the hole by his own hands.

Michael strained his eyes in the darkness, watching as the beam of light roamed beyond the first statue. He took a step forward, intrigued by the magnificent figures. He let the spot of light go to each one in turn, and then finally to the area they were centered upon. He saw huge jagged boulders piled high; it reminded him of a burial mound. Michael studied the placement of the statues in relationship to the mound. They were positioned at the compass points,

seemingly standing guard around whatever he figured might be buried there.

A sudden thump in the darkness behind him sent
shivers through Michael's spine. He turned, stumbling blindly upon the slippery, guano covered
stone floor, his light searching out the source of the
sound. A round object bounced along the ground,
past his shuffling feet, the flashlight's bright beam
trailing behind it desperately. Michael jumped in
fear, afraid that the object was some sort of mad animal, seeking his blood. He lost his footing on the
slick stones and fell heavily on his back, the flashlight slamming down to the rocks as he tried to
break his fall.

Darkness fell over him.

Panic set upon him. He sat up quickly, banging
the light against the palm of his hand violently.
Over and over again, he struck the light, until the
palm of his hand was sore. Terror edged into his
soul as he peered around in the thick darkness, his
imagination wreaking havoc with his psyche.

Michael could barely breathe under the weight of
the deep shadows and humid air. The walls of the
chamber did not seem so far away now, and neither
did the statues.

A sound caused him to stiffen, his eyes wide and
fearful, staring in the direction he knew the statues
to be, waiting for the strange sound to repeat. But it
did not. Nearly at the point of hyperventilation,
Michael remembered the Zippo he kept in his
pocket to light his cigars.

Quickly he tore it from his cotton pants pocket,
flipping it open desperately, longing to be out of
the dreaded darkness that seemed to have a life of
its own. His hands shook violently, his thumb flick-

ing over the lighter repeatedly, bringing useless yellow sparks to life.

"Light, dammit!" he growled.

He heard another sound.

This time it came from above him. Something wrenched deep within his soul as he held completely still in the darkness, afraid to look up. Slowly, his head went upward, his eyes finding the tiny hole fifty feet above his head. What he thought was a headless body disappeared into the darkness as it fell silently to the stone floor behind him with a damp thump.

Michael dared not move now, his head still turned to the right and the area where the body had landed. A shadow, darker than the blackness of the rest of the chamber, shifted on his left, sending another chill riving through his body.

Something else was down there with him.

Terror seized control of his actions, and he went at the lighter with renewed fervor, still seated on the slime covered stone.

His thumb was almost raw from his attempts to light the small silver lighter, and sweat rolled down his forehead to sting his eyes.

He flicked the lighter once more, but no flame. He flicked it again, still no flame. With every spark, he imagined a gigantic creature hovering before him, ready to devour his trembling body.

A sudden, whipping breeze, short and warm, washed across his face, causing his eyelids to flutter.

Michael froze, listening to the darkness. He swallowed the thick lump in his throat and flicked the lighter again.

The flame caught.

What Michael saw in the soft light of the yellow

flame brought tears of despair from his frozen heart. He knew in an instant that life was nothing more to him now. No scream would save him, no miracle would befall him, and no savior would rescue him—no, in that brief instant, Michael knew that all was meaningless.

Bridgette's eyes were locked open in a chilling gaze that burned deep into his heart, eyes set within a bloody decapitated head—eyes that Michael never saw. For just beyond the gruesome head, beyond the weak globe of flickering light, stood Michael's despair.

A thousand eyes stared directly into his soul, and a snake-like tongue flashed, tasting the scent of the mortal's fear.

Michael closed his eyes, unable to bear witness to the sight just as another blast of warm air whipped across his face, exterminating the light as the creature's great wings flexed.

Michael screamed as the statue advanced.

CHAPTER SEVEN

It was nearly eight PM when Alexander Glenn finally arrived at the designated rendezvous point. Enoch had been very vague in his instructions, so it was with a scowl that Glenn now stood on the empty sidewalk in front of the Archdiocese building in Center City, Philadelphia. Damn that Ebonee Lane, with her freak boyfriend and the FBI. They had nearly been successful in capturing him, but had succeeded in making him extremely tardy for his meeting.

As cars whisked past him on the wide one-way street, his eyes surveyed the building. Up the wide stairs was the revolving door that led into a dark lobby. Directly across the street from the high-rise office building was the bustling Wyndham Hotel. Tourists and businessmen smiled and chatted as they went to and fro through the side entrance Glenn was now eyeing. Taxies slowed and picked up awaiting fares, all of them seemed happy and without a care.

Glenn was just about to give up and go make a call to Enoch, hoping he could schedule another meeting, when a shiny black Lincoln sedan pulled up along the curb in front of him. Curiously, Glenn watched the white driver step out. He was dressed in a sharp black suit, complete with the chauffeur's cap and white gloves. He did not speak, but simply eyed Glenn passively as he opened the rear door to the vehicle.

Glenn hesitated, but only for a moment. He was not surprised to find the back of the car empty. The windows were tinted black in the rear to the point where he could barely see the bright streetlights outside. He remained silent as the sedan turned into a driveway beside the tall office building. Behind the building was a large parking lot, which was shared by one of the largest Catholic Church's Glenn had ever seen. The driveway continued through the parking lot, exiting on the next block over and turning onto another one-way street. Glenn stared out of the window, his eyes following the tall spires of the church, which was now passing on his right. Again the Lincoln turned into another driveway, this one next to the church.

The driver brought the car to a stop beside a side door and dropped the transmission into neutral.

Glenn sighed heavily, sitting in the thick silence. After a pregnant moment, he pushed the door open and stepped out, his eyes going to the red door on the side of the building. As soon as the car door closed, the driver pulled off, leaving him staring after it stupidly.

The red door was not locked and with a deep sigh, Glenn pushed it open and walked into the darkness.

He jumped as the heavy door closed behind him with a thump and found a man standing there, dressed in the same dark type of suit as the driver of the Lincoln. His black hair was long and swept back in a gelled ponytail. Jewelry sparkled on his wrists and fingers, and Glenn's first thought upon seeing him was of the Italian Mafia. The man nodded gruffly, motioning for Glenn to follow him.

The man led him down a narrow, dark hall with soft red carpeting. Various paintings hung upon the walls and small chandeliers hung from the ceiling intermittently down the center of the walkway, all set to their dimmest level. Glenn was not a religious man, so he felt nothing as he stepped behind the man into the cavernous sanctuary, wrinkling up his nose at the strong scent of frankincense and myrrh that clung to the room. Rows upon rows of pews lined the vast area to his left, the highly polished cherry wood glowing under the soft candlelight.

The man led Glenn to a small, shadowy alcove situated on the right of the large room where three large booths stood against the wall—confessionals.

The man silently slid back the partition in the center booth and stood, waiting. Only then did Glenn feel his pulse begin to rise, as he slid down onto the small bench in the darkness, the partition sliding closed behind him. He frowned in the darkness, the small window in front of him covered in thick screening. Below the window was a padded foot rest, apparently, thought Glenn, for kneeling.

After a few minutes had passed with nothing disturbing the silence, save for his own breaths, his thoughts began to wonder. First to his former prominence within the FBI, and then to his first meetings with the heads of The Order of the Rose. Life had been good then. None of this hiding in holes like a rat. Then came Ebonee Lane and her freak partner, Elijah Garland. Glenn scowled bitterly within the shadows of the confessional as the memories replayed in his mind. He had seen it all coming before she was even in place undercover to investigate his little operation.

But he had underestimated the beautiful agent's abilities, and had not planned on the freak's intervention. Glenn's sarcastic chuckle disturbed the silence for a moment before dropping off into a deep sigh.

"What is it, former director, that amuses you so?"

Glenn went rigid in his seat as the raspy voice filled the shadows from the other side of the small window and his hand went instinctively to the gun at his waist. He stared at the window for a long moment, before finally relaxing somewhat. "Enoch?" he whispered.

"Our business is concluded, Mr. Glenn . . . ville," the voice began evenly. "Beneath your seat you will find your payment . . . may the Lord be with you."

Glenn felt his pulse quicken at the finality in the man's voice. "No! Wait!"

There was a slight pause as both men sat in silence, waiting for the other to continue.

"Are there sins you wish to confess, former director?" the voice asked cynically.

Glenn searched for words, any words that would keep the conversation going. "Is . . . is . . . there anything else I can help with?"

Another moment of silence.

"Are you seeking employment, former director?"

Glenn swallowed hard. "Well, of course. I'm sure I

can be of some use to your, uhhh—" His eyes roamed about in the darkness, wondering exactly who it was he would be working for, "organization."

"Are you not curious as to the nature of our last transaction?"

Glenn had no reason to be. He had truly hoped to wiggle some more funds by dangling half truths, as to exactly what Mr. Corvalis had found, but upon meeting Enoch, he knew instantly that it would be useless. Whatever was in that hole in the ground was probably already acquired by Enoch and his associates. And for some odd reason, he felt that the less he knew the better.

"Not at all," Glenn said evenly.

"Interesting," came the rasping voice after a pregnant pause. "Tell me what you know of the one they call the Protector."

Glenn's eyes went wide at the mention of the title. "You mean the freak," he began, scowling as he brought images of the white haired black man into his mind. Then a second thought came to him. "I'm sure you know more than I do about him."

There was another moment of silence.

"You will need a new disguise, former director. I suggest you use your payment wisely," Enoch said.

Glenn narrowed his eyes in the darkness. "Then you have work for me?"

"Go with Vito; he will give you the appropriate paraphernalia that you will require."

"What about the freak?" Glenn asked, sitting forward as he felt the meeting coming to an end.

"Ego still scarred, former director?" Enoch asked.

Glenn's nostrils flared. He was getting tired of being referred to in the past tense.

Enoch chuckled softly, if that's what the sound

could be interpreted as. "The Protector is beyond your means. However, there is the small matter of a certain female agent named Ebonee Lane." Enoch paused as Glenn clung to his every word. "She may prove to be a hindrance to our plans . . . it would be very beneficial to have her . . . removed. But, considering your past relationship with the young woman, I am not absolutely certain that she is not beyond your means either."

Glenn absorbed the insult with some difficulty. "The circumstances were different then . . . and I had not factored in the freak."

Enoch sighed heavily and Glenn imagined his face in the shadows, twisted up in contemplation. "True enough. Very well, former director. See to it that circumstances do not apply in your next encounter . . . and as for the freak . . . we will ensure he is not a factor. God be with you."

Glenn sat still as he heard Enoch whisk from the booth. After a silent moment, his own sliding partition slid open and the large body guard with the slicked back ponytail motioned for him to exit.

"Vito?" Glenn asked.

The man nodded, his expression as rigid as a crisp new ten dollar bill.

"Come with me," Vito announced, his heavy bass voice echoing in the sanctuary.

Glenn grinned, reaching back into the booth to extract the large leather shoulder bag, and then he fell in behind the muscular man, extremely satisfied with the meeting.

He would get his revenge.

"Beware your haughtiness does not become your downfall, brother," Dalfien hissed dryly, his blood-red eyes narrowed to thin slits as he stared at his demon brother, Rathamon.

Rathamon chuckled lightly at the words. "As it was yours?" he sneered.

Dalfien's canine-like maw drew up into a scowl, baring rows of sharp teeth as the two behemoths locked gazes. Around them roared the fires of chaos that was the abyss—their astral home, which was now Dalfien's prison. Having been banished from the Earth by that damned Protector and his cursed blades, Dalfien was now forced to serve out a one thousand year sentence.

At the thought of the Protector, Dalfien's mind reached out from his terrible throne, constructed of bones, some still holding flesh. Quickly he ensnarled a tortured spirit, a sinful human male, his soul nothing more to Dalfien than a squeeze toy used to relieve stress. With a mere thought, Dalfien gave the soul substance, gave it a body.

Rathamon looked on with distaste, watching as Dalfien's mighty claw encircled the naked, faceless being.

"You would be wise to avoid him," Dalfien muttered, returning his gaze to Rathamon as his fingers slowly began to clench, drawing a blood-curdling scream from the mass of flesh, the sound mixing pleasurably with the plethora of painful wails that already filled the cavernous area.

Rathamon flashed his own wicked grin, his broad muscles flexing in his wide shoulders. "With failure comes wisdom!" he exclaimed, noting the higher pitched scream resound from the spirit in Dalfien's hand as he said the words. Rathamon was enjoying this, for so long he had sat quietly in Dalfien's shadow, accepting meaningless and trite missions from the greater beasts of the abyss, Dalfien included. "Perhaps I shall pay El'Rathiem a visit next, see what useful wisdom I may acquire from another failure!" he spat.

Rathamon frowned, watching as Dalfien roared in anger, standing from his thrown to his impressive height, the tortured soul's head popping from its body to land upon the smoldering ground, rolling along as it continued to wail.

"You forget your place, Rathamon!" he snarled, saliva dripping from his fangs as he stormed over to stand before him.

Rathamon did not back down, even as he felt the shudder in his hoofed feet as Dalfien's weight shook the ground with each step. "No . . . it is you, dear Dalfien, who has forgotten his place, banished one," he said evenly.

Dalfien stood a full head taller than Rathamon and could have crushed him as easily as he had crushed the damned soul. He seethed now, his body trembling with demon rage as he stared down at Rathamon. But his words were true. Dalfien held no influence now, not even over a lowly imp. But still, what further punishment could befall him if he were to crush the life out of Rathamon where he stood? None, there was no other punishment here.

Rathamon chuckled, feeling Dalfien's intentions as clearly as he felt the comforting heat rising from the forever burning ground at his feet.

"Come Dalfien, your anger consumes your better judgment," Rathamon said lightly. His eyes flashed out over the sea of despair and flames, silently making the call.

Dalfien heard the guttural growls almost instantly, hundreds of them, surrounding his small, smoldering grotto, Imps and fiends, lower denizens of the abyss, creatures he himself once commanded to bend to his will. Now they approached the two figures, flames lapping up around them, glittering off of shining blades, some carried long poles, others clubs with wicked spikes on them. He even recognized a few of the larger ones, grotesque fiends that he had tortured personally. In their eyes was the promise of pain and torture.

Dalfien growled maliciously, but backed away a step from his brother, keeping a wary eye on the closest fiends that had closed in the circle. His upper lip quivered, releasing a fresh line of saliva to fall to the burning ground where it hissed and dissipated into steam.

Rathamon held his purple eyes on Dalfien, waiting for him to calm. He had no other choice. A mere thought from him would bring the beasts down upon Dalfien's head with extreme malice. He knew they would not be able to truly harm the great demon, but their numbers would provide a significant amount of pain, ripping his flesh from his bones, pausing long enough only to allow him to regenerate, and then once again repeat the process, until Rathamon tired.

Rathamon held the mass of chaos in check, confident that Dalfien would come to terms. He sighed as he watched Dalfien smirk and raise his powerful arm. A spear appeared in his hand, its point barbed with a great hook. Beneath the hook, a pile of chain dangled from the spear's end.

Rathamon watched apathetically as the spear shot out from Dalfien's mighty throw, the length of chain rattling as it fed out, pulled by the force of the spear's speedy flight. One of the bigger fiends shrieked in shock, staring down at the shaft of the spear now imbedded in its leathery chest. Its eyes grew wider as it followed the length of taut chain back to Dalfien, just as the mighty demon gave a powerful jerk on the chain. The fiend rushed forward then, snatched in one fluid motion across the twenty five foot buffer zone the creatures were commanded to maintain.

Dalfien snarled as the beast landed at his wide hoofed feet, squirming and cowering as the other fiends looked on. Shouts and cries of anger arose from the chaos as Dalfien's hand slowly went up into the air. A heavy metal collar with sharp inverted spikes appeared between his clawed fingers, resting open in a c shape, a length of chain falling down to the ground where it was attached to the foot of his writhing throne.

Rathamon's lip twitched ever so slightly, but he held his anger in check, and kept the impassive expression locked upon his demonic maw as Dalfien's hand slammed down on the fiend's throat, clamping the collar in place. Rathamon could feel his tenuous hold over the large mob slipping as their anger and cries for vengeance filled his mind.

"Enough of this foolishness," he spat, waving his clawed hand in the air, dismissing the horde. He knew he would have to find another demon for them to appease their bloodlust. "I need to know everything you can tell me of the Protector and his friends."

It was Dalfien's turn to chuckle maniacally now as he bent over to snatch the spear from the poor creature's chest, bringing with it a strip of flesh. He tore the bloody meat from the end of the spear with his teeth, swallowing it in one gulp. Silently, he dropped down onto his throne, his arms draped across its arms leisurely as he glared at Rathamon with a snort.

"Bah . . . send your hordes," he stated nonchalantly, his gaze drifting in boredom.

Rathamon breathed a heavy sigh. He had hoped to get the information from Dalfien without giving up too much in return. Silently, he strode forward, reaching out telepathically to the cursed souls writhing within the ground itself, commanding them to take shape.

Dalfien watched in silence as Rathamon's own, smaller throne slowly writhed to life, arms and legs clutching together, torsos bending unnaturally, spines breaking and reshaping, until Rathamon sat before him, his elbows resting on each arm of the chair, hands crossed in his lap above crossed legs. How foolish he looked! A demonic bookworm! Dalfien chuckled heavily as he stared at Rathamon.

"You will tell me all I wish to know," Rathamon said evenly, his gaze steady.

The calmness and surety in his voice brought an end to Dalfien's mirth. "Why don't you go and ask him yourself?" Dalfien sneered.

"And end up like you? No, I have subtle ways of bringing about his end . . ." Rathamon paused, deciding just how much of his plans he should divulge. "Already I have set into motion a chain of events that will aid me in this cause."

Dalfien cocked his head slightly, taking a new look at his lesser brother. Diminutive in size, Rathamon had always been considered a weakling among the greater demons like El'Rathiem and himself. But it was slowly becoming obvious to Dalfien that he was much more dangerous than looks would imply. He was aware of Rathamon's highly influential link to the upper world and amazed by it as well. He himself had attempted to force his will upon the very same

individual, only to be fought off by his strong faith
and resolute beliefs. How had Rathamon succeeded
where he had failed? Perhaps there could be bene-
fits in aiding his brother.

"I will tell you what you wish to know," Dalfien
sneered. "But at a price."

"Name it."

"The Protector's soul will be mine!"

Rathamon chuckled lightly at the insane demand.
"That, my dear brother, is a commodity even I have
no control over. Besides, his death may not be our
master's wish," he explained, deciding to spill out a
little more of his information, realizing that it was
necessary to make his brother forget about acquir-
ing the soul of the Protector, which was indeed off
limits. "However," he continued, narrowing his eyes
in a promising stare. "There is another soul that
may be of interest to you."

Dalfien knew his words to be truth. "Name this
soul."

A wry grin found Rathamon's lips. "Ebonee Lane."

Rathamon's grin was joined then, as Dalfien sat
back in his throne, remembering his visits to the
human woman's mind. She was strong willed, and
beautiful. Yes, she would provide ample entertainment for his thousand year banishment. His eyes
drifted down to the floor next to his throne as his
smile held. The floor shook suddenly as he stomped
a hoofed foot down onto the cowering fiends hand,
crushing it into pulp.

Then Dalfien's eyes met Rathamon's once more, and
they held a bright glow. "What do you wish to know?"

Ebonee tossed and turned in the large king-
sized bed in the hotel suite. The evening's

events still weighed heavily on her mind. Not only had Glenn slipped through her fingers again, but the startling and chilling realization of Heaven and Hell being all too real would not let sleep come easily.

She turned over in the bed, kicking the quilt from her body as she stared at Elijah. A soft smile came to her face in the blue moonlight that drifted in from the slightly parted curtains. She tried to force the disturbing thoughts from her mind with images of her lover. Her smile widened against the soft pillow. She had never known a man so strong yet also graceful. Every muscle of his body seemed to move with the fluidity of a well orchestrated ballet. Even in his sleep he was smooth and controlled. Never had she ever heard a snore or an uneven breath come from his slumbering lips. But beneath his beauty and grace Ebonee realized, Elijah was cursed with a troubled spirit.

His inner pain ran deep below the flawless exterior he presented to the world, a pain he had harbored from childhood. Ebonee felt a tear leave her eye as her hand stroked the side of his face tenderly, wishing she could take away his pain, hoping that perhaps their earlier conversation proved to be the first step toward achieving that goal.

Her contemplations were disturbed by the sudden intermittent tone emitted by her laptop in the other room, signaling an incoming video call from the FBI.

Before she could move to get up, Elijah's eyes flashed open, his lips still tightly sealed as he inhaled deeply through his nose.

"I'll get it," Ebonee whispered, kissing him gently

on the lips with a chuckle, knowing full well Elijah had no intentions of getting up to answer a call from his new superiors.

Hope quickened Ebonee's steps across the carpeted floor. Maybe they had found Glenn. But her hopeful gaze changed to one of confusion as she stared at the unknown face upon the screen. His slender, pale face was ancient, holding lines of wrinkles too numerous to count. He wore a suit, that much she could see displayed on the screen in front of her.

"Agent Lane, sorry to bother you at this late an hour," the man began. "But I just wanted to update you on your case."

"Who are you?" Ebonee asked, her face still contorted in confusion.

The man ignored her question. "We will need the subject brought in for further testing," he went on, oblivious to the astounded look on Agent Lane's face. "I applaud you on your ability to manipulate him; seems we picked the right agent for the job, but I warn you, Agent, do not let your feelings get involved here. Elijah Garland is dangerous, and until we fully understand the nature of his abilities, you must stay within his circle of trust, by any means necessary ..."

"What the hell are you talking about? Who are you?" Ebonee exclaimed in a hushed whisper.

"You will be informed of the pre-determined drop point for the next tests. Until then, be safe. Director Gordon out."

The screen went blank. Ebonee stared at the dark monitor for a long moment, still baffled, until she felt the presence behind her. She turned her head to see Elijah standing in the doorway, his eyes narrowed to thin slits, staring through her like daggers.

He never said a word, simply snorted dryly and turned back to the bedroom.

Ebonee's jaw dropped open as she realized he had heard the ridiculous communication. "No, no . . . Elijah!" she shouted, her heart now pounding frantically in her chest as she ran for the bedroom.

Elijah was already dressed.

"Where are you going? What are you doing?" she asked, fear lining her broken voice.

Elijah did not say a word, would not even look at her as he draped his twin blades around his waist.

Ebonee could not find the words to say at that moment, she ran to him, pulling at his arm as he moved for the door. "Elijah! Where are you going?"

Elijah turned as he felt her hand grip his arm. He stared at her, searching her eyes for a long moment, then he snorted derisively, snatching away from her without saying anything.

Ebonee felt her pulse increase as her tears began to fall, watching him as he threw on his leather trench. She hurriedly began to get dressed. "Elijah, you have to believe me! I don't know who that man was!" she cried, running from the bedroom with her clothes in hand. "Just stop and listen to me, Elijah!" Her mouth fell open as she watched Elijah pull open the sliding door to the balcony and, without hesitating, leap right over the rail.

Ebonee crumbled where she stood, knowing she would not be able to catch him. Her body trembled as tears flowed from her eyes. How could he believe that lie?

Elijah's black trench flapped madly as the air

rushed up around him as he descended the four-story drop, landing in a tight crouch and springing directly to his feet into a calm walk. He snatched up the black helmet from the seat of his bike, removing the leather gloves he had placed inside of it. He tried to remain in control; tried to force the maddened pace of his heart to slow as his anger continued to build. A single swift motion sent the helmet flying through the night sky, landing a full block away upon the empty sidewalk.

Elijah felt the wave of emotion threatening to overwhelm him as he mounted the bike, turning the key, hoping the loud roar of the engine would drown out the hurt he felt in his heart. His foot stomped down on the gears and he released the clutch, hurtling through the parking lot at insane speeds. The bike hit the expressway already at one hundred miles per hour. Elijah squinted as the winds beat against his face, smearing the tears that streamed from his eyes as the landscape whizzed by in a blur. And still, his anger continued to mount.

"What are we doing here?" Glenn eyed Vito from the passenger seat of the black Lincoln, averting his eyes from the front of the hotel just for a moment.

Vito was a tight-lipped one. He had not spoken a word since they had departed from the church, and it appeared he was not about to yet. He simply sat behind the wheel of the car, staring at the bright lobby through the glass.

"I think we are supposed to be working together here, uhhh . . . Vito," Glenn frowned. "I can't help if I don't know what we're doing."

Vito's eyes suddenly narrowed and he silenced

Glenn with an upraised finger as he focused in on the sound. A second later a black dart streaked out of the parking lot and onto the street.

"Hey! That's him!" Glenn exclaimed excitedly, sitting up in his seat.

Vito smiled easily, flashing him a wink as he started the car and headed for the parking lot.

"Hey, you're letting him get—" Glenn let the sentence fall incomplete from his thin lips. "Lane is up there alone," he finished, his eyes narrowing as her name rolled of off his tongue.

Vito stepped out, leaving the car parked in the middle of the driveway. "FBI," he said, flashing his badge to the bellhops who approached.

Glenn followed him into the lobby. The large man looked more like a bodyguard for one of those hip-hop characters, stopping in the mirror to smooth his sharp suit, his jewelry glittering brightly.

"I need a disguise," Glenn mumbled, noting his own reflection in the wall-length mirrors as they approached the elevator. His hand held the grip of his 9 mm inside the pocket of his pea coat. "She'll recognize me on sight." He stared up at Vito, who stood almost a full three feet taller than he.

Vito simply shrugged, a wry grin spreading out on his heavy cheeks as he stepped onto the elevator.

Glenn felt his pulse increase as the doors slid closed and he found his reflection again staring back at him from the elevator door. Sweat was beginning to bead upon his forehead, despite the coolness in the air. The elevator stopped and Glenn inhaled deeply, removing his gun from his pocket.

"No," Vito said, his hand falling down on Glenn's

hand, pushing the gun down as they stepped off of the elevator into the brightly lit hall.

Glenn watched the man reach into his inside pocket and produce a set of tasers, extending one to him. He accepted the weapon with a grin, walking slightly behind Vito as they made their way to the door of Ebonee's suite.

Glenn held his breath as Vito's meaty hand went to the doorknob.

Ebonee's fingers slammed down hard on the keyboard of her laptop in frustration. Who the hell was Director Gordon? And why in the hell had he said all of that nonsense? Tears continued to stream from her lovely brown eyes, eyes that had only moments before, watched her beloved Elijah depart in anger. Surely Elijah could see past the falsehood of that fools message. He had to know that her feelings were real and that none of this had been staged in any way.

A brief thought of never feeling his warm embrace again flashed through her mind and her tears doubled in their flow. Anger flowed through her veins as she stared through blurred vision at the laptop and the blank screen. Her hand struck out, sending the computer sliding from the table and into the wall with a loud smack. Her heart raced and her eyes continued to release the tears as she stood up from the chair, her hands going to her face to wipe at the moisture. Her heavy sobs filled the room as she paced back and forth, wondering what she would do now. "*He knows . . . he has to know!*" she said fiercely, her eyes going to the front door.

The knob turned.

"Elijah!"

Ebonee ran full speed to the door and flung it open, expecting to see her Elijah. Her arms anticipated the warm embrace she would envelop him in as her mind formed the words that would reassure him of her love.

The jolt from the taser fried those thoughts and sent her arms trembling just before darkness overwhelmed her. . . .

*E*lijah's nostrils flared as his tears streamed back along his face, the wind causing them to water as he guided the motorcycle along the Philadelphia streets. The video message was still fresh in his mind, but his sensibilities cried out for him to stop and think rationally. The image of Ebonee's smile flashed into his mind, and the memory of her embrace brought his hand closed upon the bike's brake.

Elijah sighed heavily, sitting beneath an overpass in the darkness, ignoring the blaring horns of motorists who were forced to swerve around him. He turned his head to stare back at the hotel, which could still be seen only a few blocks back. Ebonee's love was real. It had to be. A wave of emotions ran through his body, bringing with it a jolting chill. He swallowed hard, his lips tightly sealed. The message was a lie. His heart knew it to be true. And even if it was not a lie, he would rather submit to whatever plans the FBI had for him than to lose the love he had found in Ebonee. But why would they send a message to her like that, knowing that the two of them were together, unless . . .

Elijah's angry growl was drowned out by the sudden roar of the BMW's 1200cc engine. The rear wheel spun in a smoky white circle, leaving a trail of smoldering rubber as the bike fishtailed in a 180-degree turn. The front wheel came up off of the ground as the powerful engine propelled the bike forward at insane speeds. Elijah's muscles flinched and contracted in spasms as he fought to keep the bike under control. He veered through the oncoming traffic like a madman out of control, swerving at the last minute to jump onto the sidewalk at an intersection. A homeless person shrieked in surprise as he stepped out of an alleyway, the black dart swerving at the last minute to miss him. Back onto the one-way street Elijah went, already at 120 miles per hour. He ignored the red traffic light as he came to the string of intersections that marked the overpass and the interstate below. Just across the interstate was the hotel, and his beloved Ebonee.

He made it across the first intersection without trouble, leaving blaring horns and screeching tires in his wake. He never slowed as he came to the next traffic light. The hotel was on the opposite corner and that's where his eyes went when he saw the light turn green. He did not see the late motorists speed across the intersection from his right until it was too late.

The bike slammed into the rear of the white stretch limo with a deafening crash. Plastic and metal twisted and went flying, as did Elijah. He tucked into a ball at the apex of his short stint as a bird and landed on the roof of an oncoming car that was stopped at the intersection. The thin metal gave way as he continued to roll, and he landed on his feet behind the damaged vehicle, already running for the doors of the hotel.

A black Lincoln Town Car accelerated as it pulled from the hotel's driveway and Elijah swore that the car was trying to hit him. He slowed as the car whisked past behind him, his eyes straining to see into the dark tint of the windows.

"*Ebonee*," he whispered the name as the Lincoln tore into the street, clipping a police car and veering around the halted traffic, with its tires screeching.

Elijah took off after it on foot, jumping clear over the same white limo he had landed on, just as the Lincoln turned the corner onto the empty street, and accelerated quickly. He knew he would never catch the vehicle on foot, and a quick glance to the side and the mangled motorcycle told him he would not be chasing it on that either. He stood for a moment, ignoring the shouts from the limo driver, watching as the police car's siren lit up and it tore around the corner in pursuit of the Lincoln. A small crowd had gathered on the corner, staring at him and the scene of the accident.

Elijah was running again, to the hotel parking lot. He hopped onto Ebonee's motorcycle and ripped the ignition housing out with his bare fingers. The crowd forming in front of the hotel driveway parted with shouts of fear as the motorcycle screamed out of the driveway, turning the corner and gaining ground quickly on the flashing lights in the distance.

The black Lincoln tore through the moderate traffic and across the Ben Franklin Bridge with the police cruiser close behind. The pretty lights decorating the bridge in red white and blue were lost on Elijah as he hit the wide, eight-lane, concrete and steel expanse that arched across the Delaware River into Jersey. He ignored the signal lights overhead on the crossing girders, flashing red to indicate that the lane he was now in was closed. He had lost sight of the police car over the arc of the bridge. His thumb hovered over the turbo button. His vision blurred by the wind, Elijah ducked low, letting his thumb come down. With a loud whine, the turbines kicked in, shooting the bike forward at speeds topping the 200 mph mark. The lights blew by him in a blur, and before he knew it, he was upon the tollbooths. Elijah's heart rate did not have time to increase, so it merely stopped, or hesitated for a moment as he watched the black Lincoln speeding along on the other side of the toll. The police car had given up pursuit, most likely handing over the chase to the Camden authorities. The black and silver streak was only twenty yards away from the toll, and all eight lanes were occupied.

"Fuck!" Elijah exclaimed in a teeth-clenching growl, anticipating a very nasty fall as he guided the bike as best he could. He guided the too-powerful crotch rocket into one of the lanes, aiming for the widest opening between the car just pulling up there and the wall of the booth.

Sparks lit up the area and Elijah cursed bitterly as the bike's handlebars bounced off the rear of the car and slammed into the toll booth wall, pinballing him back to the car. It took every ounce of strength and skill in his limbs to keep from wiping out, but somehow he did. The black dart shot out of the toll-gate and took up the chase before the final sparks could die away.

Elijah could feel the bones in his right knee reset-ting as he continued down the dark highway, the pain was nothing compared to the brutality he would re-lease upon whoever was in that Lincoln.

Glenn's eyes were the size of a small orange as he

stared back out of the tinted windows of the Lincoln. He had thought them home free when the black and white had given up pursuit back at the toll. Then he had watched a tiny object erupt from what appeared to be flames and sparks and uncannily became very large as it closed the distance between the vehicles. He was now staring directly into the freaks angry eyes as the motorcycle's front wheel came to within a foot of the Lincoln's bumper.

Glenn cursed as the car made a sudden swerve, jumping off of the highway onto a shadowy, tree-lined road. He stole a glance down to the unconscious woman slumped in the backseat next to him, then returned his gaze to the rear window, removing his Glock 9 mm.

The first shot shattered the tinted glass and the bullet tore into the Protector's left shoulder.

Elijah ignored the pain, his eyes burning into Glenn's with a fierce hatred. Glenn swallowed hard, then proceeded to empty a clip in the freak's direction.

Several of the bullets found their mark, but still Elijah held his course and his gaze. His wounds would heal. Glenn's would not.

Elijah waited until the vehicles were cruising at the same speed and hopped up onto the body of the bike, his eyes never leaving Glenn's. His leg muscles flexed and contracted, preparing for the leap that would take him to the back of the moving car. Just as he let go of the handlebars, he saw Glenn's eyes go wide. But he was not looking at Elijah; his gaze was locked on something beyond him.

Elijah felt a powerful tremor barrel through his body and a chill, unlike any he had experienced, sent tiny bumps racing along his skin. He felt, more than saw, the thing behind him as Enobe and Soul Seeker went into a fit of vibrations at his sides. He braced himself for impact, with the car, or with the thing behind him. He didn't know which would come first. Unfortunately, it was the latter.

Sharp talons, two inches long, tore into the Protector's chest and shoulders, thrusting him forward into the top rear of the car, leaving a large dent before whisking him up and into the night sky. Elijah let out a howl as the claws locked into place and he felt the rush of air. Powerful leathery wings worked at the air currents, taking the Lincoln farther and farther away with every downward beat . . . taking his Ebonee farther and farther away.

The pain disappeared in a whirlwind of rage that surged through the Protector like a violent typhoon. Bright spots flashed in his vision and he growled, his body trembling with anger. He gave no thought of the distance to the ground as they soared over the trees in the darkness. His only thoughts were of killing whatever beast this was, and sending it back to hell in little pieces. He gave no thought to how or why the thing had appeared, nor did he care. He didn't taste the greenish blood that flowed past his lips as his teeth wrended the leathery flesh from the beast's legs. His hands struggled against the thing's powerful talons, his own nails raking wildly, tearing muscle and cartilage to the bone.

Tears were blurring his vision, yet he was not aware of them. He thought he heard a shrill cry fill the night, but could not discern if it were his own voice, or that of the beast. One talon snatched away, and the Protector's right arm was free. He dangled in the demon's tentative hold, but any thoughts of snatching one of his blades free was lost in his primal state of rage. Before the free talon could again find his arm, his free hand found a hold of its clenched claw. Somehow he wiggled and writhed, turning his head and biting, scratching, kicking anything that would loosen the remaining claw. He felt the grip release a bit, and promptly tore his shoulder free. A pain-filled cry echoed into the night, drowned out by the rushing of the wind as the creature began to lose altitude, concentrating on keeping a hold of its quarry.

Elijah was blinded by the rage, and could not see for the tears. But he knew where the thing's neck was. He climbed up, grasping a handful of wing, a fistful of skin, kicking and biting on his way. He was upon the demon's back then, his arm clamped around its sinewy neck in a tight embrace. Suddenly the tears were gone; the rage had peaked. A wry grin found the Protector's lips as his muscles flexed and the demon howled in defiance.

Elijah was ignorant to the slapping branches that left welts upon his cheeks and hands as they hurtled back to the earth. They tumbled over and over, the moon dancing in a chaotic circle with the trees and ground in Elijah's vision. Internally, Elijah could sense the moment of impact arriving and he fought desperately to maneuver his body to be on top when that moment came.

He partially succeeded.

Again, bright spots filled his vision and he felt his body go numb. He landed on his side, his left arm crushed beneath the creature's weight in the soft earth. The scent of the evergreens and pine trees did not register to the Protector, nor did the otherwise beautiful sight of the bright moon shining through the thick canopy above him stir him to act.

Both figures lay motionless as the sound of breaking branches slowly came to an end above them. Leaves and debris floated down around the two . . . until there was silence.

Moments later, a shrill cry reverberated through the forest, echoing eerily, startling animals from their nocturnal activities. Elijah laid with his eyes shut tightly, a weak groan escaping his blood-covered lips, ending in a choked gurgle. His lung had been punctured in the fall and several of his ribs had fractured. His internal organs were a mess, and he knew that they would not heal properly unless he moved. His mind fought to heed the call of his physical being— the call for him to fight the pain and inhale deeply, expanding his lungs to reset the bones.

A memory flashed across his closed eyelids. The Lincoln, drifting slowly away from his outstretched hands. Ebonee, her body nailed to a cross embedded within the roof of the car, slowly disappearing into the unnatural darkness. He heard her voice, soft, sweet. *"Elijah, kiss me please . . ."*

Elijah did not feel his blood stained lips move, nor did he recognize the words whispered from them as he spoke, *"Eloi, Eloi, lama sabachthani?"*

The darkness then grew heavier around him, and he welcomed it. Without her, he had no reason to go on.

"Get up!"

Elijah felt a sudden jolt of power run through his veins as he heard the words whispered fiercely just above his face. He blinked his eyes open, catching a clear image of Gabriel, his face stern, eyes wide in anger, white hair billowing atop his head as if the very winds were conveying his temperament.

The image disappeared within a single flutter of

his light brown eyes. He stared up at the canopy of tall trees, focusing on the stars painted upon the vast azure blanket of space. Ebonee was still alive. He could believe nothing else. She was alive and in need of him and he would go to her. It was as simple as the scowl that was clearly engraved upon his father's face only moments ago.

Elijah found the resolve he needed and tilted his head to the side, wincing as he felt the snap of vertebrae returning to their normal position in his neck. His eyes fell on the demon, still lying limply upon his arm. Fire still blazed within his abdomen and chest, roaring higher with the slightest movement he made. He gritted his teeth, mentally preparing himself for the pain that was to come. Then he inhaled deeply, expanding his lungs to their maximum capacity, forcing the splintered bones to return to their place.

The pain was unbearable. He growled and writhed as the bones reset. His pinned arm was dislocated at the shoulder, further fueling the agony. The intense pain drove him near to the point of insanity. Over and over he cried out in angry shouts, saliva foaming at his lips, his free hand closing bloody digits to form a fist, with which he released the insane pain, over and over again, punching at the still form of the demon, growling like a wounded animal, which he was.

Slowly the pain in his torso lessened, and he calmed enough to push the body of the demon over and tear his arm free, falling instantly to the moss covered forest floor, shoulder first. He cried out again as the joint snapped back into place, leaving a slight numbness. Growling, he drug his face along the dirt, rolling over onto his back and then again onto his stomach, bringing his knees up. He stayed that way, upon his knees, bent over, his head in the dirt, as the fires slowly washed away and his Angelic blood brought healing.

Calmness finally fell over him, and he listened with closed eyes to the nocturnal sounds around him. The wind had picked up a slight howl as it blew through the trees. An owl hooted in the distance, branches groaned, dry leaves rustled. . . .

Enobe and Soul Seeker began vibrating at his waist.

Elijah's eyes opened slowly, focused upon the dark moss beneath his forehead. There was a difference between a leaf rustling in the wind and a leaf rustling underfoot. He heard the sound again, coming from his left, and he slowly rolled his head that way, his eyes searching the shadows between the wide evergreens. He was not surprised when the shadows came to life.

Four shadowy figures loped carefully from the darkness. They carried blunt weapons in their hands— pipes and clubs. A second rustling of leaves came from his right. Elijah sat up slowly to see what else was coming for him. Out of the shadows a large human male stepped, dressed in a police uniform, flanked on both sides by human males.

Soul Seeker, still sheathed upon his right hip, began to hum in a stronger vibration, almost to the point where it was visibly moving.

There was a Minor Demon in this group.

Closer they stalked, cautious and wary. This fact alone sent alarms off in Elijah's weary brain. Fiends were never cautious! He knew then that the Fiends were under tight mental control by this Minor Demon which now stood still, motioning the others forward

as it retrieved thick chains from behind its back.
They meant to capture him.

The feeling had yet to return fully to his wounded
arm, but the rest of his internal injuries had healed
enough and would not hamper him in a fight. The
pungent scent of sulfur drifted to his nostrils, replacing the fresh country air he was once breathing
as the possessed humans inched closer. Elijah remained motionless, kneeling in the dark clearing,
the demons now encircling him. His mind raced.
Perhaps he should allow the beasts to capture him,
and then just maybe they would take him to wher-
ever Ebonee was. No. If he did that, they surely
would take his weapons, and then where would he
be when the time came to rescue his love? If she
were truly still alive.

The last thought brought a surge of rage into
the Protector, just as the first fiend lunged at his
back . . .

CHAPTER EIGHT

Yes! This will do! thought Vakra, clenching Sam Rayburn's huge, powerful hand onto the lift's chain. This body was much stronger than the last. He knew Rathamon would reward him handsomely. The job was almost done. And how simple it had been!

Vakra chuckled evilly as the dark walls of the shaft drifted up around him. He thought of the rewards that his mentor would bestow upon him and more so the respect that would be due to one in the favor of a powerful and cunning demon such as Rathamon. Vakra was a minor demon of little renown, not overtly bright and nowhere near as powerful as his older brethren like Dalfien and El'Rathiem. But he was smart enough to grab opportunity when it passed him.

Slowly the darkness thickened as he descended down into the shaft, the silence disturbed only by the continuous hum of the lift. For a moment,

Vakra's grin disappeared and his hand released its hold of the chain. He fell nearly ten feet before his strong hand reached out and once more locked upon circular metal links.

Sam Rayburn's brief cry of anguish echoed into the tomb. His attempt to wrest control of his mind away from the vileness that was Vakra was only partially successful. His cries continued to ring out in the darkness of his psyche, forced into a dark recess within his own mind against his will.

Vakra's grin turned into a string of curses. He could sense the human's desire for death rather than servitude. This human's will was stronger than he had first believed. It would be prudent to be aware of this fact from now on.

Sam trembled in the void, watching helplessly as Vakra, using his eyes, scanned the darkness below. They were now at the end of the lift, just above the entrance to the find. It was like a weird, terrifying nightmare for Sam—huddled in darkness, caressed by fear and forced to witness his world through the eyes of the minor demon, Vakra. Minor demon? Vakra? How did he know these things?

Sam's consciousness was pulled from his speculations as he saw his own hand upon the cold metal link of chain. Instantly he knew the demon's intentions. Swallowing back his fear, Sam concentrated on that metal loop.

Vakra's surprise was complete.

Sam's body hung limply from the chain above the dark opening. Again Vakra spewed forth a string of venomous curses, glaring up at the hand that refused to release the chain.

Sam's teeth grinded in his jaw and he forced his

eyes shut. He felt Vakra's attention turn inward, searching him out in the recesses of his own mind. He could feel the demon's anger and hatred. Tears flowed down his cheeks, cheeks distorted in an angry glare. Sam huddled tighter in a ball within the darkness, trembling, sobbing. Every muscle in his body was tense, and with all the will he could muster, he focused on that chain. The grip would have crushed bone. Sam knew he could not let this creature take him down into the hell below.

A sinister presence floated above him, sending a chill so violent through his body that the veins in his wrist pulsed with the surge of emotion.

He gripped the chain tighter.

Vakra was angry. He stared at the human, hanging onto the chain in his mind as if it were his last vestige of life. Vakra spat and cursed, hissed and then lashed out at Sam, his claws raking Sam's skin viciously.

To Sam, the world was nothing more than darkness. Darkness, his tears, and the chain.

He would not let go.

Again Vakra lashed out at Sam, leaving a vertical gouge of blood in triplicate down his back. Pleasure washed through Vakra as he listened to the mortal's anguished cries. Rathamon was in no hurry that he was aware of. And his job was nearly complete anyway. All he had to do was distract the Seraphim guarding the burial mound long enough to release the spirit of Shemhazai.

Vakra chuckled as he considered the human. Blood splattered his body from the wounds he had inflicted. Yes! He was fortunate and smart to follow Rathamon! How easy this task was turning out to be! There was no downside for Vakra, and he even got the pleasure of torturing a few human souls to boot. Yes, he would take his time torturing Sam. Then he would use his body—which the Seraphim would no doubt shred to pieces when Vakra deserted it and returned to his own plane of existence—to release the spirit so coveted by Rathamon.

Within the darkness of Sam's mind, a whip materialized in Vakra's hand. It was a long serpentine cord that seemed to writhe with a life of its own, its end frayed into several shorter extensions intertwined with wicked metal barbs.

Vakra gave the whip an experimental crack, snapping it up and forward and then snatching it back in one fluid motion bred of repetition. The loud pop exploded into Sam's right ear, causing him to shudder.

Vakra's smile disappeared.

The human's fear was diminishing. But how? Was this some sort of priest who had disguised himself as a lowly mine worker?

Sam growled in defiance, focusing his thoughts on one object . . . the chain. He didn't even feel the first lash that tore across his back, the barbs ripping away his shirt and flesh.

His fear had been based upon ignorance and ignorance alone. He had no idea what or who this being was that had assaulted his mind and had killed Michael's wife. But the more Vakra thought, the more Sam comprehended what he was up against. The mental link went both ways. Stronger demons such as Rathamon and Dalfien knew this, and took precautions against it, especially when it came to dealing with mortals of faith. But Vakra's overconfidence and ambition blinded him to this fact.

Sam was no man of the cloth, but he did believe in God, even more so now. So he prayed fervently without ceasing, never relinquishing his concentration upon the chain.

Once more the whip lashed in, wrapping around his shoulder, the barbs slapping into his cheek and neck, embedding themselves there until they were ripped away by Vakra's powerful hand. Sam screamed out, the pain excruciating. His whimpers sent a momentary wave of pleasure through Vakra, until he realized there was no fear backing those sobs.

Sam didn't care who this Rathamon was, nor did he care about Vakra. What did send a shiver through his spine, was the thought of the spirit below. Shemhazai? Was that the name? Sam shuddered under the impact of yet another lashing, this one slapping across his face, tearing a piece of his lip away. But the pain was nothing compared to the ill feelings he received at the mere thought of the spirit's name.

Fear played no part in this now.

Sam gripped the chain with a determination unmatched. He knew he could not let Vakra win out.

Twenty lashes, thirty . . . Sam's body was nothing more than a skinless mass of bloody flesh. His eyelids fluttered. Thirty-one . . . an eyelid was torn away.

Vakra could not believe this human's will. He would break. He had to! Thirty-two . . . Sam's nose was ripped away in a spray of blood.

Thirty-three . . . Sam's hand began to slip. . . .

Elijah pushed himself from the moss-covered earth, grunting as he kicked out at the advancing demon. His heel sunk into the creature's belly, causing a loud exhalation of air to rush from its mouth. Its body bent over as its forward motion was brought to an abrupt reversal. The human body fell to the earth, gagging reflexively.

"*Anel nathrak doth del dienve,*" Elijah said the words evenly as he crouched in the darkness over the hurling human. He awaited the transformation to occur, noting the exact position of each of his attackers. Slowly and deliberately, Enobe and Soul Seeker were slid from their scabbards, their diamond-sharp edges glinting in the moonlight.

The forms hovered in a circle around him, seemingly unaffected by the ancient words that would bring them out of their hijacked bodies and into Elijah's reality.

Nothing happened.

Elijah focused on the single form still bent over, wheezing heavily, and his head in the dirt. These *were* human attackers! They were not demons at all. Then why the intense vibrations from the blades?

Elijah quickly reversed his hold on Enobe and Soul Seeker, snapping the blades over in his hands in one sweeping motion that brought their cutting edges up along his forearm.

Still the three goons circled him.

Three? Where was the other? Elijah scanned the shadows where he had seen the larger man dressed as a police officer last. Again the twin blades picked up a vibrant hum. He saw the body lying in the darkness between the trees, exorcised of its demon.

A sharp blue flicker of light brought his attention back to the three encircling men. They were dressed in army camouflage clothing, hunting attire. One of them had a taser in his hand. A second later and three sets of sizzling blue sparks were dancing around Elijah.

Elijah chuckled ruefully, the sound echoing into the forest as he narrowed his brown eyes and thrust the twin blades back into their sheaths at his waist, snapping them into place. Within the blink of an eye, he had removed the belt holding them around his waist and now stood with both weapons at the ready. The hard leather casing may break a few bones, but would not draw blood. A momentary scowl flashed across his countenance, relaying the disappointment he felt humming through the handles of his blades. Enobe and Soul Seeker had not tasted of demon blood for quite some time, and he could feel their desire to do so now. He concurred full heartedly.

The wind picked up. Elijah could hear the faint sound of their padded footfalls on the soft moss covered earth, just below the soft whine of the breeze. But he could no longer hear the man at his feet wheezing.

He saw the slight movement below him as the re-covered man tried silently to remove his own taser from his waist.

Elijah dropped the pommel of Enobe across his temple, rendering him unconscious. Yet still, the other three made no move toward him. He caught a flicker in one of their eyes. Was that a grin?

Ebonee.

The thought drove Elijah to action. If they would not come to him, then he would have to take the fight to them and move on. He had to rescue Ebonee. But where would they have taken her? Every second wasted here put his love farther and farther away.

That was definitely a grin, and again the silver flicker of the eye.

Elijah blew out an exasperated breath, just about to launch himself forward. There was a light clicking sound, and the flash of red. Elijah stared down at the tranquilizer dart that had pierced the black leather of his trench and imbedded in his muscular shoulder. A chill flowed through him.

The three men eased forward together from different angles.

Almost immediately Elijah felt the first signs of the chemical beginning to take effect. There was a moment of disorientation. He blinked rapidly, shaking the effects away. He forced his eyes to remain focused on the hunter in front of him.

Was it getting darker? Perhaps a formation of clouds had passed in front of the bright silver moon, casting the small clearing into shadows. Whatever the case, Elijah barely saw the man lunge forward, blue fire crackling in his hand, leading the way.

He nearly scored a hit with the taser, but at the last instant, impossibly fast, Elijah spun in a circle, his right hand swatting Enobe downward, shattering the man's wrist as Soul Seeker shot out in an arc, keeping the other two hunters at bay.

The man fell, howling and clutching at his mangled hand.

Elijah tried to come out of the simple maneuver, but faltered. Instead of halting his rotation, he continued in a circle, almost drunkenly, staggering a few steps before finally getting his bearings. The tranquilizer was working.

Again Elijah heard the light click, and once more saw the small pinpoint of red light in the shadows behind the two remaining hunters. A second dart thumped into his thigh.

Suddenly, Elijah felt something wash through his veins that he had not felt since that day in the church. Elijah felt fear. It was getting harder and harder to draw a breath. The darkness seemed to be thickening. There were many more trees around him than he remembered. The hunters had tripled, his vision blurring in and out. A knot developed in his throat, and stayed there, no matter how hard he swallowed.

Ebonee.

Elijah staggered to one knee, letting his eyelids, which seemed to be heavier than lead now, close, if only for a brief respite.

Then fire shot through his nerves, powerful and intense, waves upon waves of jolting volts fried his thoughts in place. The electricity forced his eyes open wide, and he felt his facial muscles twitching spasmodically.

Ebonee.

Somehow Elijah managed to hold the darkness at bay. His jowls clenched violently in a determined growl. He tasted his own blood washing down his throat from his bitten tongue.

He pivoted on one knee, bringing the hunter and his wide-eyed stare into view. The fire in his side did not abate; it continued to boil his Angelic blood in his veins, building a rage of pressure that begged to be released.

Rational thought was impossible at this point. Brain cells screamed and danced in a panicked frenzy, their only objective—survival.

The scabbards fell away in a single motion, the

moonlight reflecting once more off the diamond-edged blades.

The taser fell to the earth along with the hunter's arm. Enobe then found its home in the surprised man's belly.

Again there was the light clicking sound. This time, Elijah waited for the flash of red light to appear, and it did. The dart thumped into his neck just as he launched Soul Seeker into the shadows in a mighty throw.

Elijah did not wait to see if his aim was true; he would surely find out one way or another. Angrily, he snatched the dart from his neck and with an uncanny accuracy, spun in a circle and hurled it directly at the remaining hunter.

The man's arms went up instinctively, but the dart sailed high . . . as it was meant to. The hunter lowered his arms to find Elijah standing before him, head bowed, blood trickling down his remaining sword's blade. The man's head joined his arms in their downward fall.

Elijah stood alone now in the bright clearing, Enobe dangling loosely in his right hand. The world was spinning. Shadows danced their mystical gyrations all around him. He swayed as the breeze picked up once again. His pulse was nearly nonexistent. He tried to take a step and collapsed to his knees in the soft dirt, now moist with fresh blood.

Enobe fell from his limp hand and he closed his eyes, only another slight breeze away from toppling into unconsciousness.

At first he thought the sinister chuckle nothing more than his imagination, an unusually loud moaning of tree branches in the ever-increasing wind.

Until the cold steel of a chain wrapped around his neck.

Elijah fought to lift his eyelids even as he felt himself being lifted from the ground by powerful, clawed hands.

He had forgotten about the demon.

His feet were well above the earth now. He imagined the demon Dalfien standing before him, seven feet tall, and shoulders as thick as an oak tree.

Elijah's grime-covered cheeks stretched slowly into a drunken smile, which brought a rough shake from the demon.

"Why don't you go asleep?" the demon growled, its hot, fetid breath washing across Elijah's face.

Elijah could not feel the thick chain choking his neck, but his smile only widened. Not only was this demon stupid, but it had halitosis too!

"Go asleep now!" the demon commanded with an extra violent shake.

Elijah felt himself being jerked like a helpless rag doll, and that did manage to remove the smile from his face. His male ego was still intact.

Ebonee.

Adrenaline again flowed through the Protector's veins, momentarily staunching the effects of the tranquilizer. He lashed out. "Not . . . before . . . you tuck . . . me . . . in!"

The demon howled in pain as Elijah stabbed his thumb into its eye with each shouted exclamation.

Then he was playing the Angel again, flying through the air, the wind against his face, his locks flowing magically in the moonlight . . . until he hit the tree.

His face landed on something cold and hard. He

heard the demon's angry howls and felt its thunderous footsteps as it quickly closed the distance.

Elijah wanted to do nothing more at that moment than to obey the demon's commands. He was so tired and the ground felt so soft and comfortable beneath his weary body. Comfortable except for this hard thing his head was lying on.

The demon was only a few steps from his back now.

If I could just move this thing, then I could take a nap.

The demon bellowed, raising the chain high above its head to deliver the final blow. Elijah closed his hand on the *thing* that was so uncomfortable.

Ebonee.

The thing was Soul Seeker.

Its violent vibrations shook the Protector from his drug-induced delirium just enough to act.

The chain came crashing down.

The sword sliced through the air.

Elijah crumbled under the blow that crashed down across his back. He rolled over with the momentum and the demon's head fell onto his chest.

Ebonee.

The world was a spinning vortex of shadows and darkness. Clutching at a tree, he managed to stand. "*Ebonee,*" he whispered through numb lips.

He took a step . . . and collapsed into unconsciousness.

Director Moss sat silently at Ebonee's work desk in the dark hotel room. His stubby fingers tapped upon the dark cherry wood finish. Although the room was cool because of the open balcony door, sweat was beginning to bead upon his balding head. His black eyes were circled with dark rings behind his glasses. Life had once been stress-free for the fifty-three-year-old FBI director of internal affairs and paranormal activity. Routines were followed, orders given and obeyed, and there was trust . . . no worries.

Moss sighed heavily as he felt the vibrations of his cell phone on his hip. "Director Moss," he answered. "Where?" he asked, standing abruptly from his seat as he listened to the information being dished out over the phone. "What about Agent Lane?" His lips pursed as he received the negative response. "I'll be right there."

Moss gathered his blazer and ran to the hotel suites door, rushing through it and nearly leveling a surprised Father Holbrook.

"Father Holbrook."

The priest frowned and gathered himself, brushing off his new grey suit. "Something amiss, Director?"

Moss continued down the hall. "Ebonee and Elijah are in trouble—"

"I'm going with you!" Father Holbrook announced, his face filling with dread as he picked up his walking stick and rushed to follow the director to the elevator.

Director Moss eyed him curiously as they awaited the doors to open. "I'll never get used to this look."

Father Holbrook cleared his throat and stared up at the glowing numbers. "I had a date."

The two men stopped at the front desk to get directions. Apparently, Elijah had been found somewhere near a place called Blackwood in New Jersey. The sun was just above the horizon as they sped down the highway. Traffic was horrible and Moss found out why as they passed the wreckage of Elijah's FBI-issued motorcycle. A lane was closed as the clean-up crew cleared the debris from the road.

"That's Elijah's bike," Moss said, his tone downcast.

Father Holbrook craned his neck to stare at the scene. "How can you tell?"

This was a good question, because there was nearly nothing left to ID. "I just know," Moss replied flatly.

After exiting the turnpike at the designated exit, they hit a long stretch of deserted road where they were surrounded by nothing but woods. Ahead, Moss could make out a road block.

The Blackwood police department had several cars lined up along the road, which was blocked by an unmarked FBI cruiser. Moss slowed his Crown Victoria and let down his window to speak with the single guard.

"Moss," he said absently, flashing his badge. "What's with the locals?" he asked, seeing that they were all standing around the lead car staring at them.

"FBI only beyond this point, Director," the black suit answered, eying Moss's passenger suspiciously. "Who's he?"

"He's with me," Moss answered. He wondered why the locals were being kept out.

"Just a minute, sir. I have to get authorization,"

Director Moss sighed as the man walked back to his car and got on the radio. The man returned after a brief respite.

"Director Halfrey says it's okay, you can pass," he announced.

Moss let out a frustrated sigh as he waited for the

agent to pull the cruiser up. He saw a large black van pull up behind him as he accelerated away from the roadblock.

"What's all this about? Where's Elijah?" Father Holbrook asked.

"He's here someplace I'm told," Moss answered, squinting his eyes as he pulled up to where three black unmarked FBI cruisers were parked along the side of the road. An agent waved him over to the shoulder.

"What about Ebonee?"

Moss once again let out a sigh as he stepped out of the car. "We're about to find out now, Father." He stepped up to the agent and immediately noted the sub machine gun held in his hands. "Where is he?"

The guard nodded toward the woods. "They're bringing him out now."

Moss then saw the group of men exiting the tree line. "Stay here, Father."

Father Holbrook heard the command, but was not about to listen. That is, until the suit blocked his path with an upraised machine gun. "Yes . . . yes, my plans exactly," he muttered, staring after Moss.

"Director Moss," one of the suits said, turning from the group as he saw Moss approaching.

"Director Halfrey," Moss greeted the man. "How is he?" His eyes stayed on the gurney that was being carried from the woods by two more agents. Four other agents followed, all armed with silenced automatic weapons. Moss walked passed Halfrey, his gaze intent upon the motionless figure upon the stretcher.

Halfrey reached out a hand and stopped Moss forcefully. "He's alive."

Moss stared at the hand upon his forearm and then looked into Halfrey's eyes. "Why the tight security? He's one of ours."

"Routine," Halfrey replied quietly, positioning himself between Moss and the entourage.

Moss watched as the black van then pulled up alongside of the road where the men were waiting. "What about Agent Lane?"

"No sign of her."

Frustration began to seep through Moss's rock hard appearance. "Where are you taking him?"

"Need to know," Halfrey answered.

"What do you mean, need to know? He's under my jurisdiction." Moss was failing miserably at hiding his contempt.

"Not anymore, Director."

Moss could feel his heart rate increasing as he watched the men load Elijah onto the van. "How did you find him? What happened?"

Halfrey sighed lightly and turned to head for one of the cars. "You can ride with me. I'll fill you in on the way." He led Moss to the car. "I'm only doing this because you're an old friend."

"I'm not alone," Moss said, nodding over his shoulder to where Father Holbrook stood at gunpoint.

"Oh yes, the priest."

Moss felt a chill run along his spine as he stared into Halfrey's knowing smile. "You know of him?"

"Hmm? Oh yes," Halfrey said nonchalantly, "he can ride with Agent Banks."

Moss swallowed the lump of anxiousness that he found in his throat as the car began to pull away. He watched Father Holbrook as he was led to one of the cars and forced inside, still at gunpoint. "So, what happened?"

"That part's not too clear," Halfrey began as he guided the car along the road with the seven car procession following.

"How did you find him?"

"GPS."

Moss again felt the chill along his spine. "A tracking device? But how—"

"We implanted it during his 'routine' physical."

Moss felt his head beginning to spin. "Why wasn't I informed of this?"

"Need to—"

"Don't give me that need-to-know bullshit!"

Halfrey remained calm, staring out at the road ahead for a long moment before speaking again. "Calm down, Steven, before you have a stroke."

"What about Ebonee? Why hasn't she been located?" Moss asked.

Halfrey took a moment before answering. "Her transmitter beacon must be malfunctioning."

Moss knew bullshit when he heard it. FBI gadgets never malfunctioned. "Where are you taking him? Or is that classified now too?"

"Everything is, Steven—where your boy is concerned, that is," Halfrey began, "but like I said, you're a friend, and I know you were close to him and Agent Lane, so I'm allowing you to tag along."

Moss's patience was beginning to wear thin. "Where?"

Halfrey eyed him sternly for a brief moment and then exhaled heavily. "Fort Dix."

Moss felt his bottom lip fall open at the mention of the military installation. All at once it hit him. The rumors circulating on the internet, the whispers floating in the pentagon, the increased budget for the defense department . . . two words began to bounce around in his head. Two words that filled his heart with regret and remorse. He had promised Elijah this would not happen. He had given him his word as his boss, and as his friend. The words stuck in his brain like a festering wound, damning him for his foolish promises and his trust in his country. Two words . . .

Super soldiers.

CHAPTER NINE

Mentally, Sam Rayburn could never have been prepared for what his mind was undergoing at this moment. Spiritually, Sam Rayburn could never have been prepared for what his soul was experiencing at this moment. He hung on the narrow edge of consciousness now, his skin all but flayed from his muscular physique. Kneeling in a pool of his own blood, Sam cried, trying desperately to think of nothing but the chain clutched weakly in his right hand. But the pain was excruciating, and each lash of the whip tore away at his will.

The demon's raucous laughter floated upon the darkness, disturbed only by the loud snap of the leather against his torn flesh. *Hold on.* His mind tried to rally to the words floating in his brain, memories and knowledge of what lay below giving him the will to not let go. *Shemhazai.* That was the name the demon Vakra had given to his fear.

As much as Vakra was enjoying his new toy, he felt the urge to move on and end this foolishness.

There were greater pleasures to look forward to after his mission was complete. With a demonic sigh, Vakra willed the whip away and stood, staring at the surprisingly resilient human. The fool could not hold on to the chain forever. He began contemplating his next objective—releasing Shemhazai's spirit from the prison below without getting destroyed by the guardian Seraphim.

Vakra moved his consciousness back to Sam's reality, leaving the man alone, huddled in the darkness with his chain and his hope. His eyes saw through Sam's eyes and he surveyed the cavern below. Darkness was no hindrance for a demon of the underworld. He saw clearly the four statues below, along with the two bodies and decapitated head of Michael Corvalis's wife. All were motionless. Now all he had to do was figure a way to distract the Seraphim long enough for him to release the trapped spirit beneath the burial boulders.

Slowly Sam became aware of the emptiness around him. The whip had ceased to lash at him and the maniacal laughter was gone. A fire of emotion sent a jolt along his spine, causing his body to tremble violently in the darkness of his mind, and in the oval opening of the shaft entrance. Slowly his senses returned to him. The demon was gone, looking through his eyes at the darkness below. He was planning.

Sam blocked out the pain, refused to hear the raspy breathing of his own lips as his lungs drew in air and blood. Then he sought out the demon.

Vakra felt a shudder pass through the human's body and could not help but wonder if it was his own. He stared up at the hand still holding onto the chain with a tentative grip.

A finger slipped from the hold.

* * *

On the floor of the dark burial chamber, silence laid over the bodies of the dead like a thick blanket of wool. The slime-covered stones seemed to hold the silence in place, like a shivering body on a cold November day. Until a sharp intake of breath and a soft rustling tossed the silence away.

Michael Corvalis sat bolt upright in the darkness, his lungs burning as he panted heavily, still consumed by the terrible images that had driven him into unconsciousness. His body began to shudder almost immediately and tears began to stream down his face. His sobs further destroyed the silence as he hunched over onto his knees, trembling with each flash of the creature's memory in his mind's eye. Such terror was a thing of the imagination. Never before had Michael known a dread so complete. With each flash of the vision, words were engraved upon his brain. Words he did not remember hearing the thing say, yet they shouted out to him now, filling him with fear. *Run, human. Leave this place, never to return.*

Michael's eyes suddenly opened wide to stare around at the darkness. His heart threatened to explode from his chest as he scrambled to his feet upon the guano-covered stone floor. His tears never lessened and his sobbing increased when he turned about, feeling the place where he knew the statues to be.

Michael could see nothing in the thick shadows, yet he ran for all he was worth. He had to obey the voices. He was not conscious of the exit, which stared down at him over fifty feet above the floor. He was not cognizant of the bodiless head of his wife. He was completely entranced by his fear, running blindly, his only purpose, to be as far away from this place as possible.

He hit the wall with a sickening smack, falling back onto his behind. The pain did not register, nor did the wall itself. Instantly he rebounded to his feet in the darkness, his hands going forward madly, fingernails tearing off as he clawed at the jagged surface before him. He gave no thought to the impossibilities of scaling the vertical wall. Several times, in his maddened state, he defied gravity, climbing several feet up the sheer face of the wall, only to fall to his backside. The last fall came from ten feet and knocked the wind from his terror-filled body.

He lay there stunned for a moment, a moment that allowed his wild eyes to catch a glimpse of a small circle of light high above him. In that light a figure hung by a chain. A sliver of awareness fought through Michael's fear. "SAM!"

Vakra growled with annoyance. He was drawing a blank on his plan to distract the Seraphim. He was just about to turn his attention inward, to the tortured mind of Sam Rayburn, when he heard the shout from below. It was then that Sam's stamina gave in, relinquishing his hold of the chain.

Vakra was surprised, but only for a split second as the two beings, crowded into one body, plummeted through the darkness to the cavern floor. Vakra gave brief thought to exiting Sam's mind before the moment of impact, leaving the human to die a horrible death, but he knew he would need more than one body to accomplish his task. He easily shifted Sam's body, causing him to land on his feet with a loud shudder that shook the room. The landing would have crushed every bone in Sam's body if not for the enhanced strength on loan by the demon's presence.

Vakra turned in the darkness to where he had last seen the other human, a plan quickly forming in his mind. A tingle split his shoulder blades, again causing Vakra to scan the recesses of Sam's mind, searching him out. Oddly, there was no sign of him anywhere. Perhaps the beating, combined with the physical exertion had been enough to render him unconscious. Still, there was that chill in his spine.

Sam drifted back and forth between awareness and a blissful void. He was semi conscious of the powerful pounding of his heart, which had not yet returned to a normal pace after the plummet. *Shemhazai.* The thought triggered Sam to snap out of his daze. He accepted the pain that greeted him as he lifted his head in the darkness that was his inner being. His skin was still bloodied and torn from the beating inflicted by Vakra. *Vakra, what are you doing, you bastard?*

Sam forced himself to stand in the darkness, focusing his mind on the demon's neural transmissions. He saw them clearly then, like streaks of lightning against a dark azure sky. Calming himself, Sam honed into the thoughts, remaining perfectly still and quiet. He did not want the demon to be aware of him . . . yet.

Michael's heart was still threatening to implode as he stared at the figure which had fallen from the shaft. Dust glimmered in the weak shaft of light that fell down in a circle around the man. He appeared almost as an Angel to Michael. He continued to stare at Sam, his hope of escaping the damned place increasing with each breath he now took. *Run human! Never return!* The words slammed into Michael's mind louder and fiercer than before, accompanied by the horrifying image of the Seraphim. He bolted forward, running toward Sam as his fear returned tenfold.

"Sam! Help me please! Get me out of here!" He tripped several times in the darkness, scraping his knees and palms, but he felt no pain. "We must flee this place!"

Vakra grinned as he watched the human scramble into the weak light around him. His hands were bloody, his clothes torn and covered in guano. The madness in his eyes was a delicious sight to the nefarious demon.

Michael crawled forward, despair filling his pounding heart. He clutched at Sam's legs, begging, pleading, his eyes scanning the darkness behind him fearfully. Sam was a clever man, a very resourceful man. He would find a way for them to escape, Michael was sure of it.

"My dear Michael, I have found you."

Michael's heart wrenched to a stand still in his chest and his lips found no air. Confusion twisted his face into a bewildered look of helplessness. Slowly he brought his gaze up and around to stare at the grinning man in befuddlement. "B-B-Bridgette?"

Large blue eyes, magnified by thick bifocals, stared down in amazement at the marvel that was Elijah Garland. "The rate of tissue generation is remarkable."

Doctor Truman Wilford had never seen anything like this in a decade of work for the government. The bright lights of the examination room seemed to be far indisposed of the doctor. With his grey hair tucked neatly beneath his OR cap and loose fitting green smock, he could focus on nothing else but what lay before him upon the cold, translucent slab of fiberglass.

His hand carefully guided a scalpel from Elijah's sternum to his navel, leaving a trail of blood upon his dark chocolate skin. Quickly, the doctor removed the scalpel and blotted a swab near the initial incision. His eyes again widened in disbelief. The wound was gone! Once more he took up his scalpel.

"Doctor Truman!" a loud voice echoed alarmingly into the vast, nearly empty room, causing the doctor to start and drop the scalpel to the immaculate white tiled floor where it clattered loudly in the stillness. "We don't have time for fun . . . have you collected the proper amount of blood?"

Doctor Truman snarled as he turned to face Director Halfrey. "I need more time with this specimen! Do you know the possibilities?"

Director Halfrey gave the room a once over, seeing the filled vials of blood on a small metallic cart next to the operating table, he waved his men in. "No more time," he said flatly, ushering him away from the table by the arm. "You want more time? Then do what we have enlisted you to do. Make your own specimen."

The doctor tried to pull away, his eyes refusing to leave the body. "But that will take time!"

"All the more reason for you to stop bullshitting here and get to it!" Halfrey scolded, shoving the man into the wide hallway.

Director Moss strained his neck to see through the open doors as the two men exited. But a rough shove with the butt end of an M-16 rifle hindered his way. He glared at the guard, and then turned to Father Holbrook. "Elijah is in there."

The priest seemed oddly docile. "There is nothing you can do, Director," he began softly, "have faith in God, Steven."

Moss eyed the priest curiously until Halfrey stepped up. "What are they doing to him?"

"You know what they are doing, Moss . . . let's not play 'I Spy' now," Halfrey said, gesturing for them to walk with him.

"I can't let this—"

"Let it go, Steven. It's beyond us now," Halfrey said.

Moss stopped and stared back down the wide, brightly lit hallway. Armed soldiers in camouflage uniforms stood guard at each door. "The Department of Defense?"

Halfrey sighed and turned to gaze at his old friend. "Higher."

Moss was at a loss. His face was a mass of confusion, sweat beading upon his balding head as he glanced back and forth from the door to Elijah's room and back at Halfrey. Who would want Elijah if it were not the FBI or the Department of Defense? Who higher than both of these powerful agencies? And why?

The three men stood in silence, until Father Holbrook opened his mouth and shocked them both. "The Vatican."

CHAPTER TEN

lijah forced his eyes closed tighter, growling angrily at the sudden intense light that destroyed his moment of nothingness. His nostrils billowed, taking in the cool air and filling his lungs. He brought a hand up to shield his face and slowly cracked open his eyelids. Sand shifted beneath the weight of his hand as he pushed himself up to a sitting position, squinting as his eyes adjusted to the glaring sun.

He was in a vast desert. Endless mounds of rolling sand spread out before him as far as his eyes could see. He turned in a complete circuit, his white locs drifting in the breeze.

He was dreaming again.

Elijah's eyes went up to the blinding ball of golden light that seemed too close to the earth. Its heat scorched the ground, causing the very mountaintops to smolder. Yet Elijah felt no discomfort.

Ebonee.

Elijah sighed at the thought of her, his eyes closing slowly. Then, just as abruptly as the blinding light had brought him from his slumber, he turned, shouting at the top of his lungs in anger, "It's fucking meaningless!" Rage twisted Elijah's face as he stared up into the blinding globe of light. "All of it is fucking meaningless!"

Tears fell from his enraged eyes, evaporating in hisses of steam as soon as they found his cheeks. His emotions rolled through his body like a wave of thundering tsunami's. His rage was complete. How many times had he been through this scenario? How many times more? *No more!* His brain burned from the intense feelings boiling in his blood. He thought of the pain that was his life. All of the heartbreak, the tears and the suffering that seemed to plague him from birth. "To what end?" His cry was swallowed up by the sudden howling of the wind.

His white locs whipped wildly in the powerful gusts, compelling his legs to brace against its power. He staggered under its intensity, but he held onto his rage. Then it was gone. He was left standing in a complete and sudden silence.

"Will you forsake me, Elijah?" the soft whisper came from his back.

Elijah spun on his heel to stare up at the cross which bore his Ebonee. She was naked, her hands and feet staked to the wood. Blood trickled down to pool in the sand at the base of the cross.

His rage deserted him. It was replaced by a calmness that surprised even him. He looked upon the woman, her face pleading, her lips begging, and simply turned his back.

The first step was the hardest, but it came and was soon followed by several more, until he found himself walking at a brisk pace, Ebonee's pleas fading from his ears with each step. He kept his eyes glued to the sand that passed beneath his feet, holding on to his will, gritting his teeth, refusing to turn back.

An object in the sand caught his eye. He knelt, picking the small wooden crucifix up to examine it. Elijah stared at the cross for several minutes, his face retaining its expressionless, cold demeanor. Then he scowled, drawing his arm back and letting the cross go in a throw that sent it careening through the white sky. His eyes followed its flight. And it seemed to hang in the sky for an eternity. A shudder washed through his body, so powerful he dropped to his knees. Hopelessness filled his soul and once more he cried. He cried like a babe, there in the middle of his dreams, beneath the golden ball of light amid nothingness. He cried.

Miles away, a figure stood upon the endless horizon of sand, its hand outreached to the sky. The crucifix landed in the center of his palm and slender fingers closed upon it reverently.

"Wake up!" Gabriel's voice was filled with power and laced with anger as he stared down at the sobbing Protector. "Leave this place and leave in it the blasphemous thoughts your semi-human mind has concocted!"

Elijah opened his eyes and saw the crucifix as it landed in the sand in front of him. Gabriel's words ignited his own anger and he stood to face him defiantly. "Why should I?" he asked coldly. "To face more pain, Gabriel?"

Gabriel frowned as he stared at Elijah. "What do you know of pain?" he snarled.

"It is my life," Elijah began evenly, "you should know, you gave it to me,"

"I do not have the time to cater to your fragile ego, boy! I have enlisted you to a cause, and you shall carry through with it until its end."

Elijah's eyes swelled with emotion. "To what end? For what purpose? It is all meaningless!" His eyes went to the sand at his feet once more as he recalled words he could never forget.

"*What does a man gain from all his labor at which he toils under the sun? Generations come and generations go, but the earth remains forever. The sun rises and the sun sets, and hurries back to where it rises. The wind blows to the south and turns to the north; round and round it goes, ever returning on its course. All streams flow into the sea, yet the sea is never full. To the place the streams come from, there they return again. The eye never has enough of seeing, or the ear its fill of hearing. What has been shall be again, what has been done shall be done again, there is nothing new under the sun.*"

Gabriel chuckled softly as he stared at Elijah. "Ecclesiastes. I am impressed." The sarcasm in his words was not meant to be missed. He gazed at Elijah thoughtfully for a moment, never relinquishing his wry smile. "You know . . . I have always been in awe of man's halfsightedness. You see only what you want to see, only what your burden will allow you to see."

"It's the truth! All of it is meaningless!" Elijah shouted.

"The truth? You will never know the truth, for you are too blinded by your own sin to know it is with you at all times! You see only what Lucifer wants you to see! Your back is bent with the weight of his iniquity and your eyes forever cast downward at your feet!" Gabriel's smile was gone now, and his anger piqued. He closed on Elijah, who could no longer hold his gaze. "Say the rest of it! I implore you! Speak it and condemn me to hell!" he shouted.

Elijah was silent, for he had never read beyond those words.

"All right," Gabriel said, his voice calm once again, "I'll finish it for you. *Now all has been heard; here is the conclusion of the matter: Fear God and keep his commandments, for this is the whole duty of man. For God will bring every deed into judgment, including every hidden thing, whether good or evil.*"

Elijah turned from the words, slamming his eyes shut tightly. Fear devoured his anger, and then came the sorrow.

Gabriel's expression softened at once and his voice took on a calming tone. "Open your eyes, Elijah," he began softly, "You want the truth? Lay down your burden and stand erect . . . *The truth is the light and has been with you always.*"

Elijah knew that Gabriel was gone. Even as he dropped to his knees with the weight of his burden, he could feel the absence of his presence. His heart pounded within his chest, like a raging wildfire unable to be contained. His tears spilled forth as his hands closed upon the small crucifix between his knees in the sand.

Suddenly, Elijah was aware of the intense heat radiating from the ball of light high in the sky. It took several moments, but Gabriel's words finally struck through to his heart.

Elijah swallowed his fear and fought to control the violent trembling of his body. *I understand now.* And with that thought, he stood to his feet, leaving his burden behind. Slowly, he lifted his head toward the fiery ball of light. Its heat was strangely comforting. It did not scorch his skin, yet Elijah knew in his heart that it could do so at a whim. No, the warmth he felt comforted him and helped a smile slowly spread across his lips. For the first time in his life, Elijah stood perfectly still, digesting the meaning of all that he had heard from his father, Gabriel. Then, as his hands gripped the small silver crucifix tightly, Elijah opened his eyes and stared into the light . . . he stared into the truth.

Sergeant First Class Ronald Baker frowned as he guided the gurney along the wide hallway within the top-secret facility. His eyes did not bother to take in the scenery around him, for there was nothing but blank walls and shining floors. He did not know the other guards, nor did he care to. All SFC Baker cared about at that moment was getting the gurney to the transport. Once that was done, his shift would be over and he had a very hot date with a fine-ass sista that worked in the military exchange. His eyes fell down to glance at the young black man secured to the rolling metal table and he sighed.

Poor brotha, I wonder what kinda shit they got planned for you?

The hard plastic wheels of the gurney squealed as they turned a corner, making a sound that Baker found truly annoying. He took his eyes off of the patient and glanced down at the wheels. When he looked back up, cold brown eyes were locked upon him. Even as his jaw fell open in shock, the man's long black dreadlocks faded before his very eyes, until they were as white as the purest snow. Baker froze, unable to move under the eerie gaze.

The other five guards glanced at him curiously and stopped the gurney and then they too noticed the man's eyes open.

"Holy hell! The sedative wore the fuck off! Quick, get another one going!" one of the guards shouted, reaching for the IV that hung from a pole above Elijah's head. His hand froze and he stared at the IV bag in shock. It was half full and working just fine. "Get out the tasers!"

Baker could not explain the wave of emotions that ran through his body as he continued to stare down into Elijah's eyes. The look he saw there was one of complete bliss, supreme ecstasy. He watched as a tear rolled free of Elijah's eye, and he knew that there was no threat to them. "No!" He did not remember shouting the word, nor did he know why he did. "It's okay . . . he won't hurt us,"

The excited guard stared at him, one hand at his waist about to draw his weapon. After a moment of dubious glances within the group, they finally calmed down. Elijah's eyes were once again closed, and a blissful peace was etched onto his ebony features.

SFC Baker felt warmth fill him as he continued to eye the young black man. "Let's get him to the transport," he finally said.

As they began to roll the gurney along the hall once more, Baker heard a metallic clatter and gazed down to the floor beneath the gurney. There he found a small silver cross attached to a silver chain. He stopped the gurney and picked it up, wondering where it had come from. A questioning glance to the others told him it did not belong to any of them.

Smiling, SFC Baker placed the cross in the palm of Elijah's hand and felt reassured when his slender fingers closed over the cold metal.

"What's the hold up?" Director Halfrey turned the corner, seeing the men standing around the gurney. Immediately they began to move forward.

Moss joined Halfrey as the gurney passed them, heading for the elevator at the end of the hall. Father Holbrook had to be physically restrained when he saw the Protector being carted by.

"And you have no idea where they are taking him?" Moss asked, his eyes never straying from Elijah.

"Not a clue," Halfrey replied. Then he stared at his old friend and gestured for him to follow him to a door. The two men stepped into an office which contained a large desk and a small filing cabinet.

Halfrey closed the door behind them and turned to Moss. "Listen, Steven," he began softly, "you know as well as I, how cold this business can be." He paused, exhaling as if he were so very tired. "When they first offered me this position I hesitated to accept it. I didn't think I was ready to handle the responsibility." His voice became softer as he continued and his eyes went to the floor. "I had nightmares regularly during the first few years . . . all the young lives unfortunate enough to die in the line of duty . . . on a mission I assigned to them." A moment of silence filled the room. "Have you ever lost an agent, Steven?"

Moss sighed heavily, swallowing hard.

"No, I suppose you haven't," Halfrey continued, "I guess there isn't as much risk of death over in the unexplained phenomena department, eh?" He chuckled lightly.

Moss rolled his eyes. "What's your point, Director?"

"My point is this, Steven, I know what you're feeling right now, and if it were me, I wouldn't accept the codes to the security office where they are holding Elijah's belongings. I also wouldn't allow anyone to give me the GPS tracking device's frequency so that I could follow him. . . ."

Moss's heart rate increased as he listened to Halfrey, who was now grinning.

"But I warn you, Steven, whoever this entity is that has the Defense Department jumping like cockroaches when the light comes on, is very dangerous . . . my hands are clean of it as of right now," he said, holding up his palms. "As far as the girl is concerned, you have every resource we have to help you find her."

"Thank you, I'll probably be needing them," Moss said, accepting a sheet of paper from Halfrey that contained the frequency to Elijah's implant. Both men then stepped back into the hallway under the curious stare of Father Holbrook.

"Captain Morel here is in charge of things for the Department of Defense." Halfrey gestured to one of the soldiers standing next to Father Holbrook.

"Captain," Moss nodded his greeting as he moved to stand in front of the slender white male. "I would like to request that the subject's personal effects be released to me."

"Take what you like," the smooth faced man began, "we have all we need."

Moss stared at him and then cut a curious gaze back to Halfrey. "Who's transporting him?"

"That . . . is confidential information, Director," Captain Morel said. "You have all you are going to get, now I suggest you utilize the extension of my courtesy to you and the priest here and be on your way ASAP."

The muscles in Moss's cheeks clenched repeatedly as he stared at Morel. "Where can I get the belongings?"

Morel seemed to take comfort in the fact that he was getting under Moss's skin. He waited a long while before replying. "Second door that you came in, Director."

Moss turned on his heels with a final glance at Director Halfrey, and then gestured for the priest to follow.

"Director Moss," Morel called out, causing Moss to stop and turn. "The other way."

Moss and Father Holbrook stepped slowly back in the opposite direction, with Moss calmly eyeing Morel as they passed. "Thank you," he said sarcastically.

When the two men stepped into the door the Captain indicated, Father Holbrook stood with his back to the door. "Do you think the blades are here?"

Moss ignored him and went straight for the single rectangular, metal table situated in the center of the empty room. "How's this for an answer?" He held up Soul Seeker.

Former Director Glenn watched Vito from across the small cluttered room closely as the big man moved to answer the knock at the secluded shack's single wooden door. They had arrived several hours earlier, just before dawn with no signs of pursuit and no signs of the freak. Glenn's mood was foul indeed as he watched Vito escort a thin white man with grey balding hair into the room. "Who the hell is he?"

Vito offered his always-present grin and stepped past the two men. "Doctor Herman Pokalman, this is—" His gruff words fell away as he stopped to stare at Glenn in the sulky light of the shack.

"What the hell is he doing here?" Glenn exclaimed.

Vito chuckled and gestured for the doctor to follow him. "He is here to see to the required state of our prisoner."

Glenn frowned, hurrying to follow the men to the small square door set within the floor near the back of the room. "Required state? What the hell does that mean?"

Vito easily hefted the heavy wooden door and waved the doctor on. "You will soon see."

Glenn waited until the doctor was well into the sub level of the shack before grabbing Vito by the arm. "Look, if we are supposed to be working together, I would appreciate it if you let me in on a few things," he sneered.

Vito calmly turned to regard the hand holding on to his thick bicep and then gave Glenn an utterly chilling look that promised a lot of broken bones. Glenn immediately removed his hand. Vito smiled once more. "I will tell you what you need to know, when you need to know it."

Glenn fumed as Vito then disappeared down into the darkness. After a glance around the now empty room, he followed the big man down into the cellar.

"Wait here," Vito instructed the doctor.

Glenn came right behind the man in the shadows, waiting for Vito to turn on the light. A chain rattled in the gloom and then a swarthy cone of light illuminated a old wooden table in the center of the room. The doctor's eyes lit up as he stared at the woman laid out on the table and he moved closer with Glenn on his heels.

Vito eyed the doctor as he approached. "Will this take long?"

Doctor Pokalman took a moment to answer, his eyes now roaming over the ebony skinned woman's firm breasts. "N-no . . . not long at all," he whispered absently. Then he stared up at Vito. "I mean, I will need a few moments to insure the procedure is complete."

Vito turned to Glenn, who was now standing on the opposite side of the table, staring at the doctor. "Stay here with him, I'm going to go contact Enoch."

Doctor Pokalman was in his own world. He neither heard Vito's comments, nor was he aware of Glenn's cold gaze fixed upon him. His eyes seemed to glaze over as he stared down at the dark-skinned beauty laid out before him. Absently, his white, thin fingers went to her cheek, gliding softly across her skin.

"Do what you came to do," Glenn said coldly.

Doctor Pokalman flinched at the sudden words, snatching his gaze to meet the angry glare from Glenn. "Y-yes . . . yes," he stuttered. He then retrieved his small black leather bag from the floor, depositing it upon a small table next to Ebonee's head. "I was not expecting something so delicate," he said, removing a syringe and a small vial from the bag.

Glenn sighed heavily as he frowned, his eyes dropping down to woman. Here was the object of his hate. The instrument of his downfall. "Not so delicate," he whispered.

Pokalman stared up at Glenn with a curious expression, he could see the distaste in his eyes. He swallowed a lump in his throat as he looked back to Ebonee. "She will need to be conscious."

Glenn remained silent as the doctor produced a small cylinder of gauze, he then broke the ampoule inside and waved it beneath Ebonee's nostrils.

The pungent aroma snatched Ebonee from the restful darkness. Her eyes flashed open and her body thrashed, fighting against the restraints holding her to the table. The room was a blur of shadow and light as her vision slowly cleared. She saw Glenn first.

Their eyes locked briefly in a moment of mutual hatred until Ebonee noticed the second figure hovering over her. Her heart was racing and she could feel the burning around her wrists and ankles where the bindings held her securely. The lust in the doctor's beady black eyes went unnoticed as she searched the shadows, looking for some hint to her whereabouts. Her racing pulse belied the calmness she appeared to portray.

"Where am I?" she shouted at the doctor, refusing to look at Glenn.

The doctor glanced over to Glenn, expecting him to speak.

The hate in Glenn's eyes never diminished and he remained silent. He would let her bask in her misery.

"Where am I?" Ebonee screamed at the doctor.

"Shhh," the doctor began, leaning in close with the syringe in his hand, "everything will be okay in a few moments."

Fear slowly began to crawl through Ebonee as she felt the doctor's hot breath upon her skin. There was madness in his eyes, or was it simply lust? She trembled as he slid the point of the syringe across her cheek. She tried to hold completely still, afraid the needle would puncture her skin.

"Yesss," Doctor Pokalman hissed, "everything will be fine."

Ebonee jerked her head away as his face lowered closer to her, his long nose widening as he inhaled deeply, closing his eyes.

A scowl slowly developed on Glenn's face as he watched the doctor's face contort into what he figured to be ecstasy. Growling, he snatched the man's arm up, gesturing to the syringe. "What is it?"

Doctor Pokalman glared at Glenn with hatred in his eyes. He almost looked ready to strike out at him. But his rational side won out, and he lowered his gaze to the syringe. "Gamma-Hydroxybutyrate," he said flatly, attempting to pull his hand free, but Glenn did not release him.

"The date rape drug?"

Pokalman frowned. "Similar."

Glenn released his arm. "Wake her up to put her back to sleep?"

The doctor sighed as he rolled up Ebonee's sleeve. "Not quite . . . sleep would be a lesser degree of the state she will be in."

Ebonee had never known fear like the dread she felt now. She knew there would be no answers coming from Glenn, and most likely, the doctor knew little or nothing at all about her plight. No, this was something deep. Someone somewhere had it in for her. Someone powerful. And her instincts screamed out dark thoughts. Flashes of her time spent at the hands of the demon Dalfien filled her mind.

"At the right dosage, GHB will cause the subject's life signs to dwindle to the point of being imperceptible. Effectively slipping her into a coma which—"

"Kill me now."

Both men stared down at Ebonee at the sound of

the barely discernable words. A smile found Glenn's face as he watched the tears begin to stream down her ebon skin.

"You would like that wouldn't you?" he sneered. "Where is your hope, Ebonee? Have you no faith in your freak boyfriend? Will you not wait for him to come dashing to your rescue?" His laughter echoed in the small room.

"Kill me."

"No way, beautiful." Glenn smiled. "Whatever it is that is so terrible— so horrible that it has you seeking death— I'm going to send you to it. I owe you that much."

Ebonee fought to control her trembling body as she watched the doctor lower the needle to her arm. She watched it hover there, the doctor's steady hand holding completely still.

"Perhaps," the doctor looked up to Glenn, his eyes pleading, "I would be allowed a moment with her . . . alone."

However much Glenn hated Ebonee, he hated perverts that much more. It was all he could do to refrain from breaking the man's neck where he stood. "Do what you came to do and no more . . . and do it before I change my mind about letting you live."

Anger filled the doctor's heart as he stared at Glenn. "I will do her no harm . . . please . . . just a moment alone."

Glenn's hand closed into a fist. "You piece of shit—"

"Leave him, former Director."

Glenn froze as Vito stepped from the shadows near the stairs. The large man walked up to the doctor and glanced down at Ebonee. Her brown eyes glistened with tears of hopelessness. "You have an hour," Vito announced, turning to head back for the stairs.

Glenn was sickened by the disgusting grin that appeared upon the doctor's face. "You can't be serious." He moved quickly, again grabbing Vito by the arm before the man could go up the stairs.

This time, Vito did not just give Glenn a hard stare. Almost too quickly, his hand closed over Glenn's, ripping it away from his own arm. Glenn fell to his knees as he heard cartilage twisting, his face contorted in pain.

"If not for Enoch, you would be dead already, former Director," Vito began quietly, "remember your place!"

Glenn growled in defiance as Vito released his sprained hand and walked up the stairs. He paused near the top and turned back, his face now illuminated by the light of the room above. The sickening grin was there. "Well?" he called down to Glenn.

Glenn remained tight lipped, his anger building as he stared up at Vito. "Fuck you."

Vito chuckled lightly. "The second subject awaits us . . . we can be there and back within two hours."

"Second subject?" Glenn asked, forcing his anger to the rear of his mind.

"Elijah Garland."

Glenn's anger was forgotten as the name echoed in his ears. Images of "the freak" as he called him, standing on the back of their car, his eyes fierce as Glenn pumped bullet after bullet into his torso flittered in his memory. Why was Enoch going after him?

Vito's voice carried down the stairs to Glenn.

"Don't worry, former Director . . . he has been sub-
dued for us."

Glenn snapped out of his thoughts and bolted up
the stairs. Whatever this Enoch was up to, he would
find out soon enough.

Doctor Pokalman stared into the shadows near
the stairs, waiting to hear the close of the door.
When the subtle thud found its way to his ears, his
lips parted in a wicked grin.

Ebonee trembled as a chill washed through her
body when his tiny black eyes turned to her. Her
stomach churned and she felt the need to vomit as
he leaned over her, his breath smelling of stale cig-
arettes and liquor. She pulled at her bindings in
vain, stretching her neck in an effort to escape his
closeness.

"We are alone now my ebony goddess," he began
in a whisper, "when we first met I felt our bond."

Ebonee shrieked as she felt his tongue slide
across her cheek.

"Do you remember? It was only a day ago."

Ebonee's eyes went wide as an image popped into
her mind. The routine examinations, he was the
one.

"My prayers have been answered," he continued
slowly, his hand going in his bag and withdrawing a
surgical scalpel.

Ebonee held her breath as she felt the cold steel
press against her throat. Slowly he moved the blade
down to her top, his eyes mad with lust.

Ebonee screamed as the doctor's lust exploded in
a blur of action. The scalpel sliced at her clothing as
his hands grabbed at her, holding her, groping. His
breathing was ragged, coming in short gasps until

he had her completely naked. Then he climbed up onto the table, his face gliding along her legs. She could hear his deep inhalations as she stared down at his head as it moved between her thighs. Her tears began anew when his face looked up from between her legs, a sick smile stretched across his lips.

"I have always loved watching black whores getting fucked by huge black cocks." His breath was hot as he brought his head up her trembling belly. "I like to hear them scream and moan . . . watch them squirm and cry out in pain . . . you black whores enjoy that, don't you? You enjoy the pain . . . you like long hard cocks rammed into your bowels."

Ebonee shuddered, watching him as his eyes closed and his hips grinded in the air above her groin. Then she noticed the scalpel still clutched in his hand next to hers beside her head. She also saw the syringe protruding from his shirt pocket, filled with the drug he planned to use on her. She heard him gasping.

"N-no . . . not yet." His eyes opened again, staring at Ebonee. "I want to see you squirm first . . . I want to hear your pain."

Ebonee watched as he reached over with his free hand to dig around in the large black leather bag. Her heart rate tripled when she saw what came out of that bag.

Dr. Pokalman waved the object before her face slowly. "Big isn't it? Just like you black whores like it."

Ebonee panicked, struggling against the leather bands binding her to the table. This only seemed to heighten the doctor's arousal.

"Yesss, you want it don't you? How much of it will

you take before you scream?" he whispered sadisti-
cally, letting the object slide down between Ebonee's
bare breasts. "Ten inches? Thirteen?"

"Please, no," Ebonee whimpered. The doctor trembled at her childlike plea, his hips jerking spasmodically. She saw the blade fall from his hand next to
hers.

Her fingers reached out for the slim blade.

Suddenly her body went rigid and her lungs filled
with the swift, quick inhalation of air.

Her fingers brushed the cool metal of the scalpel.

Ebonee screamed.

CHAPTER ELEVEN

Michael Corvalis shuddered like the leaves of a sapling in a powerful hurricane as he fell back, staring up through tear filled eyes at Sam Rayburn. He could not dare to think about what he had just heard. He dared not think about anything at this moment except the whispered words that still resonated in his terrorized mind. *Run human . . . and never return to this place.* Michael screamed out into the darkness, the shifting shadows becoming the horrible image that shouted into his mind. The Seraphim.

"Don't be afraid, Michael," Vakra said. He did his best to hide the smile he felt creeping onto Sam Rayburn's face as he watched the human squirm on the rocks. He knew the source of the human's fear at once. He could sense the guardians of the tomb, which meant they too, could sense him. He had no time to spare. He continued to speak to Michael through Sam, using Bridgette's voice. "Michael, you must listen to me. My spirit is trapped and only you can free me."

"Shut up!" Michael's strained voice shattered the silence. "You're dead!" he cried. His eyes were wide now as madness slowly began to filter into his system. He huddled in ball, clutching his knees to his chest. "I-I-must escape . . . that's all I *must* do."

Vakra stared down at the vegetative fool who continued to mutter to himself. Then he stiffened, feeling movement from the shadows near the statues. The Seraphim stirred.

"There is a way for you to escape, Michael," Bridgette's voice said hurriedly as Vakra saw a plan take root in his demonic brain.

Michael ceased his rambling and stared up at Sam. "Escape? You can help me escape?" he marveled, crawling on his hands and knees toward the weak shaft of light where Sam stood.

"Yes, there is a way—" Vakra suddenly fell silent and both figures searched the area with fear filled eyes at the sudden rush of air and the flutter of wings in the darkness. A shadow passed the shaft of light high above their heads.

Michael screamed. "It's going to kill us!"

The powerful presence hovered in the air above them and Vakra could feel it reaching out to them, as if it were judging them. "Quickly," Vakra began in Bridgette's voice, "there is a tunnel, beyond the statues and beneath the rubble there."

A strong gust of wind disheveled Michael's already mussed hair.

"Go, I will distract them so that you may escape, my husband."

Michael was already running for the boulders before Vakra could get the last word out.

"Fool," Vakra muttered, watching the man run blindly into the darkness. He then focused his attention on the Seraphim. He knew they would all focus on him, so with a great bellow, he drew their attention, running away from the boulders and deferring their awareness from Michael.

He felt them around him almost immediately. He could sense them about to strike. But before they could, Vakra concentrated, falling back into Sam's mind and seeking out the door that would take him back to his own plane of existence. He found it, and in an instant, his spirit zipped through the dark realm, finding the door to Michael's mind in a split second.

Sam remained silent within the shadows of his own consciousness. Even when Vakra vacated his mind, he did not move. He stared at the magical portal the demon had fled through. He knew there was no tunnel; it was a lie Vakra had used to get Michael close to the boulders. Therefore, there was no exit. At first, Sam only thought of his freedom, to be rid of the demon, to have his body back. But as he stared out into the darkness of the cavern, feeling the presence of the Seraphim all around him, Sam saw the hopelessness in that. Vakra would escape this place, using that doorway, leaving Sam trapped. The door began to fade from his sight. Sam felt a tear run down his cheek as he shifted his resolutions. Freedom was no longer his objective. Sam prayed as he huddled in the darkness, for prayer was all left to him.

Freedom was gone, vengeance replaced it.

Michael ignored the shriek that tore into the silence behind him as he stumbled blindly along, his arms seeking the mound of boulders Bridgette had told him to find. His sobs echoed in his ears, louder than his shuffling feet. He tripped over a stone and fell atop the first of the large boulders. Hope brought his racing heart to an even higher pace. His arms reached around the heavy stone and he heaved. The boulder did not shift in the slightest.

Vakra wasted no time forcing his way into Michael's consciousness. The weak, fear-filled human offered no resistance as Vakra took over the task of moving the boulder. He strained against the spiritual bond holding the stone in place, ignoring the sudden terror-filled shriek that suddenly filled Michael's mind.

Michael felt the Seraphim coming.

Vakra focused on the stone until finally with a loud grating, the boulder slid away, rolling down and smashing against the wall of the cavern. But Vakra was not satisfied. Michael's screams continued to fill their shared brain as Vakra grabbed a hold of a second boulder in the darkness. He heaved with desperation, even as he felt the first Seraphim's claw dig into Michael's spine. The boulder rolled away with a second violent crash.

Vakra paused as his spirit exited Michael's body through the portal. He had done what he had been instructed to do. But had it been enough? He decided to make sure.

Sam felt the demon's presence the moment the portal opened in the shadows of his mind. He forced himself to remain calm and silent, so as not to alert the demon to his awareness.

Vakra reclaimed Sam's body and stood, staring in the direction of the tomb. He could hear the Seraphim, still tearing and maiming Michael's dead body. They would soon realize his trick and come for Sam. Even at that very moment he could already sense the Seraphim attuning to his presence. Their anger filled the darkness as they spun around, moving with all speed toward Sam.

And then it happened.

Sam was crying before the complete dread could wash through the entire cavern. The very air shivered from the malevolent force that yanked the tears from Sam's eyes in the darkness. The Seraphim froze, turning to stare at the mound of boulders. The earth trembled above them, and the shaft collapsed in upon itself, trapping all inside. But these beings were not confined to the physical world, and none of them paid the earth's rending any attention. But Sam paid it all the attention in the world. The only exit was sealed. His only glimmer of freedom, gone, and on top of all of that . . .

Shemhazai was free.

The four Seraphim cried out in a single voice as they charged the spiritual entity which now hovered in the darkness above the mound. Their great and terrible spears led the way as they sought to imprison that which should have never been freed.

Vakra turned Sam's lips up into a wide grin as he felt the dark being rise from the stones. He immediately sent a mental image to the powerful spirit, showing him the magical portal that would take him to the ethereal domain where Rathamon awaited.

Sam swallowed back his fear as he took it all in, watching from a dark recess within his own mind. He sensed Vakra as the demon fled through his consciousness, seeking the doorway that would take it back to its own dimension and leave Sam to die in the black cave. Anger replaced the fear in Sam's heart and vowed his vengeance as he saw the door's soft red glow appear.

Vakra disappeared through the portal. Sam's heart tripled its pace as he stood, his eyes holding fast to the fading doorway to hell.

Then Sam found a distant memory from his childhood, a memory he had thought long forgotten. The words of the prayer flowed from his lips as easily as if he were reading the scripture directly from the bible.

"*The Lord is my shepherd I shall not want. He maketh me to lie down in green pastures: he leadeth me beside the still waters. He restoreth my soul: he leadeth me in the path of righteousness for his names sake. Yea though I walk through the valley of the shadow of death,*" Sam closed his eyes in the darkness, taking the step that would lead him into the unknown. "*. . . I will fear no evil, for thou art with me . . .*"

The words of the prayer stayed with Sam as he vanished through the portal, leaving his physical body lying upon the cold stone floor of the black cave, still and unmoving.

Vengeance would be his.

Moans of intense anguish flowed eternally upon the deep shadows in this place, cries of pain, and whimpers of agony—these were the melodies of the underworld . . . these were the sounds of hell. The muted glow of molten lava flows cast an eerie red sheen upon the black, scorched earth. This was a place of suffering, and every shadow held pain.

Minor demons scoured the darkness, snatching up human souls, forcing them into physical forms to be mutilated, maimed, and destroyed, their painful wails drifting up to join in the cyclical cacophony of dread. Winged demons howled and swooped down from the fetid heights, their long claws snatching up damned souls and demons alike.

Within the gloom, upon a small island surrounded by the ever-flowing lava, sat an ill designed throne. The enormous seat was constructed of human limbs, stretched and bent at awkward angles. Eyeballs stared out from the mass of twisted flesh, grotesque mouths wailed in incessant agony. Upon the throne sat the enormous demon, Dalfien. His black eyes set deep within his canine skull, staring out into the abyss, contemplating his exile.

The small island would be his prison for the next one thousand years thanks to that cursed Protector and his stinging blades. The foul beast's lip quivered, sending a line of drool to hang from blade-like teeth.

A shadowy figure appeared in the gloom, moving along a narrow path that led to Dalfien's island. As it drew closer, Dalfien could see that his visitor carried something beneath its arm. His forked tongue slid hungrily across his foul mouth, anticipation surging through his dark demeanor. Banishment was his hell, but oh how easily the time would pass—with the soul of his most hated enemy's dearest beloved to torture. Already Dalfien had devised countless cruel torments to implement upon this soul, and as the figure drew closer, a thousand more came to mind.

Rathamon suppressed his mirth as he approached his larger sibling, seeing the desire in his eyes. His hunger for that which Rathamon had promised was more than evident and could be seen clearly in his posture. His great muscles flexed as he sat forward, drooling, eyes focused on the body beneath Rathamon's arm.

A toothy grin slipped through Rathamon's expression as he dropped the body unceremoniously to the smoldering earth. He studied Dalfien's expression, watching his hunger and desire quickly change to anger and dejection. Rathamon kicked the body hard in the side, clearing an area for his own throne which now began to writhe to life from the stone at his feet. Appendages stretched forth, twisting and bending, bones breaking, new cries of anguish joined with those already present, as Rathamon's throne took shape.

Rathamon continued to eye his older sibling, taking joy in his disappointment, for no action he took was without purpose. For so long he had been looked down upon by his elder kin, Rathamon the weakling, tormentor of children and fools, they would call him.

Dalfien's claws clutched the arm of his throne with enough force to crush stone bringing louder moans from the souls trapped within the dire seat. Every fiber of his body wanted to reach out and throttle Rathamon where he stood. Perhaps torturing a sibling would suffice for a thousand years . . .

"Your thoughts betray you, brother," Rathamon said evenly, his dark eyes narrowing as he stared at Dalfien, who only growled, his eyes glancing angrily back and forth between the body and Rathamon. "Oh, I see," Rathamon began, feigning surprise as he followed Dalfien's stare, "you believed this to be." He paused to place a chiding stare on Dalfien. "You know as well as I that a human can have no true physical form here," Rathamon chuckled at his own little dose of revenge, but then his demonic face drew up into a tight semblance of seriousness. "Curb your anger, brother, or our agreement will be null."

Dalfien's wide neck bulged with veins as thick as the legs of his throne. He stood abruptly, stalking forward to tower of the smaller demon. "You dare to command me?"

Rathamon remained calm, seated upon his smaller throne; even as Dalfien's hot breath flowed down upon his face. "Command the great Dalfien? Never!" he replied sarcastically. "One of my meager existence could only hope to *advise*."

Dalfien was not smart enough to discern the sarcasm in Rathamon's voice, so he backed down, his lips still quivering with anger. "What is this you bring to my—"

"Prison?" Rathamon interjected slyly.

"Your clever tongue will be the end of you, little brother."

And your stupidity has already brought about your end, big brother. "This, dear brother," Rathamon began aloud, "is my servant—"

"You promised me a soul."

"And you shall have it," Rathamon began, "when I deem it the time."

Dalfien flashed a toothy scowl. "Perhaps you shall prove a worthy replacement."

"And perhaps I shall walk away and leave you to your devices."

The two powerful demons locked stares, their black eyes seeking any weakness in stature. Rathamon's stare proved to be the strongest. Dalfien knew he could rend the smaller demon's body into a thousand pieces, but he also knew that Rathamon would be prepared for this. His black eyes fell away from Rathamon's supreme gaze of confidence to stare into the gloom surrounding his island.

"They are there, dear brother; do not doubt," Rathamon said icily, verifying Dalfien's suspicions.

Indeed, lurking in the shadows were hundreds of
minor demons, all at Rathamon's beck and call. Dalfien bristled with anger, but also with another emotion he was not familiar with—envy. Growling, he sat
down upon his throne, his eyes holding to the dark
perimeter of his prison. "If you have not come to
deliver my—"

"Be silent!" Rathamon dared to shout. He held Dalfien's stare with ease and then continued in a more
somber tone, "Shemezai is free."

Dalfien sat back and eyed his brother with an
empty stare. "Which means exactly what to me?"

"It means that I have succeeded where you have
failed, brother," Rathamon said, glancing over to the
body. "The terrible Protector whom you so dreadfully
fear is mine." He paused, insuring Dalfien's eyes were
set on him as he spoke the next words. "As is his
bitch," Rathamon rolled his eyes as Dalfien continued to sit there, staring at him blankly. Would his
stupidity go so far as to rob him of his retribution?
A sigh escaped Rathamon's wicked lips. "You shall
have the woman."

This brought Dalfien forward in his seat. "When?"
he demanded.

"When you have admitted that you are the lesser
of us!" Rathamon spat.

Finally Dalfien realized the purpose of this visit.
Once more he sat back in his seat, eyeing his
smaller sibling. "Is it not obvious?" he asked lightly.

Rathamon stood abruptly, his maw snarling with
anger. "Say it!"

Dalfien's lips twitched as he fought to contain his

rile. His chest rose and fell, swelling with the desire to crush Rathamon where he stood.

"Say it!"

"Rathamon is the greater!" Dalfien growled, his black eyes simmering with rage.

The wails of the damned souls filled the area then, as both demons were silent. And then, Vakra stirred.

Vakra was the smallest of the greater demons, dwarfed by Dalfien and Rathamon alike. His head lifted from the ash covered rock and stared up at Rathamon.

"Is it done?" Rathamon queried.

"It is," Vakra answered as he stood. He flexed his arms and clenched his fist, glad to be back in his own body. Then he saw Dalfien. Immediately his instincts told him to run away, far away. It was not uncommon for greater demons to torture lesser demons as well as the damned souls trapped here. But Vakra's trepidation left him, as he remembered Dalfien's banished status. He held no power over him, but still, it would be wise to keep his distance.

Vakra's mind was so taken by Dalfien's presence, that he wasn't aware of his legs moving as they sought to put more of a distance between him and the foul tempered Dalfien. His awareness returned to him post haste, by courtesy of a vicious back hand.

Rathamon frowned down at Vakra as he fell to the floor of the grotto, his eyes bulging as he stared up at Rathamon, whose fist was still closed and hovering above him threateningly. The thought of torturing Vakra flitted through Rathamon's mind, but it was a mere nuance. Leave the torturing and fear invoking to his brothers. Rathamon did not care to be feared. But they would respect him!

Dalfien chuckled quietly at the exchange. His mirth faded quickly when he noticed the slight shimmering in the air above his small island prison.

Rathamon saw it too, and his eyes went wide, his grin triumphant. Slowly the shimmering air began to take a humanoid form as it drifted down between Dalfien and his sibling.

Even the grotesquely evil Dalfien felt a shiver in his bones as the purest form of evil manifested before them. They watched as the image took on a definite form, human, nearly seven feet tall. Black hair, blacker than the shadows around them, rolled over its massive shoulders in silky waves, contrasting with pale, milky skin.

Rathamon stared in awe at the creature, seeing its lowered head slowly rising, black eyes, partially hidden by the silky locks, coming to rest upon him.

Rathamon fell to his knees in fealty. "Master Shemhazai," he whispered, not daring to raise his eyes.

Vakra's heart seemed near to collapse. Fear, like he had never known, forced him to his knees, he shivered as he covered his face. Terror filled his mind and he wanted to cry out. He wanted to run and hide. So completely in awe of this malevolence was Vakra, that he was not aware of the presence that suddenly joined that fear deep in dark areas of his psyche.

Sam stood in the shadows of Vakra's mind, his physical body swelling with thoughts of revenge. Here, in this place, Sam realized he could be anything he wanted to be, he could have anything he wanted to have. In the darkness, Sam closed his eyes, concentrating. It took him a moment of intense thought, but soon he felt the cold steel in his right hand. He felt the heavy armor of the roman gladiator's upon his frame. He focused on the image of his favorite movie starring *Russell Crowe*. He felt the strap of the Roman battle helmet beneath his chin. He felt the shield in his left hand.

The cries of the damned forever echoing in the gloom slowly faded into whispered murmurs of a chant.

Vakra was stunned. He heard the strange chant in his mind and looked inward. Something was amiss. He roamed the darkness now, searching for the source of this ridiculous chant which was growing louder in his head. He delved deep into his own psyche, staring into the shadows, searching.

Then he found it.

Confusion tore at Vakra like the flails of a seven headed serpent whip. He could not understand this—*thing*—that stood before him. Golden armor glimmered in the darkness, a short broad sword rested in its right hand and a shield was held by the other.

The chants grew louder.

"Maximus, Maximus, Maximus . . ."

Vakra whirled in the darkness, which suddenly gave way to weak light. His eyes darted madly at the stands that rose up around him, a huge coliseum, filled with robed figures, all shouting hysterically, pointing, cheering . . .

Vakra then heard one sound rise above the din. He whirled to face it and awareness set in. He recognized the human. There was no mistaking those dark eyes. But there was something in those eyes Vakra did not recognize. There was no fear there. Vakra stumbled back as he suddenly realized what that look was. As Sam's war cry exploded in his eardrums, he remembered . . . that look, was rage.

"*I am free?*"

Rathamon dared to look up. He watched as Shemhazai brought his large hands up before his square set jaw, clenching his fists repeatedly. "Yes, Master. I have freed you," he said.

Shemhazai's black eyes locked on Rathamon, causing him to flinch and lower his gaze once more. Then Shemhazai stared around the dark area curiously. "What is this place?"

"It is Lucifer's realm," Rathamon answered.

Shemhazai's eyes widened slightly. "Lucifer? My beautiful brother remains?"

Rathamon's attention was drawn to his side, where Vakra had suddenly begun to writhe as if he were in intense pain. He ignored the fool. "Yes."

"This place," Shemhazai began curiously, "this is what has become of earth?"

Again Rathamon noticed Vakra's movement. He convulsed wildly. Rathamon growled, kicking the smaller demon in the head. "No Master, this is the lower place, where Lucifer rules his children and tortures the damned souls of human's. This is . . . Hell."

Shemhazai seemed to take a moment to reflect. "And what of man?"

"They continue to live in the earth. *He* has remained silent, He does not answer their prayers, and their sin is deep." Rathamon watched as Shemahazai digested his words. "The Angels remain, yet our gracious father has managed to sew the seeds of war within their ranks. Even now they do battle against each other, leaving man to fend for himself."

Shemhazai's eyes darkened as he suddenly

placed a stern gaze upon Rathamon. "Show me," he said icily.

A grin found Rathamon's grotesque mouth. "Master, I, Rathamon, do profess my fealty to you—"

"Show me!" Shemhazai exclaimed. His voice reverberated in Rathamon's skull, fluctuating with power, causing his heart to flutter. Even the shadows seemed to cringe away from the square jawed entity.

Rathamon swallowed his fear. "Show you I shall, Master . . . but there are steps which must . . . be t-taken." Rathamon winced, stuttering as he suddenly felt a sharp pain in his head.

Shemhazai floated forward, oblivious of Dalfien and Vakra. He towered over his self-proclaimed servant now, scouring his mind for information.

Dalfien watched with an amused smile as Rathamon writhed upon his knees. A soft chuckle escaped his lips.

Shemhazai whirled at the sound, his black eyes burning with rage and power, focusing on Dalfien. In a flash, he hovered over to Dalfien's throne, seeming to grow in size. Great and terrible, Shemhazai loomed over the demon, his will forcing through Dalfien's meager mental defense.

Dalfien cried out a torturous and horrible scream, his claws slamming against the sides of his head as he fell forward from his throne to squirm in the dirt. The pain seemed to last for an eternity as Shemhazai gleaned information from his mind. For Dalfien it felt as though his very brain were being crushed within his skull.

Shemhazai let out a breath of frustration and finally released Dalfien from his painful hold. He then turned to Rathamon. "Where is this Protector?"

Rathamon dared to look up. "M-Master, I have already captured him for you. Even now Elijah Garland and his Angelic blood awaits you."

"I am pleased," Shemhazai began evenly, his opaque orbs lingering upon Dalfien's prone form, "you have served me well . . . and will continue to do so."

"Y-yes, yes of course, Master," Rathamon agreed. "All that remains now is—"

"Why have you promised this . . . Ebonee Lane to this pathetic creature?" Shemhazai asked, nodding at Dalfien.

Dalfien's common sense battled with his surprisingly adept stupidity as he listened. He wanted to lash out at them both. He wanted to see them dead by his hands. Anger fought to control his emotions, threatening to reveal his thoughts to the powerful Fallen Angel. Gritting his teeth, he forced the thoughts from his mind and listened.

"As payment for information," Rathamon began, "I promised my brother a simple novelty."

Shemhazai let his gaze linger upon Dalfien a moment longer. "Very well . . . how long before my earthly vessel is prepared for my ascension?"

"I will go now and insure that all is going as planned, master," Rathamon answered, his eyes straying once again to Vakra, who let out a muffled grunt and convulsed oddly.

Shemhazai took note of Vakra also and moved closer, his expression curious. He focused on the smaller demon's mind, attempting to delve into it.

Rathamon watched as Shemhazai focused on Vakra, wondering what interest could pull the Fallen Angel's attention to such a meaningless thing as Vakra.

Suddenly, Rathamon saw Shemhazai's form go rigid and a look of anger found his face. Shemhazai cried out in denial, shifting quickly to stare into the dark sky.

Rathamon followed his gaze and his mouth fell open as a bright streak of blinding light descended like lightning, splitting the darkness like a hot needle through butter. The shaft of the spear pierced Shemhazai's chest, its tip exploding into the ground, sending sparks flying.

Shemhazai howled maniacally, his hands clutching the shaft of the spear which protruded from his upper torso at an angle, pinning him in place.

Rathamon and Dalfien both stared up into the dark skies with mouths agape. Dalfien was in simple shock, for never had he seen such a sight in this place. Rathamon saw all of his plans flash before his eyes, he saw failure, and he saw what should not have been. . . .

He saw the Seraphim descending.

Shemhazai's pain riddled wail pierced Dalfien's ears. Still, the sight could not begin to register in his stunned mind. Even as the four enormous, winged Angels descended upon Shemhazai, Dalfien remained motionless.

"Impossible!" Rathamon exclaimed. He too stood and stared in chagrin. He watched as one of the Seraphim let out a great roar, which chilled him to the bone. Huge insect-like wings folded back as it dove down to the impaled Fallen Angel.

Shemhazai struggled against the shaft of the spear, but its divine hold would not give way. He stood, impaled to the ground his black eyes mad as the Seraphim alighted next to him. He howled in rage as its six hands sought to subdue him. He fought them, swatting them away, punching at the Angel's insect-like face and head. Another Seraphim landed behind him, its hands too, clutching at him, too strong.

He continued to struggle until at last the two Angels held him still in twelve vice like grips. Shemhazai cried out in denial as he saw the other two Angels descend, each carrying heavy chains.

And then shock wore off.

Rathamon and Dalfien both felt the transition simultaneously as the awe of the situation shifted. Their maniacal howls of anger filled the dark grotto as the evil of their black hearts came to understand the nature of the beings descending upon one of their own. The Seraphim's holiness ignited a hatred so deep within the two demons, they were not aware of their actions.

Rathamon charged forward, his only thoughts to rip these creatures to shreds. These detested beings, radiating the fetid aura of *His* presence. How dare they invade this place? A cruel, curved scimitar appeared in his hand as he closed the short distance. He began to hack away at the Angels, his mind clouded in rage.

Dalfien was doubly affected by the hatred. His was a primal state, much less sophisticated than his younger sibling. The rage filled him fully. He did not care about Shemhazai, or Rathamon, or anything else for that matter. There was only *His* holy presence—here—in the Father's domain.

None of the combatants noticed Vakra, who now stood, watching the violence with a blank expression.

The two Seraphim carrying the chains turned to meet their attackers.

Rathamon howled as he swung his blade in an arc, aiming to decapitate the Seraphim before him. A spear of magnificent light appeared in the Seraphim's hands as it moved to deflect the blow. It countered; knocking Rathamon's enraged attack deftly to the side and then plunging the glowing rod deep into the demon's belly.

Pain assaulted Rathamon's senses. It tore through him like red hot lava flowing through a drift of delicate snow flakes. He fell back, the wound relieving him of most of his rage.

Dalfien's fiery blade met the same resistance as a glowing spear appeared in the other Seraphim's hands, replacing the heavy chains. It too, easily deflected the hate inspired attack and countered in the same way, driving the tip of the spear into Dalfien's stomach. But Dalfien's rage was fueled by the pain. With his razor-sharp teeth grinding so hard in his jaw with hatred that they chipped, Dalfien pulled himself forward on the spear with his free hand. His anger brought the fiery blade down in a vicious chop, taking one of the Seraphim's arms at the elbow. Without hesitation, another arm replaced it, snatching the spear back as the Seraphim retreated.

Rathamon staggered back, drawing the Seraphim away from the group. His sensibilities returned, and he focused his mind on his brethren. Immediately, the shadows around the small island began to stir. Above them, the darkness came to life.

Demons came forth. Great winged beasts, diving from the abyss above. Huge fiends and the smallest of imps rushed from the shadows. The evil wave fell upon the Seraphim like a vast swarm of locust, hungry mouths biting, filthy claws raking.

Dalfien's feral shout rose up above the carnage, warning his brethren to stay away from his prey.

In a matter of moments, three Seraphim were banished from the dark realm. The fourth lay chained with all six of its arms cleaved from its body. Dalfien stood over it protectively, his fiery blade slashing at any of his brethren who strayed too close to his prize.

Rathamon watched as they encircled his older sibling, longing to taste of the holy flesh. He knew they would not be denied. He glanced down to his stomach, where the wound still festered from the divine weapon. It would heal, in time.

Sam swallowed hard as he watched the scene unfold through Vakra's eyes. He had left the creature beaten to a bloody, unconscious pulp in the recesses of its own mind. As he took in the carnage, he ventured into Vakra's memories and intellect. He knew the Seraphim and their nature then. He knew they were God's creatures. And now . . . he knew they were dead. His hope faded as the last Seraphim was bound in chains by Dalfien. They would succeed in releasing this evil Shemhazai into the world. He felt a twinge of sorrow for the poor soul they had called the Protector, and an even deeper sympathy for the one named Ebonee. What would become of the world he once knew?

Stop it, Sam! Don't give up yet! Sam stared at the large demon called Rathamon, watching as it pulled the white glowing spear from Shemhazai's torso, freeing him.

There has to be something I can do!

Seeing the demon's cruel lips moving, Sam willed Vakra's limbs to move, edging closer to hear.

Rathamon fell back as Shemhazai fell to his

knees, growling as he winced in pain, swatting him back. He turned his attention to Dalfien, who had added a dozen more bodies to the bloody mound at his feet. "Let them have their reward. Yours is forthcoming," he instructed.

Dalfien growled as he took another of his brethren's heads from its shoulders as it sought to capture the fallen Seraphim. The mention of his reward slowly brought him his sensibilities. His lip twitching, Dalfien willed his fiery blade away, and stepped back from the Angel. Immediately, the horde swarmed over it, pulling it away into the shadows as their competing snarls drifted up to mesh with the ever continuous moans of the damned souls.

Rathamon surveyed the area and then turned back to Shemhazai. "Master, I will go now to prepare the Nephilim for you," he paused, seeing no sign of acknowledgement of his words. He turned back to Dalfien. "Vakra will deliver the woman's soul to you."

Sam shuddered as suddenly both sets of black demon eyes were focused on him. Tears threatened to burst forth from his eyes as fear began to build in his very soul.

"Go . . . fetch the woman's soul and return it here," Rathamon instructed. "Unharmed!"

Sam swallowed his terror, barely able to keep his . . . Vakra's knees from trembling. They were about to find him out. "T-the woman?" he managed to croak.

Rathamon glared at him. "Ebonee Lane, you fool!" Rathamon silently chided himself for surrounding himself with complete idiots. Still, Vakra stood there with a stupid look of befuddlement upon his ugly maw.

Sam had no idea how to find the woman and his horror increased ten fold with every second that passed under the dreadful glare of the Demons. "H-how?"

Rathamon cursed vehemently, feeling his brother's stare upon him. "The mind of a damned Imp!" he swore, just before sending the mental guidance into Vakra's mind.

Sam swayed under the barrage of psychic instruction, nearly fainting. He shook a violent chill away as the way was made clear to him. He silently vowed to thank Vakra for being so stupid later. It had definitely saved his life. "Right away, Master!" he said aloud. Sam then turned his attention to the darkness of Vakra's mind. He found the creature where he left him—lying in a pool of his own blood, beaten silly. He kicked the creature in the head twice for good measure—wouldn't do to have him wake up while he was gone; God knows what would happen then.

In the darkness, a small rope dangled above his head, almost in his reach. Sam smiled weakly. Perhaps hope would be in his grasp once more . . .

CHAPTER TWELVE

"What are we looking for?" Glenn asked. He sat in the passenger seat of the black Lincoln next to Vito. They were in the parking lot of a small strip mall in a small town near Fort Dix, New Jersey. A light rain had begun to fall as they sat waiting in the parked car.

Glenn frowned as he stared over at the silent man. Vito had not spoken a word since they had left the shack, and it appeared he was not about to now. "You're a hell of a conversationalist." He chuckled dryly, staring out of the front window at the few people walking by with umbrellas.

The rain began to fall harder, beating a muffled drum upon the roof of the car. Glenn sighed heavily, longing to get back to the shack. A chill went through his body as a picture of the lunatic doctor doing unspeakable things to his prisoner, Ebonee Lane, ran through his mind. "If that sick fuck so much as harms one hair on her body—"

"What do you care? She belongs to Enoch now," Vito interrupted him.

Glenn stared at him curiously, surprised he had spoken. "What does Enoch want her for?"

The din of the rain again filled the car as Vito resumed his concentrated stare out of the window.

"I'm asking," Glenn began slowly, "if you don't know, then it would be a good thing to make sure she gets to him unharmed, don't ya think?" Glenn saw what he thought may have been the semblance of a frown appear on Vito's round face. "I mean, Enoch is a preacher—"

"Bishop," Vito corrected sharply.

"Yeah. Bishop." Glenn's eyes narrowed as he stared at him. "Suppose he wants her pure? You think that pervert back there isn't gonna try to get his fuckin' rocks off?" Glenn asked, seeing the displeasure suddenly upon Vito's expression. "I know I sure in the hell would."

A few beads of sweat formed on Vito's brow. "If he wanted her untouched, he would have made it known," he said uncertainly.

"Or . . . he would have faith in you to know that already," Glenn countered, testing the waters.

Vito's nostrils flared. "Enoch trusts no one."

Glenn smiled. "Of course he doesn't." He sat back, feeling that he had struck a nerve. "If . . . our friend the doctor happens to violate Enoch's precious cargo . . . and Enoch is under the impression that you know he wants her untouched, what do you think he would do?"

Vito growled, the sweat running down his forehead now in streams. "Shut up, Glenn."

Glenn chuckled. "Oh, I have a name now? Well,

Vito, if," he began, quietly, "it plays out that way, don't worry. We will come up with something to get you off the hook." He returned Vito's sudden angry glare with his own determined expression. "I won't say a word about you being the one who wanted to leave him there alone with her."

Again the raindrops falling on the roof of the car was the only sound.

Vito returned his gaze forward. "I could kill you." he said simply.

Glenn laughed. "I guess you're right . . . I would be expendable to Enoch, wouldn't I?" His laughter faded away as he focused on the soreness in his left hand, where Vito had nearly crushed the bones into pulp. "Nothing but a pawn in his master plan . . . whatever that is." He watched a smile return to Vito's thin lips. "A trifle fool he can use to further his ambition without getting his hands dirty," Glenn continued, not even aware of Vito any longer as he stared out of the front window. "Unlike you, Vito. He needs you, doesn't he? You're not *expendable*."

Vito chuckled. "Finally your little brain has begun to—"

Vito's words ended sharply as the 9 mm bullet tore into his temple. Glenn fired two more shots into the man's chest, point blank from the silenced pistol.

Glenn smiled as he pulled a handkerchief from his pocket to clean the blood from the driver window. He silently complimented himself for a job well done, his aim was perfect, and the exiting bullet had lodged into the hard plastic between the two side windows. After sitting Vito up so that his eyes were staring straight forward, Glenn sat back with a deep sigh. "News flash, Vito," he began humorously, "we're all expendable."

Glenn basked in his brilliance for a few moments, listening to the sounds of the rain and then calmly reached over to retrieve Vito's cell phone from his breast pocket. He stared at the device, which was not actually a cell phone, but a two-way communicator with GPS functions. His attention was pulled to the parking lot as he saw a black cargo van pull up. Behind it was a military Hummer. A lone figure, dressed in army fatigues, parked the van and got out, walking back to the Hummer. Glenn smiled as the Hummer pulled off, leaving the van parked in a slot only three cars over from him.

Glenn decided to wait an hour to be sure no one was following the van. He put the time to good use, going over to the Radio Shack to purchase a camcorder. He returned to the Lincoln and waited some more, keeping his eyes on the van.

Finally, the device in his hand began to vibrate. Glenn could not suppress his smile as he depressed the transmit button. "Glenn here," he said, his grin spreading as he waited for a response. He wondered how Enoch would take the news.

"Where is Vito?" came the icy smooth voice, barely intelligible over the now pounding rain storm.

"Vito's dead."

The drumming raindrops filled Glenn's ears for a short moment.

"Have you acquired the second subject?" Enoch asked calmly.

It was Glenn's turn to be silent. If Enoch was upset about the loss of Vito, then he certainly was doing a good job not showing it. Then again, maybe he just didn't care. It was obvious to Glenn that whatever plans Enoch had for Elijah and Ebonee, meant more to him than anything else, and Glenn decided to find out just how much it was worth. "Time to re—"

"Ten million, Mr. Glenn. No more, no less," the voice began evenly, causing Glenn's jaw to fall open. "And of course you will remain in my service after this business is concluded." The voice paused, allowing Glenn time to swallow the information. "Since of course . . . as you know, Vito's services are no longer available to me."

Glenn's mouth felt as if he had chewed on a wad of cotton balls. A chill ran the length of his spine, his mind trying to fathom exactly what or who he was dealing with here. *Ten million dollars.* "Where do I deliver them?"

"The coordinates have been transmitted to your GPS . . . go back to the cabin and gather the girl, then bring both subjects to me," once more Enoch paused, with Glenn hanging onto his every word. "And see to it that no one else in my employ meets with any accidents, former Director,"

Glenn shook the threat off and focused on his mission. "The freak," he began hesitantly, "he's in the van?"

"Of course, why else—" Enoch ended his sentence with a dry chuckle. "I see . . . do not worry, former Director. My partners have assured me that he is quite heavily sedated. But I would hurry if I were you. Who knows how long those drugs will last?" Enoch waited before finishing, "Perhaps the doctor could ensure he remains that way for you?"

Glenn sighed. "I'm on my way."

"Time is of the essence, former Director. No mistakes."

Glenn dropped the device into his pocket and stepped out into the downpour. When he came to the back of the black van he pulled out the camcorder and began to record his insurance policy. Inside he found Elijah, still secured to a gurney. Tentatively, he stepped up into the back of the van. He stared down at Elijah, afraid that the freak's eyes would pop open at any moment. He nudged him with the camera. There was no response. "Well, freak boy," Glenn chuckled to himself, "let's go pick up your girlfriend."

Sam Rayburn followed the course laid out for him by the demon Rathamon. When he found the doorway that would supposedly lead him to the female named Ebonee Lane, he pushed right through it. It was dark in her mind. Silent. He found no traces of her thoughts as he walked silently through the darkness. He thought of calling out to her, but immediately changed his mind when a chill caused him to stop in his tracks.

He was getting comfortable with this psychic traveling and knew almost instantly what the chill meant. The shadows held sadness, and as he focused on that emotion as he heard the faint sound of a sniffle. Slowly, Sam approached the sound and suddenly found himself walking in soft silver moonlight. Blades of grass, freshly cut, sprung up beneath his sandaled feet, and a large Victorian style home appeared before him. Lush vegetation surrounded the grassy yard, which was cordoned off by a white picket fence. In front of the house was a beautiful white gazebo. Inside the gazebo was an antique red cherry wood porch swing. Sam could hear the creak of the chains as he approached.

Two figures sat in the swing and as he approached he could make out a man with his arm wrapped around a sniffling woman's shoulders. The sadness flowed from here. It bombarded his senses and brought tears to his eyes it was so strong. He stepped silently up onto the wooden flooring. He froze as the man suddenly looked up. His hair was stark white, and long individual braids were pulled back into a ponytail. His skin was the color of caramel, smooth and flawless. Sam held his breath until he realized the man was looking straight through him as if he were not there.

Fear trickled into Sam's soul as he watched the man's hand caress the crying woman's lovely face in the shadows of the moonlight. He suddenly felt very guilty for intruding into this woman's special place. "Ebonee Lane?" he whispered.

As soon as the sound left his lips the man vanished. Sam watched as the woman's tears continued to fall, her hands clutching at the empty air as if the man was still there. Sam searched frantically for something to say. He realized then that he actually had no plan whatsoever. "I-I'm sorry to bother you, but I need your help," he said softly, stepping closer to the woman.

Ebonee Lane sniffled, wiping at her tears before she finally looked up. Even in this saddened state she was beautiful, her dark skin glowing in the light of the moon. Her black hair was cut short and neatly styled. Her tear-clouded eyes stared hard at Sam for a long moment and then fell back to her swing.

Sam sighed lightly as he dropped his eyes down to his own body. He was still wearing the gladiator outfit. He chuckled softly, figuring the woman probably thought she was dreaming. "Ebonee, there isn't much time . . . you are Ebonee Lane, right? The demons called you that."

Ebonee's eyes shot up at the mention of demons. "Demons?"

Sam sat down next to her on the swing, his armor fading away and his old clothes returning with a mere thought. "Yes. Rathamon and Dalfien to name them—"

"Dalfien?" Ebonee moved away from him excitedly, remembering the name and the vile memories that came along with it. "Who are you? And what are you doing here? Where is Elijah?"

"That's what I came here to talk to you about. You're both in great danger, they are coming for you . . . you have to warn him, whoever he is," Sam explained.

Ebonee's eyes closed and she seemed to be concentrating. Her face contorted into a frown. "I- I don't know," she stammered, her brow wrinkling further.

"You don't know what?"

"Something happened to me . . . I remember—" Her face suddenly lit up and her eyes flared open as she doubled over in the seat, clutching at her crotch. A sharp pain flowed through her, beginning between her legs and rolling through her belly, causing her to stiffen, slowly subsiding until it was a continuous stinging sensation. "I can't wake up . . . he drugged me,"

Sam looked worried. He gently placed a comforting hand upon her shoulder. "Who? Who drugged you?"

"A man. I never saw him . . ." Her eyes went to the green vegetation. "He works for the FBI."

Sam closed his eyes, sighing heavily. "This isn't

good," he began, going through possible scenarios in his head. "You can't warn him if you can't wake up."

"Who are you?"

"I'm sorry. My name is Sam Rayburn." He paused, knowing he had little time to explain. "I was on a dig in Egypt—"

"For Michael Corvalis?" Ebonee asked, her eyes wide.

Sam stared at her curiously. "Yes, how do you know?"

"My name is Ebonee Lane, FBI . . . we were on a case and your boss's name came up. Please, continue."

"Well, we dug up something out there, something evil . . . a demon or a Fallen Angel . . . I think . . . its name is Shemhazai."

"I remember Father Holbrook speaking of Fallen Angels . . . go on," Ebonee said.

"We don't have much time. My body was . . . possessed by a demon and used to free this Shemhazai creature. The demon thought to leave me there to die in that tomb, and my body is still there I presume," Sam stared down at his hands as he continued. "But I followed it, somehow. I don't know how, I just know I was so very angry at it for what it did to me . . . what he did to my mind. I found him in . . . Hell, I guess . . . him and his friends, the other demons I mentioned."

"I know of Dalfien," Ebonee said softly, recalling the torture she endured at the foul demon's hands.

"I beat the hell out of Vakra—that's the demon's name that possessed me—and took control of its body. I guess you could say I possessed his ass back. Then I learned of their plans. They sent me here to bring you back to Dalfien as some sort of payment... I don't know... and your friend... this Protector... they plan to use him to bring that Shemhazai fellow to our world." Sam stared at Ebonee, his face set in grim determination. "We can't let that happen... he is pure evil."

Ebonee stared out at the moon as she listened to his words.

"I planned to come here and warn you, hoping you and this Protector would be able to do something. I'm afraid I can't do anything from this side, and my body is still trapped in that tomb. But if you can't wake up, then I don't know what we will do."

The two of them sat in a long moment of silence, both minds racing for an answer to their dilemma. Suddenly, Ebonee's eyes grew stern and she stared at Sam.

"Take me back with you."

Sam gazed at her quizzically. "Dalfien means to torture you."

Ebonee seemed unfazed by the news. "We can't do anything here, and I'm sure they will grow suspicious if you do not return, in which case they will send another to retrieve me."

"I'll stay, and we can fight them here," Sam protested. "Until you can wake up."

"No, they have control over my body, and most likely, Elijah's as well." Ebonee stood, walking to the entrance of the Gazebo. "I do not fear Dalfien... we have a past, him and I."

Sam followed her. "Maybe it's not too late to warn him," he contemplated aloud. "I followed Vakra there, and was able to come here—"

"Let's not waste any more time, Sam Rayburn," Ebonee said with a deep sigh. "They don't know about you, so that works in our favor. And as long as Elijah Garland breathes and walks, there will always be hope."

Sam stepped from the gazebo and gazed into her eyes and saw the hope she spoke about. His heart fluttered at the sight, feeling the power of that statement radiating out from her being. "This Protector, this Elijah Garland . . . he must be some special guy."

Ebonee smiled a smile that would quite possibly be her last as she looked at Sam. "He's my Angel."

With no further words spoken, the two figures walked off into the sudden darkness, Sam guiding Ebonee into the hands of their enemy. Both clung to that small sliver of light that bound them together in the darkness . . . both holding on to hope.

CHAPTER THIRTEEN

The perverted man's guttural howls filled the dimly lit basement. His body convulsed violently, his hips thrusting forward as he climaxed. Sweat poured from his balding head as he fell forward in exhaustion. His beady black eyes closed in satisfaction as he felt the woman's firm, round posterior against his naked skin. Doctor Pokalman reached up his hand and took her lifeless palm into his own. Another wave of tremors washed through his lanky body as he let his limp member slide from her torn vaginal opening. Lines of blood ran down between her thighs.

The doctor's thin lips kissed the nape of her neck before he pushed himself up. He stepped back, admiring her shapely body that was draped across the table face down. He glanced at his watch, wondering when Vito and his friend would return. Silently he stepped forward, again closing his eyes as he brought his crotch into contact with the unconscious woman's backside. His expression was one of extreme bliss.

"We gotta move—" Glenn's words fell from his lips as he stared at the perverted scene.

The doctor's eyes flashed open as he stumbled back away from Ebonee, staring fearfully at Glenn.

Enoch's words repeated in Glenn's head as he stalked forward. *No more accidents to anyone in my employ.* His nostrils flared in the dim light as he spotted the enormous black dildo on the table. He saw the blood between her thighs.

Doctor Pokalman struggled with his pants. "I-I did not hear you—"

His sentence was cut short as Glenn's fist slammed into his temple, dropping him to the cold stone floor. Glenn fumed as he stood over him watching him squirm and whimper, covering his head like a child. Before he realized what he was doing, Glenn had snatched up the heavy sexual instrument and had begun beating the man in the face and head viciously. He wished the dildo were an iron pipe.

Glenn beat the man with the odd weapon until he was exhausted and the doctor laid squirming, blood flowing from his lips and whelps covering his face. Glenn dropped the bloodied instrument and stood back.

"Get up!" he growled in anger as he watched the man struggle to get to his feet. Glenn helped him with a rough grab around his neck, shoving the man toward the table with a swift kick in the posterior. "Get her dressed and put her in the van," he instructed. "And make sure you put some of that shit you drugged her with in the other captive . . ."

Glenn watched the doctor in silence for a moment and then finally stalked up the stairs.

It took every ounce of willpower in Elijah's body to refrain himself as he heard Glenn step into the back of the van, but he did so. He was glad he did too, when he heard Glenn's chuckled words about picking up Ebonee. He kept his eyes closed in mock unconsciousness until he felt the vehicle lurch into motion. Fifteen minutes into the trip, Elijah strained against the restraints securing him to the gurney. His right hand snapped the thick leather as easily as if it were paper. He then quickly undid the other restraints, pausing to drop the cross pendant around his neck. There were no windows in the back of the cargo van, so he sat in silence upon the edge of the gurney, contemplating his next move.

Who's pulling your strings, Glenn?

Elijah stared at the walls of the van, his hands clenching into fists repeatedly, longing to feel the grip of his blades, Enobe and Soul Seeker. He remembered the confrontation in the woods and recalled the presence of the demons. They never acted alone. Something or someone had sent them with a strict purpose. But who? Dalfien? No, Elijah was confident that the demon had been destroyed. Another Demon perhaps?

A deep sigh escaped his lips. It was obvious to him that Lucifer had indeed marked him well. He knew in his heart that none around him would ever be safe. As the steady hum of the tires gliding swiftly across the paved roadway suddenly shifted and became a bumpy affair, he vowed that after this, none of his loved ones would ever be put at risk because of him. There was only one way to get to the bottom of this current predicament. So with a grim determination, Elijah settled back onto the gurney, reaffixing the restraints to all but his right hand and waited.

Dr. Pokalman's guttural growls preceded him as he struggled with the woman's one hundred and thirty pound weight. He carried her draped over his shoulder, and in his hand he carried an IV bag. Glenn frowned as he watched the man walk to the back of the van to come to a stop, staring at him hopefully. Glenn rolled his eyes and stepped over to open the rear doors.

The thin man dropped Ebonee heavily on the floor of the van, sweating from the effort. He then set up the IV, hanging it from the roof of the vehicle.

"Him too," Glenn reminded the doctor gruffly.

Pokalman sighed, hopping down from the van to disappear into the shack. He returned with his bag and trench coat. The two men stared each other down for a moment, until Glenn motioned for him to get in the van.

Pokalman eyed Glenn for a moment longer, his hatred showing clearly in his beady black eyes. Then he hopped up into the van, opening his bag to retrieve a second IV bag. The doors slammed closed and a moment later the engine revved to life. Pokalman grunted, bracing himself as the vehicle suddenly lurched into motion.

Elijah felt the prick in his arm and focused his mind on Ebonee, who now lay unconscious beside him. He could easily have freed them both at any moment he choose, for neither Glenn, nor the man next to him showed any signs of demon possession. But instead, Elijah waited. He could only hope, as he felt the drugs effects beginning to set in, that his body would soon adapt to the poison, like it had done with the tranquilizers the military men had used. His mind slowly drifted into a dark abyss, and as always, Elijah found his comfort in Soul Seeker and

Enobe. The blades appeared in his hands as soon as he left reality behind. He walked in the shadows of the dark cavern that was his mind now . . . waiting, brooding. His hands clenched the hilts of the twin swords as he brought up his rage, releasing his hold of his newfound faith. He knew in his heart that faith could conquer mountains, but there was no enjoyment in that. No, that was not his nature . . . for one such as Elijah Garland, there could be no greater pleasure than to carve out his name in all that opposed him and threatened those he loved. His was the way of the blade.

CHAPTER FOURTEEN

By all appearances, the woman was too fine a creature to be walking through such a horrid and festering place. Too beautiful. Her delicate obsidian skin, the subtle curves of her body and the tender falls of her steps, were more than out of place here. An Angel in the pits of hell.

Ebonee Lane held her chin high as she moved calmly across the smoldering ground, bare feet leaving not a trace of her passing. Fiends and Imps, ugly and grotesque creatures born of this place, hovered close, yet she showed them no fear. Sweat covered her ebon skin, causing her naked body to glimmer red in the light of the flowing lava around her. The foul creatures hissed and spat, longing to devour her soul, knowing they dare not touch a hair on her head, for she was marked by Dalfien.

Ahead of her in the gloom, a small island rose above the ever-present mist that clung to the ground, making it appear to float on the air itself, it was her destination. Her expression remained stoic as the large demons slowly came into view.

"From where does your ire rise?"

Dalfien considered Shemhazai's words as he stared at the fallen Angel from upon his decomposing throne. The wounds Shemhazai had suffered at the hands of the Seraphim were gone. He stood squarely now, his back to the silent and brooding Dalfien. "From a hundred years of banishment," Dalfien said.

Shemhazai laughed easily, turning to look upon the pitiful demon. "A hundred?" he repeated mockingly. He let his attention leave the silent form of Rathamon, who stood motionless in a trance-like state. "Perhaps your ire would be better suited after one thousand years."

Dalfien shifted uncomfortably under the dark Angel's intense gaze. He could feel the power in those black eyes, eyes similar to those of another, the father of lies.

Shemhazai took stock of Dalfien for a moment as the sounds of the damned souls swirled around them chaotically. "But do not doubt, little demon, your fate is indeed an unhappy one." Shemhazai looked away from him then, his eyes gazing toward the darkness above and he imagined he could see what he had long ago forgotten in his prison of earth and stone. "It is pleasurable, is it not?" he spoke reverently now. "An hour among mortal men is well worth a lifetime in *his* presence." His lip twisted in a brief sneer as he spoke of *him*. "Humans are so very fragile . . . easy to break . . . their minds weak . . . and their daughters," Shemhazai's eyes closed as he smiled, "sodivine." He let the thought linger for a while and then stared at Dalfien once again. "I shall taste of their flesh once more."

Dalfien sat idle, his forlorn gaze focusing on the swirling, mist-filled shadows beyond his island. Shemhazai's words meant less than nothing to him. A chill caused him to shudder as he felt Shemhazai suddenly in his mind, reading his memories, his thoughts.

"Take heart, Dalfien. Your banishment shall soon be no more."

These words did register in the dark demons ears. He stared at Shemhazai suspiciously. "My banishment is beyond your power, it is beyond anyone's power, even the Father cannot change this." His forked tongue flicked out, licking at his black lips. "Only the one who cast me from the world with those damned blades could ever reverse my sentence," he said dryly, watching as a smug grin spread over Shemhazai's square face. Then it hit him like a gigantic boulder falling from a mountain one thousand miles high. His eyes went wide and he sat forward upon his throne. "The Protector . . . you will break him?" he asked excitedly.

Shemhazai laughed. "As if he were a twig beneath my feet."

Dalfien suddenly had hope. He knew of the Protector's soul and its great tenacity, but against a power such as Shemhazai, surely that soul would wither and fall. His black eyes glimmered with the newfound possibility of freedom. He sat back in his throne, staring over at his smaller sibling, Rathamon. A renewed vigor coursed through his veins for his brother's plans. And he held him in a higher regard than ever before. He felt the edge of anticipation eating away at him. Each moment that passed, he found himself willing Rathamon to awake, longing for him to return to lead Shemhazai to the Protector so that his banishment would end.

Nothing in the seven levels of Hell could have brought Dalfien more joy than the thought of his freedom so close at hand than the slender, beautiful figure of Ebonee Lane stepping from the swirling mist.

Vakra shuddered in the darkness, his subconscious mind battered and broken. Images flittered in his brain. A coliseum, dust, and hundreds of faces staring at him. He heard the chant, "*Maximus, Maximus, Maximus.*" A groan escaped his lips and he saw the human, Sam Rayburn. Pain assaulted his mind as memories of the short, wide blade cutting into his flesh came back to him. "NO!" he screamed, forcing his eyes to open. He saw Dalfien, his eyes locked in a wide, shocked gaze at something in the distance. He saw Shemhazai, great and terrible; he too stared off in the same direction curiously. "Humans! Here! In my mind!" Vakra shouted deliriously, hoping to warn his brethren.

He staggered forward then, clutching at his grotesquely shaped head. He fell to the ground, feeling the presence of the human return.

Sam screamed out a battle cry as he found the demon's subconscious. He charged through the darkness, his sword leading. He could only hope the fool had not given him away.

Dalfien ignored the foolish Vakra, knowing that it was the stupid demon that had brought the human here in the first place. He paid no attention to his antics, as Vakra collapsed to the floor, writhing in pain. His eyes remained locked on the human woman who continued to walk forward. His joy was weathered by uncertainty and left him speechless. For the woman's steps were not taken by trembling limbs. There was no fear in her soul and this confused him greatly. Her chin was held high, her eyes strong and filled with a determination he could never comprehend.

Even the damned souls' everlasting cries of anguish seemed to diminish as they took note of the woman's passage. Fiends and Imps scurried from the shadows, daring to get a closer look at this soul that held no fear.

Shemhazai watched impassively as the delectable treat passed by him without a thought. He licked his lips, tasting of her essence, which flowed from the very pores of her naked skin. Curios, he watched as the woman walked right up to stand before Dalfien.

Ebonee relied upon her bitter hatred and anger to suppress the deep fear she knew to be in her heart. Every step she had taken in this place had been a battle between the emotions. But so great was her hatred for the demon that she was able to stand before him now, with no fear to show. Even as the great and horrible beast stood suddenly, scowling down at her, she remained unmoved.

"Tell me, Dalfien," her words dripped with contempt as she spoke slowly, freezing the enormous demon in his tracks, "when Elijah takes your foolish head from your shoulders in this place," her eyes were cold, piercing through him like daggers, "what will become of you then?"

Dalfien's anger bristled as he stared down at the insolent human. Her words grated into his mind, remembrance of the Protector's divine blades forging into his heart, casting him into banishment. Then he shifted his gaze to Shemhazai, and suddenly his head reared back, maniacal laughter spilling forth between razor-sharp teeth.

The eerie laughter sent a chill through Ebonee's body, chipping away at her resolve. She felt her fear take a foothold in her soul.

Then she felt pain as Dalfien's sudden backhand nearly took her head from her own shoulders. She crumpled to the ground half awake, half unconscious. The dark world became a blur around her.

"We shall see whose head it is that rolls this day, dearest Ebonee," Dalfien said through clenched teeth. He moved to stand over her, his large claw slamming downward to the back of her neck.

Ebonee could make out up from down in her dazed state. She could hear his voice, filled with a confidence that further heightened her fear. Again she felt intense pain as sharp points of metal dug into her neck as her face was driven into the ground. The heavy collar of inverted spikes weighed almost as much as she did.

Dalfien grinned as he pulled the woman up by her short black hair, watching with pleasure as lines of blood began to snake down her chest. "I shall enjoy breaking you."

Ebonee moaned and felt the ground rushing up as the demon slammed her face into the stone.

Sam kicked Vakra in the head one last time to ensure the fool was out cold. Then he turned his attention to his surroundings. He shuddered as he watched the large demon's backhand send Ebonee tumbling to the ground. It was all he could do to refrain himself from running to her aid. Growling, Sam focused on the greater problem. Somehow, he had to warn Elijah. His eyes fell on Rathamon, who stood, motionless. A thought occurred to Sam then as he stared the demon's trance-like state. He would be near Elijah. He would need to be in order to carry through with his vile plans.

Perhaps if I could do to him, what I did to Vakra . . .

Sam felt Vakra's shoulders sag in the shadowy gloom as he thought of invading Rathamon's mind. Rathamon was powerful and he feared he could not pull it off. Sam forced Vakra's body into motion, stepping boldly up to stand before Rathamon.

A chill caused Vakra's body to tremble as Sam stared into the lifeless black eyes of the powerful demon. He swallowed, sensing the mental power Rathamon wielded. *No . . . I will fail. He is too strong.* Sam felt a tear roll down Vakra's cheek as he slowly began to give in to the hopelessness that had floated on the edge of his sensibilities since the beginning of this ordeal. He saw Ebonee Lane, lying unconscious, blood flowing from the wounds inflicted by the heavy collar. He shook his head, sniffling as his tears increased. *It's hopeless.* He saw Dalfien, great and terrible, holding the end of a chain connected to Ebonee's collar. He heard his maniacal laughter. His sobs lifted above the wails of the damned souls. Then he saw Shemhazai's eyes—eyes burning black as pitch, eyes that were focused, eyes that were enraged . . . and eyes that promised pain.

Eyes that were staring directly at him.

Sam's heart went still within his chest as the black daggers held him frozen in fear. The Fallen Angel's ire preceded its mental presence into Vakra's mind, and Sam knew that all was lost. He fell to his knees in the darkness of Vakra's mind, waiting for the foulness of the Fallen Angel to come and destroy him. There was no fighting this thing; Sam knew this in his soul. To do so would be foolish.

Sam whimpered like a baby as he felt the cold grip of Shemhazai's large hand fall on the back of his neck, lifting him up to bring him face to face with his fear.

Sam's fear reached the apex of its culmination and his tears fell freely. His mind snapped, the fear triggering the instinctual drive in every human being—the instinct of survival. He howled and cried, lashing out madly, kicking and punching, his feet nearly five feet off of the ground.

Shemhazai held the wild human at an arm's length, completely intrigued by the sudden turn of events. What was it doing here?

Sam's wild blue eyes caught one last sight before the madness took him fully. In the darkness of Vakra's mind, he saw the window to the demon world, the image of Rathamon still there, standing, motionless. Sam closed his eyes, concentrating.

Shemhazai blinked in confusion as the human suddenly disappeared and left him holding nothing but air. He stared around the bleak mind of Vakra, searching for the human, but found only Vakra's torn and battered subconscious. Then he was aware of the image in Vakra's sight. He stared at Rathamon from inside of Vakra's mind, watching as the once still and unmoving demon suddenly trembled, its face contorting with a frown.

He knew where the human had fled.

Father Holbrook struggled to remove the seatbelt from around his wide waist as Director Moss slammed the gearshift of the blue Crown Victoria into park. The rain pelted down upon the car's windshield in front of the small, non-descript shack the signal Moss had been following had led them to.

It was dusk and the forest around the small building was creeping into shadow. Father Holbrook growled at the annoying device until finally it snapped free. He threw the car door open and promptly fell face first into a mud puddle.

"Oh my, I will definitely have to write to the manufacturer of these confounded things," he muttered as he found his footing in the slick earth.

Spitting grit and dirty water from his mouth, he carefully made his way to the front door of the cabin, Enobe and Soul Seeker clutched protectively under his arm. He said a silent prayer to Saint Michael, longing to find the Protector and Ebonee safe inside. As he stepped into the threshold he saw Director Moss coming back up from the apparent hole in the floor. His expression was grim, bordering upon anger as he stalked back toward the old priest.

"They're not here, Father Holbrook," he said through clenched teeth. His agitated steps brought him to the open door and he stared out at the pounding rain as if it were to blame for this travesty. Sighing heavily, he pulled out his cell phone and made a call.

"Brown? They're not here," he said into the phone, removing his glasses to rub wearily at the bridge of his nose. "What information? Why would I care about an ex-mafia hit man from Sicily?" His face twisted up in confusion as he listened to the words on the other end of the phone line. "Just tell me where the signal . . . the Archdiocese? Are you certain? Still . . . what made you think it was something I needed to know?"

Father Holbrook leaned against the door, staring at Moss curiously.

The agent on the other end continued to explain. "W-well . . . just so happens that the cops traced the tags on the car back to the very place where your signal has turned up."

Moss flipped the phone closed and grabbed the priest by the arm, pushing out of the door and into the rain.

"Calm yourself, sir! My word! You are worse than the Protector . . . are all of you Americans so pushy?" Father Holbrook complained as he was ushered all the way to the car door and pushed roughly inside.

"Just wanted to make sure you didn't fall and brain yourself, Father," Moss said as he slammed his door closed, turning the key and slamming his foot down on the accelerator. He eyed the priest's soiled suit quickly with a grin.

"It was the seatbelt!" Father Holbrook cried, holding on as mud slung up into the air behind the vehicle and it tore out onto the wet, bumpy road.

"Whatever." Moss squinted as the heavy rain continued to wash over the windshield in waterfalls.

"You have found the signal again?" Father Holbrook asked.

"Yep . . . and your friends down at the Archdiocese may have something to do with this."

"I have no friends in America, other than the Protector and Ebonee Lane." Father Holbrook paused and stared at Moss hesitantly. "And perhaps I'd be able to add you to that list . . . if your driving were to improve."

In answer, Director Moss slammed on the gas and spun the wheel hard to the right, bringing the car careening up onto the roadway from the dirt trail and bouncing the priest about unmercifully.

After righting himself in the seat, Father Holbrook stared down at the twin blades resting across his lap. He remembered first seeing Elijah wield those magnificent blades. A spectacular sight indeed! He felt a pang of remorse creep into his heart and quickly forced it away. Elijah would be fine. Ebonee would be fine. He just had to heed his own words— words he had spoken to Elijah this very day. *Have faith, young Protector . . . all will be well.*

Moss cut a quick glimpse over at the silent priest and saw his eyes closed and head bowed. "Say one for us all, Father . . . then pray we don't need them."

Glenn frowned as he guided the black Econoline cargo van along the wide lanes of Ben Franklin Parkway. The huge greenish dome of Saints Peter and Paul Basilica loomed before him like a gigantic wart on the tip of his nose.

"I'm tired of churches," he muttered, glancing at the GPS device that indicated he was at last at his destination.

As if on cue, the device chirped and Enoch's voice disturbed the pounding rain. "The rear of the parking lot . . . back the van up to the dock and bring the subjects, along with the doctor, into the lower level. I will meet you there."

The lot was empty, devoid of any vehicles at all. Glenn wondered if the Bishop slept on one of the pews as he slowed the van, his hand fishing into the seat next to him for his palm recorder. He aimed it up at the breathtaking copper dome, now worn to a greenish color, and the golden cross at its apex and began taping. The marvels of the historic building were lost on Glenn. The magnificent architecture of the oldest building on the parkway meant about as much to him as the tires on the van he was driving, as long as they were there, he didn't care.

He parked the van and slammed his fist on the wall behind him, letting the pervert know they had arrived. Before climbing out, Glenn took the small tape from the camera and slipped in into his blazer pocket.

He was soaked two seconds after stepping from the van. Growling, he hurried to the back of the van and flung the doors open. "You get that IV started on him?" he asked, waiting for the doctor to assist him with Elijah's Gurney.

"Y-yes . . . yes of course," Pokalman answered, grunting as he pushed the gurney forward.

Glenn walked backwards, holding up the stretcher until the legs extended to the ground. "Throw the girl on top of him," he said in reply to the doctor's curious stare.

Pokalman struggled with the woman's dead weight, but finally managed to get her onto the gurney. His glasses were fogged and large water droplets caused him to squint, his face distorting in ugly grimaces as he stared at Glenn, waiting.

"Come on," Glenn said, pushing the Gurney toward the door.

The doctor hesitated. "I-I'll be fine here."

Glenn stopped to look at the man. "No, you will bring your perverted ass in here with me," Glenn pushed the cart forward again. "Besides . . . the bishop wants to see you."

That was just what the doctor did not want to

hear. Grudgingly, he took up pace behind the former FBI director.

A small hallway brought them to the lower level of the large building. Glenn sighed heavily as he pushed the gurney into a dark hallway, lit only by candles that burned low in decorative candelabrums spaced down the wall. They came to an intersection and he saw a large burly man dressed in a suit much like Vito's. Even his slicked back hair was the same. Glenn let out a heavy breath as the man motioned them toward a wide doorway in the middle of this hall, his hand going to the knob and pushing the door open wide.

Glenn ignored the big man as he pushed the stretcher over the slight hump up onto the hard, white marble floor of the dimly lit room. He was not surprised when he looked to the rear of the spacious room to find a robed figure sitting solemnly in a large, red, velvet, throne-like chair. Behind the majestic seat was a large mural, probably a Michelangelo, Glenn thought as he stared at the scene. It was actually a DiVinci.

Around the room, spaced in intervals were several vaults set within the white marble walls. Upon these were inscribed names. Glenn shook his head as he turned back to the small, simple, white altar made of Carerra marble that stood between himself and the robed man. "Please tell me these are not what I think they are."

And indeed they were. The tombs held several of the former bishops of the city. Glenn focused on the man sitting in the large chair. A chill flowed into his limbs, causing him to shudder as the man's hollowed eyes slowly blinked open. The sagging skin around his face denied the youthful glimmer in the ancient priest's gaze. The bony set of his shoulders, drooping and frail.

A surprised look found Glenn's face as he watched the old bishop suddenly stand. His movements seemed too fluid for one of his age.

"Enoch, I presume?" Glenn said easily, not showing any signs of his thoughts.

Rathamon moved quickly and silently, sending another chill along Glenn's spine as he flowed past him to stand before the gurney. He brought the bishop's wrinkled hands from the folds of his overly large robe. They hovered over Elijah's arm, almost reverently.

Doctor Pokalman forced his eyes to remain affixed to the lone source of light in the room, a large white candle that sat high upon the west wall. Shadows flickered and danced upon the mural behind the chair, making the doctor imagine that the figures in the painted scene were alive. He nearly fainted when the bishop whirled suddenly and stared him in the eye.

"How long will this last?" Rathamon asked, his voice barely above a croaked whisper.

"T-t-two to t-t-three hours," Pokalman stammered, his heart pounding rapidly in his chest. "You received the r-rest I presume?"

Rathamon turned away form the man, his eyes returning to the gurney. He waved a hand, motioning for the lone guard to enter with a second stretcher. He had indeed received the shipment of the drugs required to keep Elijah and Ebonee sedated for the next several years if need be.

"I c-can change them whenever they r-r-run out," the doctor offered eagerly.

Rathamon continued to stare at the two figures as

the guard finished positioning Ebonee on her own gurney and then made his way to stand behind the nervous Dr. Pokalman. "Show me," Rathamon whispered softly, never looking up.

Pokalman swallowed the lump of fear in his throat and glanced repeatedly back at the huge man fearfully. His hands were trembling and sweat was pouring from his forehead as he tried to think of an excuse not to show Enoch what would inevitably render himself—expendable. "I-I-"

"Show me!"

Pokalman's heart nearly burst as Enoch's strong voice suddenly reverberated in the cold marble chamber. He wanted to roll up into a tiny ball and cry so great was his fear. Somehow, his feet shuffled forward, his body trembling with the chills as he continued to stare back over his shoulder at the expressionless guard.

Glenn remained silent, taken aback by the unnatural gestures coming from the supposedly ancient bishop. He watched as the doctor stuttered through his instructions on changing the IV with trembling hands. He knew what would come next.

Rathamon listened carefully to his words and when he had at last finished he motioned to the guard. "Kill him."

Pokalman's face went white with terror. "N-no . . . please!" he cried, falling to his knees as the large man stalked up behind him, a thin, barely perceptible cord extended between his meaty hands.

Then something caught Rathamon's eye as he glanced at the dried blood between Ebonee's thighs. "Wait," he commanded, halting the guard's movements. He inspected the wounds in her vaginal region and then turned upon the doctor. "You did this?"

Pokalman's eyes lit up and he groveled at the Bishops feet. "Forgive me! I am a sinner! I can't help myself!" he wailed pitifully.

Rathamon smiled, an action that stretched the many lines of wrinkles in the old Bishops ancient face. "Leave him," he said, waving the guard away.

Glenn snorted derisively, not really understanding just what had just taken place. The bishop seemed pleased with the pervert's actions! His astounded gaze followed the guard from the chamber. When he turned back, Enoch was inches from him, his cold eyes even with his own, piercing through him like daggers. Glenn trembled, seeing in those eyes something he could not name, something evil. He backed away cautiously under that gaze. "You have your bodies," he began, feeling his nerves unsettling, "you promised me—"

"Ten million dollars," Rathamon said softly, releasing his stare from Glenn to look upon the Protector. "It will be arranged," he added absently.

"Arranged?" Glenn's greed forced him to take a step closer. "It better be, because if you try anything I'll give this tape to the authorities."

Rathamon never looked up as he chuckled dryly. "Give your tape to whomever you wish ... give it your savior if it so moves you to do so, now be silent!" Rathamon urged, focusing his thoughts on Elijah's mind.

Glenn frowned, dropping the tape back into his pocket as he moved to stare at Enoch in the soft light. From this angle, Glenn could not see beneath the shadow that clung to the priest's aged face, but he saw those eyes. Glenn fell back a step, fear coursing through his veins as those eyes, black as pitch, rolled up into the bishop's head.

Then the bishop's body collapsed to the marble floor in a heap.

Elijah felt the vibrant hum of his twin blades in his hands as he crouched silently in the darkness of his own mind. He felt the demon's presence immediately and knew that this was no ordinary fiend. Its physical aura was not as great as some of the others Elijah had faced, namely Dalfien and El'Rathiem, but its intellectual psyche marked it as much more dangerous than the other two.

Elijah's skin prickled with tiny goose bumps as he saw the creature manifest in his mind. It was short for a demon of its stature, only six-foot-five-inches tall. Its red skin glistened with an unnatural sweat. Elijah got the impression that even if they were in the bowels of frozen tundra the unholy beast would still perspire. Its canine-like maw was shorter than Dalfien's, more human-like in appearance, but ugly nonetheless. Its horns were by far its greatest and most notable physical feature. The immense adorning's were twice the size of Dalfien's, extending out from above its ears in looping arcs to come to a point nearly a full foot from the creature's sloped forehead.

Elijah held his breath, fighting the urge in his soul to lash out at the obscenity that stalked through the shadows of his mind like it was his domain. But there were still too many unanswered questions in his head. He knew there was a bounty out on his head and all of hell was trying to collect it, but this demon seemed to have more on his plate than just killing Elijah. There was Father Holbrook's spiel about Fallen Angels to consider. Could this have something to do with that?

Elijah frowned in the darkness. He was thinking too much. Better to just cut the beast down now and let the chips fall where they may. He would deal with whatever situation arose when it reared its ugly head.

Elijah stood in the shadows, spinning the twin blades deftly in his hands to hold them in a reverse grip. He felt their vibrations increase as the sentient blades sensed his desire to destroy the demon. Before he could take a step in Rathamon's direction, the beast did something that caused Elijah to pause.

Rathamon stumbled.

His grotesque face twisted up in confusion for a moment and then a loud, bellowing voice echoed in the darkness.

"Elijah! My name is Sam Rayburn! This demon plans to use your body as a host for a Fallen Angel named Shemhazai." Sam's voice wavered then and it sounded to Elijah as if the man were battling some unseen force. "I don't understand all of this, but somehow I managed to follow one of them back to its domain . . . Ebonee Lane is here with me, on the other side . . . she needs your help! My body is trapped in—"

Elijah bristled as the voice suddenly fell away and Rathamon stiffened. His eyes flared in the darkness and he let out a powerful bellow.

Elijah ran forward to meet the demon in combat, Enobe and Soul Seeker leading the way. He didn't know who this Sam Rayburn was, but if Ebonee was with him, then he figured he better act now. He would not kill the demon, but beat it to a pulp and then force it to give him some answers.

Rathamon grinned as he watched the Protector stalk forward from the shadows, and the darkness around them slowly transformed into a bleak rocky cavern.

This was Elijah's home. This was where he had first learned to battle the demons in his dreams. This was where he was invincible.

Rathamon considered the strange human for a moment. His white hair flowing back in long locks that fell to his slender shoulders with a few strands masking part of his brown face. He found it hard to believe that his older sibling had fallen to such a skinny thing!

Elijah's blessed silver chain mail shirt glinted in the dim light that came from nowhere at all. Corded muscles flexed in his slender arms as he brought the twin blades up before him.

Rathamon grinned devilishly in the Protector's face and then simply disappeared.

Elijah rolled forward immediately, anticipating the attack that he knew would come from his back when the demon reappeared behind him, but the attack never came. Neither did the demon manifest again. It was gone.

Elijah stared around the rocky plateau curiously. He growled in anger, seeing nothing. Then a faint shimmer caught his eye far to the west in the darkness. He quickly ran across the uneven ground until he stood face to face with a shimmering doorway. Sam's words repeated in his mind, *Ebonee is here with me . . . on the other side.* Elijah inhaled deeply and let it out through flaring nostrils as he pursed his lips in determination. Ebonee was on the other side of this gateway.

Setting his nerves, Elijah took a step forward.

Before his foot could strike the ground, Elijah felt

an intense pain in his chest and felt the world sailing by him. He caught a glimpse of the huge fist that had suddenly appeared from the shimmering surface of the portal just before his body impacted with the rocky terrain. He tumbled a few feet; the force of the blow had shattered several of his ribs. Darkness threatened to overtake him as he struggled to lift his head, the agony burning in his chest almost causing him to lose his hold on his consciousness. Blood rolled from his mouth as he forced his head up, staring to the doorway. The fire in his chest was forgotten as he laid eyes on the biggest man he had ever seen.

Shemhazai stepped through the portal and straitened to his gigantic seven-foot-five-inch height. His pale skin rippling with muscles, arms thicker than Elijah's waist. Black hair flowed around his handsome face, silky and beautiful. But it was his eyes that betrayed that beauty. Elijah shuddered as the pools of black bore down on him, and the Fallen Angel laughed maniacally.

"This is the Protector that strikes fear into my brother's children?" He placed a scornful look on Elijah as he moved forward. "You cannot be Nephilim," he said, standing over Elijah, watching the puny man squirm and try to get to his feet. Shemhazai knelt and lifted Elijah's head by his hair. "Before I destroy your will . . . tell me . . . who is your sire?"

Elijah remained silent, his anger building as his pain slowly ebbed. The violent hum of Enobe was still in his right palm, Soul Seeker lay six feet away, dropped in his tumble.

"Very well . . . I shall see for myself," Shemhazai said flatly.

Elijah's eyes suddenly slammed closed as he felt the Fallen Angel's presence tearing through his memories.

"Inconceivable!" Shemhazai roared, his face twisting into a wide grin as he let the Protector's head fall to the stone. "I will enjoy breaking you that much more, knowing that you are the offspring of my jailer, Gabriel!" Shemhazai's head rocked back in laughter.

The pain in his chest now no more than a dull throbbing, Elijah gritted his teeth and sprang into action. His rage surfaced as he hooked his right foot behind the laughing Angel's ankle and then kicked out hard with his left foot, catching Shemhazai in the knee and forcing him off balance.

Shemhazai fell on his back, still laughing.

The sickening sound drove Elijah's rage into a maddened fury. He ran past Shemhazai, Enobe slashing viciously at the Angel's face, leaving a deep gouge along the right side of its nose from its eye to his chin.

The laughter ceased as Elijah tucked into a roll, scooping up Soul Seeker in the process. He stood and spun on his heel, facing the Fallen Angel.

Shemhazai growled in pain, pressing his left hand up against the wounded area of his face. Black blood ran down his arm as he regained his feet, his good eye finding the Protector.

Elijah charged in, dancing skillfully around the halfhearted swats from Shemhazai's right hand. Soul Seeker and Enobe went to work, slicing into the Fallen Angel's flank repeatedly, stabbing and thrusting at Shemhazai's pale skin, leaving lines of blood in their wake.

Still the giant kept its hand pressed to its face. Elijah ducked a clumsy backhand and sprinted forward, thrusting both blades into Shemhazai's belly. He immediately felt the wave of satisfaction flow into his arms as his twin blades drank deeply of the Angel's tainted blood.

Shemhazai howled in anger and pain. He finally released his hold of his face where his eye had been dislodged from its socket. The terrible wound had healed enough to keep it from dangling upon his cheek. The burning in his stomach fueled his rage and he lashed out at the Protector, but found nothing but air.

Elijah danced just out of Shemhazai's reach, forcing his own rage to simmer down as he tried to think. He held no hope of defeating this giant in this manner. He knew the minor wounds he inflicted wound heal no sooner than he had dished them out. His brown eyes went up the beast's immense body and focused on its broad neck. This was where he had to strike. Unfortunately, even the added length of the four foot blades would not reach this height. Elijah darted forward again, meaning to keep the creature off balance until he could come up with a plan to take its head from its broad shoulder.

Shemhazai growled as Elijah again came within swatting distance. His hands came together, forming a massive hammer and he slammed it down where the Protector stood, only to find the annoyingly fast-moving man gone once more. In his wake he left several fresh wounds along Shemhazai's huge arms.

Elijah circled the giant, his eyes going to the beast's massive legs. He picked out a target that would drop the giant to the floor and bring his neck within range. He feigned a move to the right and the Angel fell for it hook, line, and sinker, swatting with anticipation where he thought the Protector would be. Elijah altered his steps deftly, ducking back to his left behind the creature, Enobe slicing into its achilles tendon, severing it cleanly.

Shemhazai cried out in agony as his leg gave way beneath his weight. He fell to his hands and knees, closing his eyes, waiting for the protector to strike.

Elijah seized the moment and rushed forward, Soul Seeker swinging in a vicious arc, its diamond edged blade aimed for Shemhazai's neck.

Shemhazai saw the movement and a slight grin found his lips. Too quickly for its size, the Fallen Angel lunged forward, his left hand swatting Soul Seeker out of Elijah's grip and his right hand slamming into the Protector's throat, closing with a death-like grip.

Elijah's surprise was complete. His eyes bulged as he felt the Angel's hand tighten around his throat. Enobe clanged to the stone in the darkness as he began to desperately claw at the huge fingers cutting off his air.

Again the maniacal laughter resounded off the walls of the dark cavern. Then Elijah once more felt the world sailing by him.

Shemhazai lifted Elijah high and then slammed him down to the hard stone, feeling the vertebrae in his neck pop. He grinned evilly, his powerful hand still squeezing the puny man's throat.

Elijah's vision blurred and he felt his senses momentarily leave him as his hands continued to claw at the Fallen Angel's powerful grip. His eyes bulged and black spots appeared in his vision. He reached out with his left hand, his nails scraping against the stone, searching for something, anything to fight the beast off him with. Amazingly, he found the hilt of Enobe.

Shemhazai was still chuckling, enjoying the squirming man's dying antics when he felt the tip of the blade pierce his belly once more.

Elijah howled like a crazed man as he stabbed the blade forward, again and again, his eyes wide as death sought him out. Tears fell from his cheeks, tears forced from his eyes by the lingering knowledge that his death was at hand. He still could not breathe, and the croaked cry had expended his last bit of oxygen.

Shemhazai growled in annoyance, his left hand catching Elijah's and snatching the blade from his grip. It burned in his palm, but it did not seem to matter to the Fallen Angel.

Elijah watched helplessly as Shemhazai brought the tip of the razor-sharp blade to rest on Elijah's belly. Then with a grin, Shemhazai shoved the blade downward.

Elijah's eyes rolled up into his head as the agony assaulted his senses. The pressure was too much to bear.

Shemhazai stared down at the blade curiously, for it had not punctured the subtle mesh armor of Elijah's shirt. The tip of the blade was well beyond the threshold of Elijah's skin, which remained unbroken.

Elijah's hands instinctually lashed out at Shemhazai. He stared up at the Angel with rage in his tear-filled eyes and saw the demon grin just before he put all of his weight on the pommel of the blade.

The armor gave way, split by the power of the Fallen Angel and the razor-sharp tip of Enobe. The blade exploded through Elijah's stomach and continued its downward plunge. The sound of stone grating filled Elijah's mind as Enobe's blade sunk deep into the earth, impaling him to the hilt of the blade.

Elijah cried out, choking upon his own blood as he stared at Shemhazai with wide eyes. Then he swooned, feeling the darkness overtake him.

Shemhazai released the blade and stared down at his badly burned hands. The skin was raw and blistered, but he didn't care. "Now," he began coldly, "what is yours shall be mine."

CHAPTER FIFTEEN

Steven Moss felt an uneasy feeling creep into his soul as he stared up at the golden cross sitting atop the greenish dome of the Basilica. Lightning flashed overhead as the torrents of rain continued to assault the earth. Father Holbrook sat silently, caressing the hilts of Enobe and Soul Seeker which he held in his lap.

The blue Crown Victoria veered through the light traffic on the parkway and cut a hard right turn into the parking lot of the church. The tires screeched to a halt beside the black cargo van.

Moss wasted no time jumping from the vehicle to run for the back door. He was very surprised indeed to see the accident-prone priest sprint past him, his usually cumbersome stride moving with the agility of a sportsman. He followed Father Holbrook into the dark hall that descended down into the building's lower level.

"I suspect we will find our enemy beneath the altar of the main chapel," Father Holbrook explained, his cheeks glowing red with exertion. "There is a tomb there, where several—"

"A tomb? In a church?" Moss asked as he turned the corner behind the quick moving priest. He almost ran him over as he suddenly found the Father standing still in the center of the hall. A large burly man with oily skin and a slicked back ponytail glared their way before his hand dug into the small of his back for a pistol.

Moss was faster; his first bullet split the man's eyes just above the bridge of his nose. He collapsed to the floor, dead.

Father Holbrook stuck a pudgy finger in his ear in an effort to lessen the ringing left by the loud blast. He decided it would be safer and more prudent if he let Moss lead the way from here on out.

Glenn stiffened as he heard the gunshot, and brought his own 9 mm service pistol to bear. Doctor Pokalman stared at him fearfully, still sitting with his back to the gurney upon the floor of the chamber. Glenn eased silently to the door, his heart racing.

Moss stormed into the room without hesitation and both men suddenly found themselves at the end of similar weapon barrels. Moss cocked his head to the side, his eyes narrowing as he stared at Glenn, a sour taste filling his mouth. "I'm not surprised to see you here."

Glenn's finger trembled as he returned Moss's stare. He stepped back from the doorway, switching his aim to Father Holbrook as the man rushed into the room. "Glad you could make it, Steven," Glenn began sarcastically, his arm shifting the aim of the gun between the priest and Moss repeatedly. "I see you brought your own priest to send you off into the afterworld."

"What makes you think I'm the one going?" Moss asked coldly.

Glenn laughed, lowering his weapon. "You don't have the heart, Steven... I know you," Glenn watched the old priest as he gently laid the weapons upon Elijah's chest. "Now... this is what is going to happen—"

The single gunshot echoed off of the cold, white marble walls of the tomb, and Glenn stared down at his chest in disbelief. Father Holbrook too, stared in amazement at Director Moss.

Moss had seen the dried blood between Ebonee's thighs and his anger alone had caused his trigger finger to flinch. "That's for what you did to her, you son of a bitch."

Glenn fell to the floor, still in shock. He realized he was still holding his own gun and slowly brought his gaze up to meet Moss's angry glare. "You never were a good detective Moss," he whispered weakly, feeling his life slowly drain from mortal wound. "I didn't do anything to her... that bastard there did." He nodded to the cowering Doctor, who had begun to slide closer to the door.

Moss swallowed hard, cutting his eye at the man.

"I caught him and beat the hell out of him... even scum like me can have some morals, Steven," Glenn's words were interrupted as he choked on his own blood. He stared down at the 9 mm pistol and then looked back to Glenn, wondering if he could still get a shot off.

Moss was silent for a long moment, his guilt deepening with each passing moment. Then in a blur of movement, he ran over to the doctor and pummeled him into unconsciousness with the butt of his gun. When he looked back to Glenn, he was staring down the barrel of his 9 mm pistol.

Silence filled the tomb.

A tear rolled from Glenn's eye and Moss could see the man battling with his own inner demons. Glenn's hand trembled and his face contorted violently until finally he dropped the gun to the marble floor.

"Where did I go wrong?" he whispered through his tears, letting his head lean back against one of the bronze doors that marked it as a tomb. He looked at Moss, a smile spreading on his blood stained lips. "I wanted to be like you at one time . . . I don't know where I went wrong . . . somewhere along the line I guess I got lost, buried myself in this bullshit."

Moss silently walked over to the man he had once called a friend and knelt next to him. "It's over now," he said sympathetically. "You can make it right by telling me what's going on here."

Glenn swallowed and then turned his head to look upon the unconscious Bishop. "E-Enoch . . . it was him—" His words were again interrupted by a chilling death rattle.

Moss watched as death came to take Glenn. His eyes became glossy and his lips ceased their movement. In his last action, Glenn reached into his pocket and put the small tape in Moss's hand. Then he took his last breath.

Moss didn't have time to think as he suddenly heard Father Holbrook gasp. He turned to see the priest on his knees, his head bowed reverently and his hands clasped before him as if he were praying.

Moss then stood, his eyes following the direction in which the old priest was kneeling. "Who are you?" he asked curiously.

The figure stood, white hair long and radiant, shining. His face was beautiful, yet held an edge to it. Something about the man caused Moss to tremble and fall to his knees. His world spun too quickly upon its axis and Moss felt the first waves of darkness roll over him. He continued to stare at the man in awe, knowing in his heart that this man was far much more than a mere mortal. Moss's lips worked silently up and down, the man's presence taking his very breath away.

Gabriel walked silently into the room, his eyes focusing on the body of Elijah, his son. "Get up, Father Holbrook," he said softly, his fingertips gliding gently across Elijah's arm.

Father Holbrook obeyed and moved to stand next to the Archangel. "I have done what I could, Gabriel . . . but the Protector moves too fast for these old legs to keep up with."

"You have done well Father, and I thank you," Gabriel replied, sighing as he took a deep breath.

"Is it as I fear?" Father Holbrook queried.

"It is," Gabriel began softly, turning to glance at Moss. "Shemhazai is free."

"W-w-who are you?" Moss interrupted them from his seat on the floor, his eyes never straying from Gabriel.

Gabriel absently waved a hand in his direction. "Sleep . . . and forget."

Father Holbrook watched as Moss's eyes instantly closed and he slouched down in a deep slumber. He turned to Gabriel, curious. "Forget?"

"You know fully that the time of miracles has long

been over," Gabriel chided the priest, "Seeing me and knowing me, must not influence man's faith."

"But Ebonee . . . she has seen you . . . she knows you."

"The female's conviction is set in stone. Her faith shall never waver . . . his is still in question," Gabriel offered.

Father Holbrook sighed and watched as Gabriel looked to the ceiling of the tomb. He was suddenly blinded by an intense white light that forced tears from his eyes, sending him to his knees once again. The presence of the two Seraphim filled Father Holbrook with awe of his Father's glory. He cried, praising God's name over and over again.

Gabriel silently nodded to the great guardians and then turned back to stare at Elijah. Then the three Angelic beings simply disappeared.

"Come out!"

The angry exclamation sent a chill through Dalfien's demonic spine and he watched as Rathamon's still body suddenly sprung to life. His right hand shot forward, gripping the smaller demon, Vakra, by the neck, lifting him up off of the mist enshrouded ground easily. In the same instant, Dalfien saw Shemhazai disappear and his heart began to pound in his chest. Anticipation and confusion threatened to tear his senses to shreds as he saw a look of sheer rage upon his smaller sibling's face. Never had he seen Rathamon so riled. Thick veins bulged from his red neck and Dalfien thought for a moment that he would snap Vakra's neck right then and there.

Dalfien fidgeted uneasily in his throne. Shemhazai would soon inhabit the Protector's body and

then Dalfien would be freed. But what could so en-
rage his brother?

Sam Rayburn cowered in the dark recesses of
Vakra's mind, shuddering under the weight of the
command that resounded in his ears. He cried from
the intensity in those words, unable to deny them.
He prayed his warning had been enough. His body
convulsed as he felt his spirit being forced from the
safety of the darkness.

Dalfien's eyes widened further as he saw the
human manifesting a few feet away from Rathamon
and Vakra. Sam fell to the smoldering earth in defeat, his large shoulders trembling as he sobbed.

Rathamon continued to throttle Vakra, shaking him
unmercifully until at last his eyes fluttered open.
"Mindless fool!" he exclaimed, seeing Vakra's eyes
focus. Without a thought, Rathamon then hurled the
minor demon away from him, sending him skidding
across the black rocks and bouncing into a lava flow
with a fiery splash. Then he turned to Sam, the palm
of his clawed hand opening as a fifteen-foot whip
suddenly appeared in his grasp. Serpents danced at
the end of the whip's length, hissing and spitting,
their wrath focused on the cowering human.

Dalfien chuckled as he watched the scene unfold.
So Rathamon, the great and clever demon, had
been duped by a mere human! He sat back upon his
throne, his hand tugging carelessly at the chain,
which led to his captive's collar. He would enjoy the
show.

Ebonee winced as the spikes dug into her open
wounds, her slender fingers working up between
the metal, desperately trying to lessen the pain. She
saw Sam, and her eyes narrowed to thin slits of

rage. His defeated posture sickened her to the stomach. He knelt there, sniveling like an infant, ready to accept whatever fate these brutes dished out to him.

The whip cracked the air and Sam howled in pain, feeling the fangs of the serpents dig into his back and rip his flesh away. Again the whip lashed in and Sam was pulled over onto his side, writhing in agony. He caught Ebonee's disgusted glare and his body stiffened. He held onto her eyes, focused on them, even as the whip once more tore at his neck. Sam's tears increased ten fold as his guilt hit him like a runaway train. He wilted under those strong brown eyes, not able to bare their rebuke. He closed his eyes, seeking solace from his guilt under her penetrating gaze, but before he did, he saw the woman's mouth move. The unspoken words rang out as if she had shouted it for all to hear. It beat at his heart, jumpstarting it, igniting the fires of life once more in his soul. *Fight them!*

Sam's teeth grinded in his jaw as he felt his shame building. How could he simply roll over and die, while only a few feet away a fragile woman sat chained to a demon's throne, her will far from beaten. It was Ebonee's strength that flowed through Sam's heart now. His tears ended and he focused on the whip.

Rathamon snarled as he sent the snakehead whip lashing out yet again, but this time it did not return. There was no yelp of pain and no whimpering.

Sam let the end of the whip wrap around his arm, ignoring the stinging, venomous bites of the vipers as he stood to his full six-foot-three inch height. His broad shoulders were set with a grim determination. In his mind he could again hear the subliminal chants spurring him on, *Maximus, Maximus, Maximus!* A bronze breastplate appeared, covering his wide, barrel-shaped chest. A short broadsword then appeared in his left hand. He peered through the narrow opening of his Roman war helmet, hateful blue eyes falling upon the demon Rathamon. In one swift motion, he sliced the blade's edge through the whip's chord, shaking the vipers free of his arm. His boot slammed down, crushing one of the serpents into mush. Sam then turned and eyed Ebonee Lane. Seeing her approving nod, he returned it with his own and then stalked forward toward Rathamon.

Dalfien saw the subtle gesture and glanced down at his captive. He growled in annoyance as he saw the look of fearlessness that she shot back at him. He jerked the chain, sending torrents of pain through the woman's body as her face was pulled violently up to meet the hard back hand he delivered. He snarled viciously, seeing her body fall limply to the smoldering floor. Then he turned his attention back to his entertainment.

Rathamon chuckled lightly as he watched the human transform into some type of armored warrior. He dropped the severed whip, and it was immediately replaced by his wickedly edged sword. He met Sam's charge, ignoring the heart wrenching battle cry the man let out as the two combatants slammed together in heated rage.

The demon outweighed Sam by at least one hundred pounds, which said a lot considering that Sam tipped the scales at a muscular two hundred and forty-five pounds. Sam grunted, swinging his short sword in a chopping overhead attack, which clanged loudly as Rathamon easily parried the blow and countered with a slash of his own. Sam fell back as the demon's enormous blade battered down upon his round shield, sending a wave of numbness up his arm.

The two warriors exchanged mighty blows until sweat poured from both of their bodies. Sam labored for every breath and his sword arm was heavy and tingled with fatigue.

Rathamon's wide chest rose and fell sharply, and his mind was still at its end on how this human could stand against him. He stumbled back from his last attack, it too being defeated by the man's stalwart defenses. Rathamon found he had no more heart for this fight.

Sam tore his helmet from his head, seeking more air. He could barely breathe now. Fatigue forced his sword to drag in the dirt, and he dropped his shield. His hair was matted to his scalp from the sweat that poured from his head, dripping down to sting his eyes. He staggered drunkenly before Rathamon, who made no move to attack. Sam knew he could not give up now. He looked back to where Ebonee lay beside the powerful Demon's throne, limp and unmoving. He pulled up the memory of her eyes, so strong and full of pride. His lips sealed in resignation and he turned back to Rathamon.

Sam's sudden cry pierced the darkness, as he hefted the short blade over his head and charged madly forward. His eyes were maniacal; there was no reason in them, no thought, no pain, no emotion. There was only blind rage.

Rathamon fell back under the wild string of attacks unable to lift his heavy blade to fend off the madman; his blade was knocked aside by the viciousness of the attacks.

Sam howled insanely as he saw the beast's sword clamor to the ground and he rushed forward, bringing the tip of his blade in line with Rathamon's' black heart.

Rathamon's eyes went wide, staring at the blade as it punctured his skin.

Suddenly, Sam's forward movement ceased and he felt tightness around his throat. He whirled to see Dalfien standing, his whip extended from his hand, the vipers snapping at his face and eyes.

Sam collapsed to the ground. He had no more strength left. He watched Dalfien descend from his throne, his whip disappearing and a magnificent flaming sword taking its place. This time, there was nothing Ebonee, nor anyone for that matter could do, to get Sam to stand once more.

He knelt in silence, his limbs like concrete, as Dalfien slowly stalked forward.

Blood bubbled up and rolled out of Elijah's lips to snake down his brown skin. He continued to writhe in pain as he lay impaled by his own blade. He could vaguely make out the image of Shemhazai kneeling over him as he fought to retain his hold on consciousness. Delirium had begun to set in and he moaned aloud, seeing visions of his past blur before his eyes every time he blinked.

Shemhazai grinned wickedly in the darkness, knowing he would roam the realm of man once more in this Nephilim's earthly vessel. He closed his eyes, seeking the path that would lead him to Elijah's physical body.

"Free time is over, Shemhazai," a bellowing voice shouted from the shadows.

Shemhazai's eyes flared open in anger upon hearing the familiar voice. He whirled around in search of it.

Gabriel stepped forward in his Angelic battle attire. Black bloodstains were splattered upon his golden vest of dented plate armor, remnants from his battle in the heavens with his lost brethren. "Time for you to go back to your hole."

Shemhazai roared in defiance, his black eyes filling with the flicker of intense hatred. He rushed forward, his hands longing to throttle the life from the Archangel. A blinding light halted him in his tracks and Shemhazai cowered behind his upraised hands as the Seraphim descended behind Gabriel.

"Coward!" Shemhazai cried, backing away as the two guardians approached. Great shafts of golden light were held in their hands, divine spears that Shemhazai had seen more than enough of this day. Shemhazai's anger now teetered on madness as he halted to stand his ground, his black eyes glaring at Gabriel. "Your God is an unjust fool! Lucifer remains in the world! Yet His wrath falls upon my head!" Veins threatened to explode beneath the behemoth's skin as the Seraphim closed on him. "Why?" he cried out, struggling as the Seraphim's many hands grabbed him and held him between them. "Why has His vengeance overlooked my beautiful brother?"

Gabriel remained silent as he walked forward, his white hair flowing before his eyes.

Shemhazai ceased his struggles as he felt the tight bindings of shackles upon his wrists. A smile then found his pale, square face. "It is because Lucifer's power is beyond him," he began icily through his grin. "Enjoy your time here, Gabriel, for I shall be free again . . . my brother shall free me and together we shall destroy God's precious kingdom . . .

and you . . . you shall know darkness and pain." His eyes narrowed to thin slits as he was forced to his knees by the Seraphim. "I shall bury you in the very pit your God has prepared for us."

The words flittered around Elijah's consciousness like flies buzzing around feces. One moment they were loud and clear, the next they were far away and incoherent. The delirium continued to torture his mind as the pain from his wound increased with every breath he took. The images mixed with Shemhazai's foul threats. He saw Kenyatta, standing over a casket in which his own body lay. The vision caused him to thrash about, further increasing the pain of the wound, which triggered more visions. He saw his grandmother, smiling down at him as a child, her brown eyes rich and full of life before she was suddenly and violently snatched away from him, her eyes becoming wide and terror filled. Tears fell freely from Elijah's eyes as his hands found the hilt of the blade impaling him to the stone. Peg by peg, vision by vision, his rage slowly began to build once more. Again he saw an image, this one of a beautiful young woman, her braided hair long and framing a full brown face. The moonlight glimmered in her large brown eyes, eyes that were filled with sadness and tears. She stared at Elijah as the tears broke free and she spoke . . . "I love you, Elijah . . . kiss me please."

Gabriel's attention was pulled from Shemhazai as Elijah's lustful cry filled the cavern. It shook him to the core so guttural and filled with emotion was this cry.

Elijah pulled at the hilt of the sword, straining with the pain of his memories. A final image appeared to him as he closed his eyes, seeking the strength to free himself from the blade's hold.

Ebonee Lane, her body beaten and broken, hanging limply from a cross, the demon Dalfien stood beside her, his great and terrible tooth-filled maw grinning wickedly at Elijah.

Once more Elijah's soul-shredding cry filled the cavern.

The sword ripped free of the stone.

Elijah stood, his face dark behind blood stained white locs. Enobe hung loosely in his right hand as he turned to stare at the gathered Angels. Slowly, his heart took up a steady rhythm and he denied the pain in his belly as he took up a deadly pace. He paused only to pick up Soul Seeker from the cold stone.

Gabriel watched Elijah with warm smile. He was happy to see him back on his feet and well. His smile disappeared a second later as the Protector drew closer and he could make out the set of his face. He knew Elijah was beyond reason then. "Elijah, his judgment is reserved for—" Gabriel's words ended abruptly as he watched Shemhazai's stunned head roll from his massive shoulders. "So much for that," Gabriel muttered, watching as Elijah then snatched up the Fallen Angel's head and turned to walk solemnly away.

The Seraphim vanished, leaving Gabriel to stare at the Protector as he slowly disappeared into the shadows of his own mind. Gabriel shrugged helplessly and chuckled, before he himself vanished.

Elijah's emotions were a sea of pure rage. Only one word broke through that rage as he stalked forward towards the shimmering doorway that would take him to Hell. One name repeated constantly in the dark sea of ill intent that was his demeanor. *Ebonee . . .*

CHAPTER SIXTEEN

Rathamon's anger could not have been greater. He lay beaten and winded upon the smoldering rocks, in this, his greatest hour. As his black eyes watched, Dalfien and his mighty flaming blade descend upon the human that had bested him. *A human!* Whatever respect he had gained from his larger sibling was surely lost. He growled angrily as he struggled to his feet.

Sam knelt crumpled on his knees, trying desperately to search for the strength to stand and face Dalfien. He urged his body to move, to stand. His fatigued limbs offered only a stumbling attempt in reply.

Dalfien brought the fiery blade up over his head in both hands, ready to cleave Sam in half where he lay. He paused, watching the human stumble drunkenly about in an attempt to face him. Dalfien chuckled lightly and brought the sword back down. With one clawed hand, he snatched Sam up by the throat and held him up for inspection. His black eyes stared at Sam and then shifted to Rathamon and then went back to Sam. With a disgusted snort, Dalfien dropped the puny man to the ground and watched him squirm some more.

Dalfien let his blade fizzle and disappear. "Some sport while we await Shemhazai's victorious return?" His lips turned up into a mischievous sneer.

Rathamon seethed with anger as he watched Dalfien kick the human in the ribs, sending the man tumbling across the rocky ground. To Rathamon's surprise, Sam still fought to stand, blood trickling from his mouth, his body battered, yet still he held onto life.

"You son of a bitch," Sam whispered feebly, collapsing to the soot covered stone as the pain of fractured ribs tore at him. He was beyond fatigue, beyond weariness; everything seemed to be playing out in a strange, dream like state for him now. Somehow he managed to stand, staggering back and forth, the dark landscape fading in and out of his vision.

Dalfien closed on the staggering figure all too quickly. His fist rushed forward, slamming Sam in the chest and sending him flying backward to land in a broken heap at the foot of Dalfien's throne.

Before Dalfien could move to continue his torturous deeds, a powerful chill racked his body from horn to hoof. The electrifying jolt stopped him cold in his tracks and turned, eyes wide in search of the presence that had suddenly manifested somewhere in the shadows.

Rathamon also felt the sensation and his eyes scanned the borders of the scarred rocks and the wall of shadowy mist which marked Dalfien's prison. At first, his heart fluttered, thinking that it was Shemhazai, returning to lead them into the world of men. But then he saw the truth of the matter as Elijah stepped through the clinging mists, Shemhazai's head dangling in one hand, Enobe in the other.

"What madness is this?" Rathamon shouted insanely, unable to pull his gaze from the Fallen Angel's head.

Dalfien stood, frozen in shock and boiling with rage, gazing at the Protector, who continued his determined march directly for his island.

Rathamon snapped from his trance and called forth his brethren, unleashing hell upon the Protector.

Elijah's primal state sensed the first wave of minor demons approaching him in the darkness and with a great heave he loosed Shemhazai's head in a mighty throw and then snatched Soul Seeker from its sheath at his waist. The head bounced several feet after landing, coming to a rolling stop at Rathamon's hoofed feet, just as the first of Rathamon's horde lost its head.

Enobe and Soul Seeker carved a bloody trail directly to Dalfien's throne. Chaotic cries of pain rose up above the eternal cry of the damned soul's as Elijah hacked and slashed with a viciousness that bordered on insanity. There was no thought to his movements, no aimed attacks, no well-timed parries or strategies. There was only his rage. The sea of demons grew thicker between Elijah and his goal, yet his forward pace never diminished. The faster they came, the quicker they died. Blood soaked the Protector from head to toe. He did not know if any of it was his own, nor did he care. He could see his goal. He could see Ebonee.

Rathamon's black eyes lifted from the decapitated

head, enraged and full of hate. He stared at the Protector, watching as those terrible blades cut through his brethren with an ease that seemed unnatural. He followed Elijah's trail, looking to Dalfien's throne and the unconscious woman chained beside it. "I will die before you have her," he whispered through clenched jowls, seeing clearly the Protector's goal. He moved quickly, hoping the horde would slow the enraged being long enough for him to get to the girl and take her life.

Sam groaned as he endeavored to lift his head. He had felt the strange sensation and now he too sought to see what it was. He struggled briefly, but finally managed to lift his head from the stone and turn it. He saw the chaos, but more importantly, he saw the source of the chaos. Tears fell anew from Sam's eyes as he felt the fires of hope rekindle deep within his heart. His chest began to rise and fall sharply, as adrenaline pumped through his veins. *Kill them all, Protector!* He smiled through his own pain, forgetting it like it was simply an old lunch pail that he didn't want anyway. Rathamon flashed across his vision, stealing his smile and capturing his attention. He watched the demon as it stood over Ebonee Lane, its wickedly sharp blade lifted above her heart.

Dalfien remained motionless, until his eyes saw Rathamon. "No!" he bellowed, seeing the sword aimed at her heart. She was his to torture for the rest of his time in banishment, which he plainly knew would indeed be served now that Shemhazai's head lay only a few feet from where he stood.

Elijah faltered, seeing the blade rise slowly above his beloved's chest. He knew he would not make it to her in time.

Rathamon sneered, flashing a grin at the Protector just before he drove the blade down. He felt the soft flesh give way as his sword plunged deeper, filling him with a sick satisfaction. He looked down to take in the pleasurable sight.

Rathamon's face then twisted in confusion and denial, unable to comprehend the impossible sight. When he looked up again, Enobe and Soul Seeker flashed before him. He saw the dark eyes of the Protector, full of rage and an undeniable hate. He saw his clawed hands fall from the hilt of his blade, no longer attached to his body.

And then Rathamon's head fell from his shoulders.

Elijah slowly let go of the rage as he stood, staring down at Sam, who looked up at Elijah with a weak, blood tainted smile.

"I-It was . . . good to know you," Sam whispered as Elijah knelt next to him.

With Rathamon dead, the demonic horde held no further desire to taste of those stinging blades and so they dispersed, leaving Dalfien, the Protector, Sam, and Ebonee Lane, alone on his island. Dalfien remained still; even he did not wish to feel the bite of the Protector's blades.

"Y-y-you make sure and take care of that girlie," Sam continued under Elijah's saddened gaze. He winced as Elijah touched the hilt of the blade impaled in his heart. Darkness closed on Sam and his eyes lost vision. "She's a tough one . . ." Sam's words trailed away into silence.

Elijah let his tears fall as he gently reached down to close the lids over Sam's blue eyes and then watched as his body slowly disappeared. He looked upon Ebonee then, her life saved by the actions of

Sam Rayburn. He reached down to free her from the cruel device about her neck.

Then the world began to fade away.

Elijah cried out in denial, the vision of Ebonee slowly drifting away from him as he was pulled into the shadows. Her form grew smaller and smaller in his sight. His hands reached out for her desperately as he tried to fight whatever force it was that pulled him away.

Then there was only darkness.

CHAPTER SEVENTEEN

"Nooo!"
Director Moss and Father Holbrook shrank back from the Gurney as Elijah suddenly sprang up, his eyes wild, staring around the room in confusion.

"Ebonee!" Elijah rolled from the gurney and took her lifeless hand in his. His eyes filled with moisture as he continued to call out to her, shaking her roughly. "Wake up, damn it!" His eyes roamed to the IV bag hanging beside her and then to the bag attached to his own gurney. Both were empty.

Moss and Father Holbrook watched in silence as the Protector then began a search of the tomb. He found another IV bag full of the clear liquid and quickly replaced his empty one with it. He then lay back onto the gurney, closing his eyes, willing himself to sleep.

It took a moment for the drug to take hold; Elijah's Angelic blood was now nearly immune to it.

He awoke in the dark cavern that was his mind's place of safety and immediately began his search for the portal that would lead him back to Dalfien's plane of existence. But he found no traces of it. He scoured every inch of the cavern until finally he collapsed to the rocky ground in futility. He growled in anger, pounding his fists into the stone until they were numb and bloody.

He opened his eyes and found the cold, white walls of the tomb around him once more. Silently, he rose, going over to Ebonee's gurney. "I'll find you, I promise you that on my life," he whispered softly, his hand gently brushing the side of her cheek.

Moss turned to Father Holbrook with a curious glance. "What's going on?"

Father Holbrook did not answer.

"Elijah . . . what happened?" Moss asked, daring to move closer. "What do you mean you'll find her?"

Elijah ignored Moss's words as his eyes roamed along Ebonee's naked body, stopping at her thighs. He saw the dried blood there and whirled on Moss. "Did Glenn do this?" His eyes skipped over the dead man's corpse and then fell upon the doctor, who moaned lightly, semi conscious.

Moss followed his gaze to Glenn and then sighed. "No, it was him."

Elijah's inability to aid his beloved left him in a highly volatile state, and he now found a release for that building rage. His eyes narrowed as he followed Moss's gaze to the dazed doctor.

Moss saw the murderous intent in Elijah's brown eyes and grabbed him by the arm. "No! Let justice run its course."

Father Holbrook moved to stand behind Moss. "He is right, young Protector . . . it is not your place to pass judgment...vengeance belongs to the Lord."

Elijah stared at the priest and then placed a cold look on the hand holding his arm. "If you want to keep that hand I suggest you remove it from my arm." His tone left no room for compromise and Moss reluctantly released his hold. "And as for vengeance belonging to the Lord," he added, scooping Soul Seeker from the floor of the tomb as he spoke softly, his eyes focusing on the doctor, "Well, this day," his eyes were cold and lifeless as he stepped forward, his jaw set in grim determination, "vengeance is mine." With that said, Elijah pulled the man up by the collar and forced him to stare into his eyes. "I know you're going to Hell," he began, whispering fiercely into the man's terror filled expression, "and when you get there tell Dalfien that I will be coming for him."

Father Holbrook wanted to speak up, he wanted to yell for the Protector to stop, but the look in Elijah's eyes held him paralyzed. More than anything, he feared for the Protector's soul. He knew how vicious sin could be. Even as he watched Elijah slam the doctor face first into the cold marble wall and listened to the man's screams as Soul Seeker tore into his backside and continued up into his lungs and finally his throat, he knew that iniquity would tempt Elijah again. He knew how tantalizing the cleansed soul was to Lucifer.

Father Holbrook shuddered as Elijah twisted the blade so that the cutting edge faced the ceiling. It was not the act that brought the bile into Father Holbrook's throat, but it was the satisfaction he saw etched into the Protector's visage as he ripped the blade upward, severing the man from his anus to the base of his skull that sickened him so.

Moss turned away as blood splattered across his face, dotting his glasses with specks of red as Elijah continued to hack at the dead man, setting loose his frustrations.

But it was not enough. For the next three months Elijah searched for demons, hoping to release more of the rage and to find a portal back to the realm of Lucifer's children. He sought them out in every corner of Philadelphia, in the dismal ghettos, in the crack houses, and strip clubs. He searched the churches and the synagogues. He looked everywhere, but the demons avoided him as if he were Jesus Christ in the flesh.

Ebonee remained in a coma, unresponsive to any stimuli, her soul trapped in Hell, held prisoner by the demon Dalfien. She was admitted to the University of Pennsylvania Hospital by Director Moss, who stayed by her side, along with Father Holbrook and Kenyatta Garland, for the first month of her stay.

Elijah would come by often, sitting beside his beloved, holding her cold hand in his own.

"If this bitch don't wake up soon, I'mma crawl up inside her head and kick her fuckin' ass," Kenyatta muttered dryly, relaxing in the chair next to Ebonee's bed on one rain soaked evening.

Elijah could not help but chuckle at his sister's remark. He knew Kenyatta had found a place for Ebonee in her heart and cared almost as much about her as he did.

"How such foul language can find the mouth of one with a pure heart I will never understand," Father Holbrook said, shaking his head at Kenyatta. He walked over to stand next to the Protector beside Ebonee's bed. He stared at Elijah for a moment in silence, noting the dark rings around his eyes and the hollowness of his cheeks. "You do not look well, Protector."

Elijah ignored the comment, keeping his gaze locked firmly upon Ebonee's still eyelids. Sadness radiated from his very being. Tears threatened to fall from his brown eyes as his heart rate increased. His nostrils billowed softly as he channeled the sadness into rage. He was wasting time. Time he could put to good use searching for a way back to the realms of hell, where he could free his beloved.

Director Moss stood at the foot of the bed watching the two men. He turned and looked up at the television as the local news came on.

Sergeant Dietrich Wells returned to his Ben Salem home today amid a swarm of happy family and friends who were all there to welcome the soldier home. Sergeant Wells was serving with the US Army infantry in Afghanistan when his platoon was ambushed by Taliban loyalists, just south of Kabul. Sergeant Wells received the Purple Heart award and says he owes his life to the Special Forces team that rescued him.

Moss stared at the television as the news reporter's face was replaced by the scene of desert fighting among US forces and Taliban extremists. His eyes went wide as he watched the American soldiers storming into desert dwellings while around them gunfire could be heard. His eyes narrowed as he saw the insignia on one of the soldier's uniforms before the screen went back to the reporter's face. *The black eight.* Two darkened circles sitting atop one another. Moss strained to remember where he had seen that insignia before. Flashes of memory flittered through his mind—the army base where he had traced Elijah to. The Captain he had spoken with briefly. He had worn that same insignia.

Elijah could not bear to stand there any longer and stare at his helpless Ebonee. He ignored Father Holbrook's call as he stormed from the room, fighting away the tears that longed to fall.

"Father Holbrook," Moss began, as he too moved for the door, "you have my number . . . call me if there is any change in her condition."

"Yes, of course."

Moss exited the room and immediately took out his cell phone. He would need to get the address for this Sergeant Wells.

Elijah stepped out into the chilly night air in front of the center city hospital. The thunderous storm had dwindled into a meager misting. The occasional car sped along the street, its tires slashing through the soaked streets loudly. Elijah began his walk, his head bowed, the weight of Ebonee's predicament heavy upon his heart. *It's all my fault. I wish I would never have met her.* A rush of emotion caused his body to tremble as he moved along the dark streets in silence. A flash of memory brought him face to face with Taysia, her beautiful brown eyes full of moisture, staring up into his own eyes before her full lips parted in a final request . . . *Kiss me, Elijah.*

Elijah stumbled to the side under the weight of the memory, his face contorted into a semblance of pain and agony as he reached out a hand to steady himself. The cold, damp brick wall the palm of his hand found gave him no respite from his cruel past. He saw Ebonee, her arms outstretched, hands impaled by stakes, driven into the large wooden cross

situated in the vast underground compound belonging to the Order of the Rose.

Her voice echoed in his mind. *Fight them, Elijah!*

Elijah slid along the wall, his hands desperately
clutching at his tormented head as the lightning
above flashed anew. Heavy raindrops slowly began
their descent as the storm once again roared back
to life. Elijah staggered drunkenly along the wall
until it gave way to a dark, shadow-infested alley.
He welcomed the darkness, moving deeper into the
cul-de-sac to lean his back up against the rear wall.
Leaning his head back, Elijah let the huge, pelting
raindrops wash away his flowing tears, taking comfort in the coolness of the water against his ebon
skin. The incessant drum of the driving rain soothed
the memories away, leaving Elijah alone in the darkness to contemplate his life.

*Why? Why do you let this happen, Lord? Why give
us free will knowing that we are weak? I don't understand! Why?* His hand came up to take hold of
the shining crucifix hanging about his neck. *Why let
us endure the hardship? Why the pain? Is it some
sort of joke to you?*

Elijah's thoughts were interrupted by a brilliant
flash of lightning and a deafening crackling of thunder that reverberated through his skeleton. A chill
writhed through his body feeling like a drill hitting
a nerve inside of a molar. He stared around the dark
alley then, taking account of his surroundings for
the first time in the flashing lightning.

Water flowed loudly from drains high above the
tall buildings, saturating fire escapes high above
along the opposite wall. Dumpsters echoed the
sound of the splashing water in the shadows, mix-

ing with the rapid thumping of heavy drops falling on plastic trash bags. The sky above, between the brick buildings, was a mass of chaotic, swirling dark storm clouds, belching flashes of light as they hurled rain down onto the city.

Elijah chuckled ruefully as he blinked up through the rain, staring at the maelstrom above. "We're all just a form of entertainment to you, aren't we?" he shouted at the tumultuous heavens. He felt the edges of the crucifix digging into his palm as he closed his fist around it tighter, his emotions on the verge of exploding like the thunderous booms filling the air above.

"Everything I have ever loved in this fucking world you've taken from me!" His voice fluctuated as a heavy sob escaped his lips. His body trembled, remembering the warmth he had felt when he was in God's presence. His tears flowed down his cheeks in rivers, washed away by the rain. Guilt and anger ravaged his very soul, tearing him apart internally. A guttural growl slid from his wet lips as he fought with the contradicting emotions. His hand snatched the crucifix from the thin chain around his neck and he hurled it against the far wall with a soulful outcry.

The moment the crucifix struck the wall a resounding crackle of thunder exploded above, sending shockwaves through Elijah. A brilliant flash of lightning streaked across the rooftops ending in a boom that he felt in the soles of his feet.

Every light in the city died instantly as a blackout stretched across Philadelphia.

Darkness devoured the alley, leaving Elijah staring open-mouthed at the surreal scene that flickered before him in the flashes of lightning.

Time stood still. Elijah found himself paralyzed,

as if he were in some sort of vacuum, sealed from the outside world. The splattering of the raindrops seemed thousands of miles away. He suddenly felt small, like a tiny insect surrounded by a massive world. He stared out into the intermittent flashes of light in disbelief. Every raindrop in the alley was frozen in mid air. He could see the tiny fragments of the silver crucifix, hanging in the air before the brick wall, motionless.

Fear began to seep into Elijah's heart as he watched in awe as the fragments slowly revered their momentum amid the frozen drops of rain, reforming into a cross.

The air around Elijah suddenly became thick and he could feel his lungs heaving, laboring to take in oxygen. He knew immediately the significance of the cross as it hovered now in the air, upside down.

Thunder boomed, announcing the return of motion within the dark alley. The raindrops crashed to the ground and the sound exploded into Elijah's mind. Goose bumps traveled across every inch of his body as his muscles drew taut, sensing the evil that now occupied the alley with him.

The black shadows drew in upon a central point around the cross as it hovered in the air until a dark figure formed.

Lucifer.

In the brief flashes of light, Elijah saw the dark figure take on the appearance of a man. Smooth olive skin, firm jaw and jet-black hair that flowed like silk down his shoulders, untouched by the pouring rain. Elijah found he could not move, although every fiber of his being was screaming for him to run like hell. His heart pounded within his chest, threatening to break free and escape without him.

Lucifer's head hung down, his black hair falling to cover his face as he slowly stretched out his arms, imitating Christ crucified. Behind him, in the brief flashes of lightning, Elijah saw the brick wall. It writhed with a life of its own, and he saw souls screaming, twisting, and bending as if they were in agony.

"Why do you fear me, Elijah?" Lucifer's honey-dipped voice pierced the darkness, filling Elijah with a dread unsurpassed. "Why do you hate me so?"

Elijah could feel his muscles twitching around his heart as he watched the shadow slide closer. Water welled up in his eyes, tears forged by the greatest fear any man had ever known. He was powerless to move. The shadows shifted slowly as they drew to within inches of his face, morphing into the image of a man. His facial features were without flaw, a strong jaw line with olive skin that looked softer than cotton. A perfect nose, dark brown eyes, and full, pink lips.

Elijah trembled as those lips hovered ever so close to his face. There was silence all about him now. The storm was a memory, the cascading raindrops had disappeared, and there was only this man . . . this demon . . . this *Devil*. Power he had never before felt washed through his body, emanating from Lucifer himself. It bathed Elijah, caressed him, and sent goose bumps along his skin. He knew not the restrictions of time, for this moment seemed endless. Lucifer's honey dipped lips inched closer, Elijah closed his eyes. Sparks erupted inside of Elijah's brain as he felt the soft skin of those lips against his own. Growling in defiance of the mental intrusion, Elijah forced his eyes open and found the strength to shrink back from Lucifer's kiss.

"Get away from me, you son of a bitch," he growled.

Lucifer's lips twisted slowly into a grin as he leaned back, taking stock of this man . . . this . . . Nephilim. Elijah wilted under the malevolent gaze and once more closed his eyes. The next voice he heard succeeded in bringing yet another chill to his spine.

"Perhaps this would better suit your corrupted morals," the woman's seductive voice whispered as Elijah opened his eyes to see the most beautiful, voluptuous female this side of the equator.

But the eyes did not lie. They remained those of Lucifer, The Great Pretender. Elijah's heart fluttered madly as the woman's grin held him motionless against the wall of the alley.

"Just another testament to an uncaring God . . . your morals are . . ." Lucifer began in the female's voice, her lips sliding up Elijah's cheek, grazing the sensitive skin below his ear, "Give man a lustful heart and then proclaim all pleasures sinful."

Elijah trembled, feeling the warm breath upon his earlobe. Bile rose up in his throat just as he felt his arousal stretching the material of his pants.

"You count me as your enemy, you have named me evil . . . Me! The one son who has fought for mankind since the beginning," Lucifer hissed, his eyes flaring a dim red as he leaned back to stare into Elijah's tearful eyes. "I watched your God create Adam upon the plains of dust . . . I watched Him as He manipulated him; played with him as if he were a toy . . . it sickened me to my soul . . . 'You may partake of anything within the Garden of Eden, Adam,'" Lucifer spat the words as he related his story, mocking God's commands. ". . . 'But do not eat the fruit of this one tree.'"

"Lies!" Elijah managed to blurt through his fear. He forced himself off of the wall in an attempt to flee past in the darkness only to feel a steel grip close upon his throat.

Lucifer slammed Elijah into the wall forcefully, sending bright glowing orbs dancing inside Elijah's mind. He watched Elijah squirm, grasping at the slender hand that pinned him to the wall as he struggled to draw breath.

"Lies?" Lucifer's black eyes narrowed as he twisted Elijah's head upward. "To what purpose?"

Elijah continued to struggle against the death grip upon his throat. The darkness of the alley seemed to be growing even darker despite the now constant string of flashing electricity overhead. He could feel death's hands tugging at his soul—a growl escaped his lips.

Lucifer paused for a moment, burrowing into the Protector's pain riddled mind. "You do not need me to teach you of truth . . . no, I see you already know." Thunder exploded overhead, yet Lucifer's words rang clearly in Elijah's head behind his tightly closed eyelids. "That nagging doubt that has festered in your feeble little mind for so long," he began slowly, a grin coming to his feminine lips, "that unyielding pessimism that for so long has been buried by mankind with false beliefs and blind, foolish faith!"

Elijah's body trembled under the weight of those words and he jerked about wildly in denial.

"The truth is in you, Protector! It has always been so!" Lucifer suddenly exclaimed. "Embrace it! For it will set you free! You and all of your kind have been created upon a whim! And by that same whim you shall be allowed to die! You mean nothing to Him! Thousands of you die every hour! Children starve by the millions, loved ones die prematurely. Death knows your kind so well...disaster falls to the faithful as well as the faithless! Yet you hold on to His love...enrapture yourselves within it. You cower behind it because your feeble minds cannot comprehend beyond it!"

Anger burned in the black pools of Lucifer's eyes. Then suddenly, Lucifer calmed and seemingly with his placidness, the thunder and rain slowed also. "I ask you again, Elijah...why do you hate me so? Perhaps because it has been bred into your genes for thousands of years, planted like a seed and watered by false prophets until it has grown into your futility."

Elijah's tears flowed like the cascading waters from the roofs above. He felt air return to his lungs as the grip upon his throat loosened. Lucifer's words filled him with a deep sorrow he could not comprehend. His mind now swam in a sea of confusion more than ever before.

Lucifer removed his hand from Elijah's throat, but the seductive woman did not move an inch from where he stood. "I can sense the struggle within your soul, my dear nephew...I have always sensed it."

Elijah found he could not look away from those lucid, mystifying eyes, eyes that shifted in color as Lucifer's words glided into his mind like honey, intoxicating, soothing. The rain seemed to add to the calming effects of those words, its once torrid downpour now a placid drizzle, tiny drops softly peppering Elijah's face.

"I am not your enemy, Elijah," Lucifer began once more, the female body inching ever closer, "I offer only love...always this has been my way." His

slender hand glided gently across Elijah's jaw, sending a chill along Elijah's spine. "That is the truth of
your burden . . . that is the torment of your soul. My
love beckons you . . . can you feel it?"

Elijah's head lolled back drunkenly as he felt a
mesmerizing wave of emotion flow through him.
His tears ended their fall and he basked in the
warmness these words offered.

"Throughout time I have sought to love man. I
have comforted him when no others would, when
their prayers to an uncaring God went unanswered.
I listened and I gave them pleasures and riches. I
gave them power and glory only to have my love
and my gestures twisted into something it was
never . . . and will never be . . . temptation." Lucifer
paused as his lips drew to within a breath of Elijah's
lips. "I give love and ask for nothing in return, and
what does He give them? Ultimatums? Love me or
burn in Hell for eternity? Follow my commandments
or perish in the lake of fire? Open your eyes, Elijah,
and see the truth of my words."

Slowly, Elijah obeyed. As he blinked through the
moisture of the softly falling raindrops, his heart
froze—before him stood Ebonee Lane. Her lips were
full and glowing with moisture, begging for his
kiss. Her brown eyes seemed brighter than he had
ever remembered. "E-E-Ebonee?" he whispered, daring to hope the vision was true.

"*Kiss me, Elijah,*" she said softly, the words smoldering with an undeniable draw he was almost
powerless to resist.

Again Elijah felt a tremor rock his body and he
shuddered. *No!* The mental shout echoed in his
mind as he sought to refute the sweet poison that
was penetrating into his soul.

Within the shadows of the dark, rain-soaked alley, silence suddenly enveloped the two figures standing so close together. Elijah opened his eyes and stared at Ebonee Lane.

Lucifer seemed confused for a split second as he gazed into the Protector's eyes, eyes that were no longer consumed by fear, but eyes that were cold and lifeless. Slowly Lucifer's gaze went downward to the hilts of the twin swords, Enobee and Soul Seeker, whose blades were buried deep within his belly.

Elijah's hate fought to overcome the unyielding fear still burning in his pounding heart as he twisted the blades cruelly, watching as Ebonee's impersonation began to writhe and moan in pain. Her face shifted eerily, morphing back and forth between Lucifer's lies until finally only the original face remained. The moaning and squirming ceased as though it had never began and Elijah found himself staring into the eyes of the devil.

"She will suffer mercilessly," Lucifer promised softly, ignoring the blades that remained deeply imbedded in his abdomen. His eyes burned fiercely as the thunder above the narrow alley seemed to shake the world. "I can give her to you; all you have to do is ask and it shall be made so."

Temptation brought new tears to Elijah's eyes. What if he was telling the truth? What if all he had to do was simply ask?

"I do not fault you for your ignorance, child," Lucifer continued calmly, glancing down at the black lines of blood that spilled from the wounds in rivers. His eyes came back up, scrutinizing Elijah, seeing the confusion etched upon his dark skin. Then slowly a grin found his beautiful face as he outstretched his arms, once more, mocking the crucifixion of Christ. "I suffer for the sins of man."

Rage filled Elijah as he heard those words and watched the sick grin spread upon Lucifer's lips as lightning exploded above, bathing the scene in electric blue light. A sound broke free of Elijah's lips, a sound that was foreign to him for it held more emotion than he had ever felt in his life. Rage, terror, confusion, temptation, and hope escaped his lungs in a cry that out did the booming thunder. Desperation forced his hands to move, propelled him to act. Violently, he ripped the blades outward and brought them both up in a semi circular arc, Soul Seeker and Enobe's cutting edges aimed for Lucifer's neck.

And then there was darkness.

Black and complete. No lightning filled the skies. No thunder boomed overhead. Elijah's arms had come to a complete stop in front of him, the points of his blades unable to complete their gory chore. Elijah could only hear the sound of his heart pounding. The air seemed to be charged with electricity, making his skin tingle. He strained against the unseen force preventing the blades from closing but found he was powerless to move them. He continued to struggle against the force, unaware of time and his surroundings. Soon he felt the burn of fatigue in his biceps and his burst of rage quickly died.

Lightning flashed.

Elijah's world shattered in one brief moment of time. He saw Lucifer, his expression bored as he stood before him, Soul Seeker and Enobe held easily in the palm of each hand. Before the split second of light could fade away, the blessed blades were snapped like Popsicle sticks.

A wave of dread careened into Elijah's heart as the sound of the metal striking the concrete filled his ears. As the lighting once more filled the alley, he stared at the broken remnants of his one true source of comfort. The twin blades had become an extension of his inner self; they were as much a part of him as were his feet or hands. Sorrow forced a new wave of tears to his eyes.

Enobe and Soul Seeker were no more.

Blindly, Elijah flung himself from the wall, staggering in a rush for the lighter darkness he prayed was the alley's entrance. He could not think, he could not speak. He could only run, with moisture clouding his vision of the darkness every step of the way.

"You cannot run from my words for long, Elijah!" Lucifer shouted after him, grinning. "You will find no sanctuary that will shelter you from the truth!"

The exclamation burned itself into Elijah's mind even as he slammed into a parked car as he burst forth from the alley. It repeated over and over again like a broken record, driving his legs to move faster. He had to escape those words. He had to escape the sorrow of the lost blades. He had to escape the pain of a lost love. He had to escape the temptation.

He never looked back.

Epilogue

A heavy sense of foreboding loomed like a hundred-foot tidal wave over Father Holbrook's head as he stepped from the entrance of the hospital. The dire sense of loss seemed to fill the very air he was breathing as he scanned the rain-soaked sidewalks in both directions. The chaos of the blackout was over, and the city was once again bathed in artificial light. His eyes caught and held on the narrow entrance to a small alley a few yards to his right. Before he realized his feet were moving, Father Holbrook found himself staring down the trash-littered cul-de-sac. What premonition guided him he did not know; he only knew that it was undeniable and dark.

He found his heart beating at a frantic pace as he stepped into the shadows. Water from the lingering storm cascaded down rusted drain pipes along the alley's narrow walls, filling his ears with an incessant splash. A flicker caught his eye along the wall of the alley among the litter and trash and his breath held at the sight.

The remnants of Soul Seeker and Enobe lay at his feet, both blades broken at the hilt. He said a silent Hail Mary and knelt down to retrieve the broken fragments. He also found the silver cross that belonged to Elijah, lying in one piece on the opposite side of the alley. He dared not ponder what force could have broken that which could never be broken. Silently, the old priest stepped from the shadows of the alley, his eyes sadly looking down the empty streets.

"May the Lord watch over you and keep you in your time of need, young Protector," he whispered into the wind, and then he dejectedly walked back into the hospital to sit beside the comatose Ebonee Lane to pray some more.

About the Author

TL Gardner was born and raised in Philadelphia PA. He currently resides in Hinesville, Georgia. Comments or remarks can be sent to TL at the following: www.myspace.com/tlgardner

COMING SOON FROM
Q-BORO
BOOKS

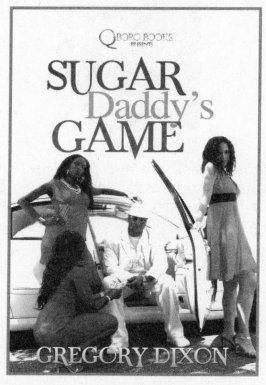

Jamell White is known as Sugar Daddy. Most of the people who know him assume that his nickname "Sugar" is a by-product of his cash-friendly habits with several beautiful, well known females. But they couldn't be more wrong.

MAY 2008
ISBN: 1-933967-41-2

NOW AVAILABLE FROM

NYMPHO
$14.95
ISBN 1933967102

How will signing up to live a promiscuous double-life destroy everything that's at stake in the lives of two close couples? Take a journey into Leslie's secret world and prepare for a twisted, erotic experience.

FREAK IN THE SHEETS
$14.95
ISBN 1933967196

Ready to break out of the humdrum of their lives, Raquelle and Layla decide to put their knowledge of sexuality and business together and open up a freak school, teaching men and women how to please their lovers beyond belief while enjoying themselves in the process.

However, Raquelle and Layla must learn some important lessons when it comes to being a lady in the street and a freak in the sheets.

LIAR, LIAR
$14.95
ISBN 1933967110

Stormy calls off her wedding to Camden when she learns he's cheating with a male church member. However, after being convinced that Camden has been delivered from his demons, she proceeds with the wedding.

Will Stormy and Camden survive scandal, lies and deceit?

HEAVEN SENT
$14.95
ISBN 1933967188

Eve is a recovering drug addict who has no intentions of staying clean until she meets Reverend Washington, a newly widowed man with three children. Secrets are uncovered that threaten Eve's new life with her new family and has everyone asking if Eve was *Heaven Sent.*

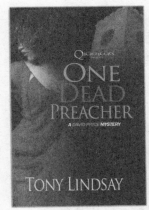

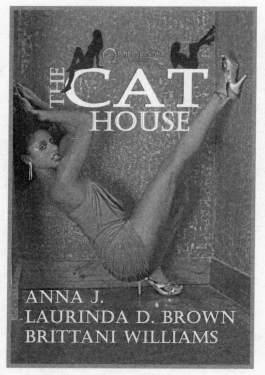